Rick Held studied creative writing at Victoria University before taking up a position at Crawford Productions, then Australia's premier producer of television drama. He has since had a long career as a TV screenwriter and editor, working on numerous series including the critically acclaimed *A Place to Call Home* and the popular family drama *Packed to the Rafters*. Since 1997 he has been based in Sydney. *Night Lessons in Little Jerusalem*, inspired by his father's wartime memoir, is his first novel.

Night Lessons
in
Little Jerusalem

RICK HELD

hachette
AUSTRALIA

hachette
AUSTRALIA

Published in Australia and New Zealand in 2020
by Hachette Australia
(an imprint of Hachette Australia Pty Limited)
Level 17, 207 Kent Street, Sydney NSW 2000
www.hachette.com.au

10 9 8 7 6 5 4 3 2 1

A catalogue record for this
book is available from the
National Library of Australia

ISBN: 978 0 7336 4166 4

Cover design by Christabella Designs
Cover photograph courtesy of Marta Ostrowska/Trevillion Images
Typeset in 12.2/19.2 pt Minion Pro by Bookhouse, Sydney
Printed and bound in Australia by McPherson's Printing Group

The paper this book is printed on is certified against the
Forest Stewardship Council® Standards. McPherson's Printing
Group holds FSC® chain of custody certification SA-COC-005379.
FSC® promotes environmentally responsible, socially beneficial
and economically viable management of the world's forests.

*For my father, whose memoirs inspired me to write this book,
and whose embrace of life continues to inspire my days.*

Prologue

The hero of this book was not a saint, nor even a tzadik – the nearest Jewish equivalent – but he was a hero. Someone who risked his own life to make a difference to the life of another.

Were his motives selfless? No. He was after all flesh and blood. A man. And a very young one. But life is not black and white. Heroes are not without their flaws.

This, as well as I have been able to piece it together, is his story.

1

Technically, Tholdi – pronounced Toldi – had been a man already for exactly three years. Since his barmitzvah when by Jewish law he became accountable for his own actions. But according to Alex, Tholdi's best friend, there was another rite to be performed, another threshold to be crossed. And so it was, on a mild evening early in the European summer of 1941, that Tholdi found himself on a tram travelling towards an appointment to surrender his virginity.

Tholdi was younger than Alex by almost two years, but they were like brothers. They'd grown up in each other's homes, in the same apartment building with a shared courtyard. Their fathers had done business together. Their mothers had swapped recipes and secrets. And Alex, who lost his virginity at fifteen, had no doubt it was time for Tholdi to lose his. It had been useless for Tholdi to try to resist. After all, it made good sense. A man should have some knowledge of these things before his wedding day. Should not be inept. And if his family were still allowed to employ a maid, as most good families once did, she would no doubt have tutored Tholdi by now in subjects that his schoolteachers could not. That was how Alex had received instruction, as had Tholdi's father, Nathan, when he was a young man. Alex had made the appointment for Tholdi with Nathan's tacit blessing. If it weren't for his poor vision, even worse at night, Nathan might have accompanied Tholdi himself.

As the tram descended the main hill towards the Prut River, Tholdi took in the passing streetscape of the busy Hauptstrasse. Ringed by the fabled Carpathian Mountains, a place of wolves and castles and legends, and surrounded by the lush rolling farmlands of the Bukovina, Czernowitz had been for nearly a century and a half a jewel in the crown of the Austrian Empire. A large rural village that had flourished into a prosperous and enlightened university town with grand public buildings where royalty visited to watch plays and operas, and where famous musicians, performers and poets were born and celebrated. Its cobbled streets boasted long rows of elegant shops and handsome townhouses, three and four storeys tall. Adorned with Juliet balconies, fanciful domes and decorative turrets, they rivalled the architecture of Vienna itself. But at the end of the First World War the jewel, Little Vienna, was snatched by Romanian hands from the south. And now, less than a year after the start of yet another world war, it had been snatched again by its eastern neighbour, Russia.

In the Ringplatz, the city's central square, the tram stopped. Outside, the heavy presence of Soviet soldiers eclipsed the usual confetti of lively young university students on summer break, and the city's walls were plastered with giant posters of the soldiers' iron-fisted leader, Joseph Stalin. With his lustrous black hair and walrus moustache he projected the presence of a stern but heroic father. There was no hint of the tyrant responsible for the sudden disappearance of thousands of Czernowitz's citizens. Those 'bourgeois capitalists' of conspicuous wealth who had, without trial, been found guilty of oppressing their workers and deemed enemies of communism. Not that any of this was spoken of. Certainly not on a tram. Not when Stalin's informants were everywhere among them, and the possibility of exile to a barren Siberian gulag was only a malicious whisper away.

'Tholdi, did you hear me?'

Alex spoke in German. Despite the best efforts of the Romanian authorities, who'd spent the inter-war years of their rule trying to stamp it out, German remained the lingua franca of the educated, who never adopted the Romanian word Cernăuți for their city. The Jews of Czernowitz peppered their speech with Yiddish, as you'd expect in the place where Yiddish had been first recognised as an official language. That event had earned the city its other nickname: Jerusalem on the Prut.

'I heard you, Alex. Zaftik. She's zaftik.'

Voluptuous.

Alex wasn't speaking of Tholdi's girl, but the one he'd reserved for himself. The woman, though neither of them could possibly have known it then, who was destined to change everything.

'I think she's tsigayner.' Gypsy. 'But she's clean. All the girls there are, if that's what you're worried about.'

It wasn't. Nor was Tholdi worried, really, that his shmok – another Yiddish word, meaning penis as well as fool – might not rise to the occasion. What Tholdi was worried about, though he knew Alex would consider it weak and womanly, was that afterwards instead of pride he would feel regret. That he had not saved himself for a girl worthy of his desire. His love.

Was it his passion for music that had shaped these feelings? Those grand, sweeping operas full of exquisite, star-crossed longing? Or was it the other way around? Was it in his nature? Is that what drew him to the music? In any case the shameful truth of his anxiety remained unspoken.

'Tholdi, trust me, you won't have a problem,' Alex said.

What a day this achievement would crown. The news that Tholdi had been named top of his class *and* been awarded the school's most prestigious music prize – yet again; he'd won it every year – had filled his parents with the sort of pride an only child, worse still an only son, could not hope to evade. Particularly when it coincided with a birthday. In anticipation Tholdi's mother, Lina, had saved ration coupons for months. Had queued half a day to redeem them. Toiled for hours, happily, at her wood-fired oven to prepare the feast. Nathan had found a dusty bottle of Hungarian Tokay wine. Even Alex's younger sister, Peppa, had been allowed some.

Nathan raised his glass. 'L'chaim!' To life!

'To our young genius!' Jakob, Alex's father, proclaimed, a touch too loudly for comfort. A reminder to them all that Tholdi's scholastic accomplishments put Alex's in the shade.

Alex, who was usually quick with a clever retort, for once remained silent. But not because of any resentment. He was proud of his friend; if there was any envy between them it ran the other way. Tholdi, for all his success, looked up to Alex, and not just literally – Alex was a good head taller than him – but in other ways, too. Tholdi wished he possessed Alex's confidence. His athletic physicality. His swagger. No, Alex held his tongue because he had no interest this evening in a fight with his father, nor the time for it. He and Tholdi had plans.

'So, Nathan, what say you?' Jakob continued. 'I say doctor.'

Mira, Alex's mother, placed a cautioning hand over her husband's. 'Jakob, please, enough.'

He ignored her. 'Or a lawyer. Lawyer is good, too.'

'He's going to be a conductor.'

Peppa's words, spoken softly, landed like a grenade. An act of open rebellion. Jakob frowned. 'Was it you I asked?'

She opened her mouth to speak again, and then decided better of it. It was Tholdi's day. She didn't want to ruin it. Nathan stepped in to smooth things over. 'My son, whatever you decide we will be proud of you.'

In that moment Tholdi could not have been more grateful for his father's love. Unwavering, unconditional. They all raised their glasses, swallowed the sweet wine.

Leo, Tholdi's grandfather, clapped his hands.

'Berthold!' he commanded, signalling an imminent announcement demanding the gravitas of Tholdi's full name. 'I have a gift for you.'

From his pocket he produced something that since the arrival of the Soviets none of them had seen. His heavy gold signet ring. The one he'd had made when he was a young man. The one Tholdi had coveted almost since the day he had first sat on his grandfather's lap and touched it with his tiny infant fingers.

'Papa, no!' Lina cried.

'Bubala, why?'

Lina was now in middle age, but she remained Leo's bubala. His little darling.

'Because it's yours. Until the day you . . .' She refused to utter the word. 'It's too soon.'

'If we wait till then, I will never have the pleasure of the giving.'

Mira knew what lay behind Lina's outburst. Her fear that her father was inviting bad luck upon himself. She knew also how little patience Nathan had for superstition. It belonged, he felt, to the peasant classes. Mira tried a more rational approach.

'If Tholdi was seen wearing it in the street . . . People these days are taken away for much less.'

Leo shrugged his shoulders and everted his palms – the distinctive Jewish gesture of turning your hands palm up to prove they are empty; of surrender to the inevitable. 'So for now he does like me. Keeps the ring somewhere safe.'

Lina looked to Nathan – as always, the final arbiter, the judge – hoping for his support. Nathan looked to Leo's face, and to Tholdi's, before delivering his verdict.

'So long as he keeps it hidden.'

And with that it was settled.

Leo passed the ring to his grandson, who examined its familiar design. The rampant lion on top and, on the sides, the delicately carved edelweiss flowers. Symbols of a legend Leo had told him so many times. A legend that was now his.

'Thank you, Opa.'

The two men, from opposite ends of life, shared a smile. Lina felt an ominous shiver, a dark premonition she would later recall, run through her.

'Another bottle?' Jakob asked Nathan.

Alex caught Nathan's eye. Urged him to resist.

'One was all we had,' Nathan said.

Jakob knew his friend was holding out on him. 'Always with the hard bargain,' he complained. 'It's a wonder we ever made a deal at all.'

Alex broke his silence. 'We can't.'

'At last! He speaks!'

'They're expected,' Nathan reminded Jakob.

'At Friedl's place,' Alex added quickly. Cementing the small lie that had been agreed to among the men.

Jakob realised his mistake and was embarrassed by it. 'Of course. I forgot. My apologies.'

'What time will you be home?' Lina asked.

The question was for Tholdi, but Alex answered it. 'By ten. No later.'

'I still don't understand why I can't come too,' Peppa said.

Another moment of defiance. Directed this time at her brother, it was more strident. Alex's response was blunt, allowing no space for discussion.

'Because you can't.'

When, Peppa wondered, would they all stop treating her like a child? Acknowledge that at fourteen she was already a young woman?

At the front door Lina pressed a woollen scarf into her son's hands. Implored him to take care. Kissed him on the cheek before she watched him go with Alex. Prayed to God no harm would come to them.

———

'Hey, Jew boys! Isn't this your stop?'

The voice, Tholdi realised, had come from a group of four youths who'd boarded the carriage.

'The rabbi is that way!'

The youth jerked his head in the direction of the synagogue that was two streets over. It wasn't the only synagogue, nor even the oldest, but it was by far the most known. Its magnificent Moorish dome made it famous.

Tholdi and Alex exchanged a glance.

Another youth joined in. 'What's the matter? Can't hear us?'

This, not the weather, was what Lina had feared. The Jewish population of Czernowitz was large, some forty per cent of the city's total. More than half of them had arrived during the Austrian era, from territories to the west. For the most part they had been accepted, or at the very least tolerated; without them there would have been no Little Vienna. But there were those Czernowitzers who had long harboured envy and resentment. They wished the city was still part of Romania, which had allied itself with Germany and was now dealing decisively with 'the Jewish problem', just as Hitler had been doing for years.

Tholdi understood that he, not Alex, had attracted the unwanted attention. If Alex were blond he could easily have passed as Aryan – his blue eyes and broad shoulders helped him blend in. Tholdi's features – his dark, deep-set eyes, his pale complexion and slender frame – as well as his reserved nature fitted the myth of the typical sensitive Jew of books and numbers much more neatly.

The third youth found his voice. 'Maybe he hasn't cleaned the shit from his ears lately!'

And then the fourth: 'Maybe he couldn't get past his beak!'

It was a weak joke – neither Tholdi nor Alex had the exaggerated hooked nose the fascists liked to caricature – but the youths all laughed anyway.

Tholdi saw the clenched fists in Alex's lap. Weapons that Tholdi knew his friend wanted to use. He thought of Lina, the hand that would leap to her breast if they came home covered in blood. *Alex, please, don't*, his eyes implored. In the end, Alex remained in his seat. Said and did nothing.

The youth who had spoken first had the last word. 'Same as all your lot,' he sneered. 'Cowards.' He turned to the others. 'Come on!'

As the tram lurched forward again, resuming its descent, they leapt from it, another burst of their laughter cutting coldly through the warm night air.

2

Lyuba. Her name meant 'love'.

She sat now before the mirror, thinking about that. About love. It was a beautiful word, but it fell too easily from people's lips. It couldn't be trusted. It was almost a relief that in a place like this it was rarely heard. She didn't care that the work she did was looked down upon by other, supposedly respectable, women. If anything, she felt sorry for them. For the interminable negotiations, the need to ask or beg their husbands for whatever they wanted. The constant seeking of approval and permission. She was glad she'd escaped that life.

Sometimes the men who hired her got swept up in the moment. Fell back on saccharine clichés, allowed the line between sex and affection to become blurred. She found that orgasm, once the brief exhilaration of it had passed, generally fixed the problem within a matter of seconds.

Lyuba also liked that where she worked was safe. The streets were cold and dangerous. More than once she'd been bashed or robbed. Or both. Here, in a building that was once a splendid hotel patronised by the wealthy and titled, there was heating, hot showers and security. Even the coarsest of their clientele these days, the soldiers, knew to respect the girls. Any transgressions were swiftly dealt with.

Shame? She had none. Nor did she ever dream of the day a rich and handsome client might rescue her. Not even a rich and plain one. She didn't delude herself with the fairytales so many of her fellow workers secretly tucked under their pillows each night to help them sleep.

She was grateful she'd been blessed with the sort of physical assets that men desired. It gave her a measure of power over them, even if she had to exert it slyly, without ever threatening their pride or sense of authority. It was a game at which she'd become adept. And which, after all, she only had to play for an hour or two at a time. Her circumstances could be far worse. She often reminded herself that they once had been.

Reapplying the mask of her make-up, preparing for her next customer, she paid special attention to the subtle touches of rouge that simulated arousal. That made her clients believe their presence excited her.

'Lyuba?'

The door opened. In the mirror, over Lyuba's shoulder, the brothel's owner appeared. A slight woman of advancing years who dyed her hair a bright rust red and went by the alluring faux-Parisian name of Madame Denile.

'Your next customer is here. Alex, the boy.'

Lyuba remembered him well. She knew that he saw himself not as a boy but as a man. And that, despite the years between them, he saw her not as a woman but as a girl. It didn't bother her. She had clients who expected her to play more demanding roles. Mother, daughter, virgin, victim, torturer. She was a versatile actress. Victim was the part she liked least, but she would willingly play even that, for the space of an hour or two, on her own terms. She had only one rule she never broke: no kissing.

'Hurry, please. We are busy.'

'Yes, madame,' she obediently replied.

—

In the lounge, Tholdi and Alex sat waiting. The décor, like Madame Denile, had seen better days. It reminded Tholdi of the stage set for an opera – *La Traviata*, the tale of the fallen woman. Only in an opera house you wouldn't need to endure the loud, foul-breathed customers, full of vodka and bravado, stumbling past.

Alex whispered to Tholdi. 'Here she comes.'

As Lyuba approached with Madame Denile, Alex rose to his feet. Tholdi also stood, the habit of manners.

'Alex,' Lyuba said. 'Good to see you again.'

'You too.'

It was said that Roma have the power to hypnotise. There's no doubt that on the night Tholdi met Lyuba she cast over him a kind of spell.

I think she's tsigayner.

The thick coal-black hair that softened her angular features – the prominent cheekbones, the deep hollows beneath them, the broad, sharp jaw – confirmed it, but her skin was a pale, almost golden shade of Romani olive and her eyes, a vivid green, reminded Tholdi of unripened Bukovina plums. Was she beautiful? By the demure conventions of her day perhaps not. But, whatever her heritage, she was without question exotic. Different. Other.

Tholdi was also struck by the way Lyuba carried herself. Against Madame Denile's advice that men preferred women who looked up to them, who knew how to make themselves seem lesser and subservient, Lyuba walked with her shoulders squared and her chin held high. It seemed to Tholdi a deliberate display of strength and poise. He wondered what was behind it.

Alex saw none of this. His attention was fixed upon the undulating contours of Lyuba's form, its promising delights. Madame Denile did not fail to notice his eager anticipation.

'I see she's made an impression. I should charge you extra.'

Alex regretted his indiscretion.

Madame Denile reassured him. 'Relax, Alex, I was teasing you.'

Alex remembered Tholdi was with them. Pleased for the chance to deflect attention, he introduced him. 'This is my friend. The one I told you about.'

Tholdi felt naked. He knew they were all aware of his inexperience. As he was often prone to do, he blushed.

Lyuba's eyes found his. 'A pleasure to meet you,' she said.

Tholdi had never met a Roma before. He was familiar with their music – it was vibrant, full of joy – and Romani men were sometimes seen in the town, where they were employed as labourers, but socially the two groups never mixed. Although they might not often have said it aloud, Jews generally regarded Roma as inferior. A tribe of outsiders even less accepted than their own.

Lyuba waited for Tholdi's reply.

'And for me,' he finally managed.

With an air of chivalry, as if he were escorting her to some gala occasion, Alex offered Lyuba his arm. 'Shall we?' He was impatient to be alone with her.

Lyuba farewelled Tholdi. 'Enjoy your evening.'

Then she and Alex, arms linked, left the lounge and made their way down a dimly lit hallway lined with many doors. Tholdi's eyes followed them.

Madame Denile studied Tholdi's still-flushed cheeks. He had a boy's face, one that had never seen a razor. Had he really just turned sixteen, as Alex had said? He looked younger. Not that it mattered. She patted his wrist – a kind, motherly gesture. 'Let me see what's keeping your girl,' she said, and left in a rustle of silk skirts.

Tholdi looked back down the hallway as Lyuba opened one of the doors. It threw a shaft of light into the corridor, making her glow like an apparition. Lyuba sensed that she was being watched, felt the touch of it, and turned to see Tholdi staring. Not with lust, a desire to have her, but something else. Something that, in this house of illusions, was far more unsettling. The desire to know her.

Alex, too, noticed Tholdi's spellbound gaze. He placed a possessive arm around Lyuba's waist, guided her into the room and closed the door, plunging the hallway back into darkness.

3

Three weeks after their meeting at the brothel Tholdi received a visit from Lyuba, in a dream. They were together in an alpine meadow surrounded by snow-draped mountain peaks. Their bed was a profusion of white, star-shaped edelweiss flowers, as soft as a down-feather mattress. Despite the altitude, the air was warm on his skin, and from a cloudless blue sky came the incongruous thunder of an approaching storm. Lyuba's extraordinary green eyes were open wide, gazing into his.

It was from this dream that Tholdi woke to a pre-dawn morning of damp, sticky sheets, the wail of air-raid sirens and distant explosions. His parents were not in their bed. In the dim rooms of his home, Tholdi searched for them.

'Mama? Papa?' he called out.

There was no reply. Tholdi looked down to the street and found his parents among a small crowd that had gathered. Alex and his family were there, too.

Rushing down the stairs, still in his nightclothes, Tholdi ran past Doina, the widowed gentile who lived in the ground-floor apartment. She followed him outside.

'What's happening?' Tholdi asked Nathan.

A German bomber swooped low over the rooftops, and roared towards the airport. Anti-aircraft fire, bright as lightning, flashed up in the sky. The sound of it was deafening. Moments later the bombs hit their target and another round of distant explosions was followed by thick columns of smoke, illuminated by sweeping searchlights.

'We're at war.'

No-one had anticipated it, not even Nathan, who'd defied the ban on radios the Russians had imposed. With help from Tholdi he'd hauled his down into the basement and concealed it artfully behind a false wall. There, with the volume kept low, he listened each day to the long-wave broadcasts from London and Berlin, and news of a war which, until this morning, had not directly touched Eastern Europe. Overnight that had all changed. Hitler had torn up his non-aggression pact with Stalin and launched his ill-fated quest to conquer Russia. It was only a matter of time before the Romanians returned to reclaim Czernowitz – bringing the Germans with them.

'Maybe,' Mira said, 'it will be better than the Russians.'

Doina looked at Mira as if she were mad. 'Have you not heard what's been happening to your people?'

Mira had heard but didn't want to believe. Germany, like its cultural cousin, Austria, still symbolised for many Czernowitzers a civilised world of art and music and poetry. And so much of what Nathan reported to them had to be propaganda. When all sides broadcast such different versions of events what else could you conclude?

—

Almost immediately the killing began. From inside her apartment Doina heard banging on her door. She flung it open and confronted the young Romanian soldier standing before her.

'I'm a Romanian citizen! And a Christian!'

Without waiting to be asked, she thrust her identity papers at the soldier. A second soldier arrived and looked up the winding stairwell.

'Are there Jews up there?'

'There were. They left.'

The soldiers exchanged a glance. Doina retrieved her papers. 'Go see for yourself.'

They did. The doors were unlocked, and inside they found wardrobes emptied of clothes, drawers wide open, hangers tossed onto the floor. They'd found the same in other apartments where Jews had made the decision to flee the city. It wasn't a wise one; in the nearby villages hardly a single Jew survived.

The soldiers returned to the ground floor. 'Let's check the basement!'

Behind the radio's false wall, squeezed together with the others, Tholdi heard the basement door open and, a moment later, the flick of a switch. A strip of electric light burst in through the gap at their feet.

Tholdi thought he could hear his own heartbeat. Fearing his mother might faint, he held onto her tightly. He heard the soldiers' footsteps advance. The woodstack tumbled to the ground.

A voice called from the stairwell. 'We found more of them! Come!'

The soldiers' footsteps receded and moments later Tholdi heard them on the footpath outside, thumping past the basement's wood hatch. Only then did he and his family allow themselves to breathe again. And to accept Doina's offer of refuge.

For four days and nights Doina hid them in a room that had once been her son's. On a dresser was a photograph of him, not much older than Tholdi, wearing a uniform from the last world war. The one they said would end all wars.

When the horror outside – the ceaseless pounding of boots, the relentless gunfire, the screams of men, women and children hunted and slaughtered like animals by civilians and soldiers alike – when it all finally ceased, it was replaced by a terrible calm.

Doina came to them with news. 'They say it's over.'

Lina didn't believe it.

'Bubala, we can't stay here forever.' Leo was right. He gave Doina their heartfelt thanks.

'What did I have left to lose?' she replied.

After the rotting bodies were cleared from the streets – over two thousand had been butchered – a semblance of normality returned. Shops re-opened, farmers returned with fresh produce, and new ration cards, Romanian ones, were distributed. For Jews, the allowance was meagre but it was something. Better than a bullet. Afraid for their safety, Jakob insisted that the women stay home, and went to collect the coupons himself. Tholdi and Alex went with him. From those who lived close to the river they heard about the German SS squads that had rounded up their community's leaders – the rabbis, intellectuals and other trouble-makers – and lined them up along the bank. Machine-gun fire had echoed across the water. The rabbi of the city's famous Moorish synagogue had been made to watch its marvellous dome reduced to ashes before he, too, was shot.

Under the previous Romanian government, before the Russians came, citizenship for Jews had been revoked. Now, one by one, their remaining rights were dismantled. New edicts prohibited them from holding positions of authority and from attending places of education or worship, as well as libraries, cinemas and theatres. They were allowed outside for only three hours a day and only with a yellow star pinned to their clothing. They were also made to apply for a new Romanian identity card. It, too, bore the yellow star. All of it was enforced by gendarmes, armed military police, who were everywhere in the town, at all hours.

Walking the street one day, Tholdi and Alex were stopped by soldiers. At gunpoint they were ordered to get onto a truck full of other Jewish men and boys wearing yellow stars, and driven down to the river. Tholdi was sure they were all about to be shot. But instead they were put to work repairing the bridge the fleeing Russians had destroyed. It was back-breaking labour but Tholdi was glad to have Alex beside him, and grateful that they were both fed more than the watery soup their two families were barely surviving on at home.

After two months, when the bridge was finally finished, a last convoy of trucks and tanks and ambulances rolled across, pushing ever deeper into the territory through which the Soviets had fled. And in the so-called Jewish ditch just up from the bridge, where the city's poorest Jews lived, another construction project took shape – a three-metre-high fence.

Walking home one day, Tholdi and Alex paused to watch it going up. They both understood its meaning.

'Now,' said Alex, 'it really begins.'

4

The fence, three metres high and topped with barbed wire, formed a triangle around a spider's web of smaller, roughly cobbled streets and alleys – Gassen – lined with squat, beaten-looking dwellings that were a world removed from the elegant neighbourhoods up the hill.

On a sunless morning in early October, ten days after Yom Kippur, all of the city's Jews, those who had survived the first few months, were told to make their way down to the ghetto. The orders were delivered street to street by gendarmes shouting in German and Romanian. Those who disobeyed were shot.

Closing up their home, locking the doors and windows, Tholdi wondered if securing their apartment was futile. 'Won't they come anyway?'

They. Those who would now feel entitled to appropriate the wealth they had for so long envied. Nathan locked it all up anyway, and for luck kissed his fingers and touched the mezuzah attached to the doorframe.

On the street, Doina farewelled her neighbours with hugs and tears. Wishing there had been more she could offer them, she watched the two families depart on foot, taking with them whatever valuables they could carry. Anything more was forbidden.

At the Hauptstrasse they joined the river of yellow stars flowing slowly up and over the city's main hill. It was still autumn but a delicate drift of early snowflakes fluttered down, giving the procession a strangely festive look. People gathered on the footpaths as if it were a parade. Tholdi saw that many were barely able to look, but many others watched without pity.

The ghetto's fence was patrolled day and night. Inside it, where four thousand had once lived there were now more than ten times that many. For a fair price Nathan arranged accommodation on the Berggasse with the family of a man who had once been his employee. Room was also found there for Mira, Peppa and Leo. Alex and Jakob were taken in by neighbours opposite. Everyone made sleeping arrangements wherever they could in the dank little cottages, on furniture as well as under it, ten to a room.

After sharing a first, sombre meal with their new hosts, Tholdi and Alex met out on the street. The night was cold but the snow had stopped falling and the air was still. The two friends were grateful for a moment alone. Beneath a clear, star-filled sky they discussed what their futures held. Ghettos had existed in the German territories for more than two years, and their prisoners were transported to the so-called detention camps from which no-one these days returned – Dachau, Birkenau, Auschwitz and the rest. But where would they be taken? Had the Romanians constructed camps for their own Jews? No-one believed what they were being told – that they were to be 'resettled'.

Alex said he hoped it was somewhere sunny. 'I could do with a tan.'

It was the bleakest of jokes but Tholdi understood that his friend was looking for a way, any way, to resist the overwhelming despair. And that it was humour that in the end would be more valuable to them than any of the possessions they had carried from their homes.

Demonstrating the improved efficiency they had learned from the Germans' methods, Romanian troops, assisted by gendarmes, began the exodus without delay. For three days coordinated dawn raids saw whole streets of the ghetto descended upon and cleared. Terrified souls were ordered from their beds at gunpoint and then marched, sobbing and shaking, to the freight yards on the northern edge of town, down by the waters of the Prut. Some paid from their own pockets to ride on farm wagons, usually used for carting produce to the town's markets. Local farmers discovered that carting bodies – the old and the sick, as well as corpses – was a lucrative sideline. At the trains everyone – men, women, young, old, babies – were prodded with bayonets and guns up the cattle ramps and crammed inside the bare wooden cars. In the first three days, more than fifteen thousand were taken.

To maintain control, no warning was given which street would be cleared next. On the day that the Berggasse was chosen, only the east side was emptied. No doubt the decision was based on arithmetic. A calculation of how many bodies could be fitted into that day's trains. Watching her husband and son being taken from across the street, just metres away, Mira howled like a wild animal. Tholdi had to help Lina drag her away from a soldier's cocked pistol. Alex shouted that he would one day return. A promise that only a mother could persuade herself he might be able to keep.

It was a bitter mercy that Leo didn't have to witness it. He had died on their second day in the ghetto, of a heart attack. Lina recalled her father giving Tholdi the ring, and the premonition that had sent a shiver through her. They were not permitted to bury him immediately, as Jewish custom dictated, and the Kaddish could not be recited, but Lina covered her father's body with his prayer shawl and stayed with him day and night, reading aloud to him from the psalms in his prayer book. Three days later a farmer's cart arrived to take his body away, along with a heap of others, for a group interment in an anonymous piece of ground that the approaching winter had not yet frozen over.

Then, soon after Alex and Jakob had gone, barely more than two weeks after the ghetto had been established, a rumour spread like wildfire through the streets. News so good that even Lina, still grieving the loss of her father, saw hope.

'Can it be true? Has there really been a change of heart?' she asked.

'There is no heart in this,' said Nathan. 'They need us.'

On this occasion, Nathan was wrong. The city's mayor did have a heart and seeing what was happening to the Jews of his city was breaking it. Desperately, he put it to his new masters that if all the city's Jews were evacuated – the word they used – the economy would collapse. In the end he convinced them to cease the transportations and let him draw up a list of twenty thousand skilled Jews who could be returned to useful work.

With Tholdi by his side, Nathan made the journey to the school on Landhausgasse, now used for the ghetto's administration, where applications for release were being considered. It was chaos. A desperate frenzy of people clamouring, shouting, shoving to get to the front and have applications approved. For those drawing up the lists it was yet another wartime business opportunity. Merit was a minor consideration; bribery, endemic even during peace time, flourished unchecked. Long ago, before the Russians came, Nathan had started hoarding American currency, which was still the most sought after in Eastern Europe. The official he dealt with, a municipal clerk, made it clear that getting his family on the list would take most of it. To have Mira and Peppa added would require all of it. Nathan emptied his pockets of every last dollar bill. To prove he'd done so he turned them inside out. The clerk slipped the notes into his own bulging pockets and nodded at the wristwatches Nathan and Tholdi wore. Those, too, were handed over. Only then did the clerk dip his pen into the inkwell and add their names. Would they be approved? They had to wait.

In the meantime, the ghetto became a stinking cesspit. Two of the city's three pumping stations had been destroyed by the retreating Russians. Without any proper sanitation and denied fresh food, it became a place of famine and disease. And then finally, five weeks after that first long walk, Tholdi and his parents, together with Mira and Peppa, were among the lucky twenty thousand who filed out of the ghetto and made their way back through the city's streets, back through eerie neighbourhoods full of vacant buildings, to reclaim their homes.

5

Tholdi had been right about the locks; they had been useless. The thieves had smashed their way in and removed anything of obvious value. His most prized possession, the upright piano his parents had bought for him when he was just five years old, lay in pieces halfway down the winding central stairway.

Doina tearfully recounted how the thieves had swept through the city. Powerless to stop any of it, she had locked herself inside her apartment. It was some consolation that Nathan's precious long-wave radio remained, undiscovered behind its false wall in the basement.

Among the broken glass and scattered possessions of her home, or what remained of it, Mira found her photo album full of black-and-white memories of everything, everyone, that mattered to her. Most of the pictures had been taken with Alex's camera which, it turned out, was no longer where he had hidden it. Tholdi found Mira and Peppa sitting together, trying to separate the pages of the photo album without tearing them apart. They stank of urine. Tholdi recalled the youths on the tram, the ones Alex had wanted to fight, and pictured them unzipping their trousers to desecrate the images. Could it have been them? Maybe. There were many more like them now – people who took pleasure in humiliating the 'filthy Jews'.

Somehow, life had to go on. Together, they swept up the glass and did their best to create some sort of order, some semblance of domestic normality. Nathan insisted that Mira and Peppa, two women without a man, should not live alone. Peppa moved into Leo's old room and Mira took the quarters where once a maid had slept. A clock was found – why the looters had not taken it no-one understood – and its time re-set. From the photo album Mira selected pictures of Jakob and Alex, cleaned them as best she could, and made a shrine where she would light candles daily and pray for the safe return of her husband and son. The piano was turned into firewood.

When it was all done, Nathan took Tholdi aside.

'My son, it is a heavy burden I must now ask you to carry. One you should not have to shoulder at so young an age.'

'Papa, I know. I understand.'

This was the moment when Tholdi truly became a man, responsible not only for himself but for two families now living as one.

The first challenge was to put food in their mouths. Doina knew of a man, a buyer and seller of used goods and chattels, who had also managed to secure release from the ghetto. Into a broken leather suitcase Tholdi packed anything that might be saleable and hauled it nearly two kilometres, on foot, to a small house, a run-down villa, on Fabrikgasse. It was one of the few houses that the looters had left untouched. When Tholdi drew close, the reason became apparent. From within came ferocious barking, a terrifying sound. Tholdi, who'd never been comfortable around dogs, was about to walk away when an old man opened the door. His beard was greying and unkempt, hair sprouted like weeds from each of his nostrils, and his eyebrows reminded Tholdi of two wild blackberry bushes.

Moritz didn't need to ask the purpose of Tholdi's visit. The suitcase, as well as the yellow star pinned to his shirt, told him everything.

Through bared teeth, the dogs snarled at Tholdi, smelling his fear, sensing their owner's natural distrust. 'Ladies, settle, settle,' Moritz said, and the dogs sullenly obeyed as he ushered Tholdi in.

As he entered, Tholdi noted the brass mezuzah attached to the doorframe, inside which, presumably, were words from the holy Torah. It signified that Moritz had a covenant with God. Or claimed to.

Inside, there was barely room to move. In every direction Tholdi looked there were household goods – clocks, vases, Persian rugs. Moritz's was another enterprise enjoying a wartime boom. Tholdi wondered if that was a second reason the looters had left Moritz's house untouched. He was the kind of man who paid cash, without asking awkward questions about the provenance of his purchases.

'So, show me what you have.'

Tholdi untied the rope that held the suitcase together and laid out what the looters had left behind – a set of fine bed linen, a hand-embroidered tablecloth, an ivory manicure set, two hair combs, a fox-fur stole.

Moritz felt sorry for the boy, but he was not running a charity. 'Come, let me show you,' he said.

Through a room with refrigerators, crates of wine and all kinds of mouth-watering luxuries, savoury and sweet, in jars and tins and boxes, Moritz led Tholdi to the rear of the house. Moritz flicked a light switch, and the naked bulb revealed another room crammed with exactly the kind of items Tholdi had hoped to trade. Shelf upon shelf, stacked all the way to the ceiling.

'I can't sell any of it,' Moritz said. 'And I have no more space.'

Tholdi saw the problem.

'Have you nothing else?' Moritz asked.

Tholdi had anticipated this possibility. After all, it was word of mouth that had led him to Moritz's door. Common sense had told him that many others would have come bearing similar items. From a pocket he produced Leo's ring. He had kept it safe, as Leo had asked him to, and been relieved that it had not been needed at the old schoolhouse on Landhausgasse. Moritz's eyes, Tholdi saw, lit up at the sight of it.

'It's gold. Eighteen carat,' Tholdi said.

Moritz's tangled eyebrows levitated with mock surprise. 'You're a jeweller's son?'

The haggling had begun.

'My grandfather told me. It was his.'

'I see. May I hold it?'

Reluctantly, Tholdi gave Moritz the ring. Watched him examine it, turn it in his hand. Silently admire the fine crafts-manship. Feel its weight.

'It's almost two ounces,' Tholdi said.

Moritz didn't question it. His fingers traced the designs etched into the ring. 'The lion, I assume, is for courage.'

Tholdi nodded. It was. He told himself to be brave.

'And the flowers?'

Tholdi was reluctant to answer. Moritz raised a questioning eyebrow. *Do you want a sale or not?* it seemed to ask.

'Edelweiss.'

'I thought so. Your grandfather was a romantic.'

Maybe that's where Tholdi got it from. Why Tholdi's visit to the brothel had gone so differently to the way Alex had planned it.

'You know the legend?' Moritz asked.

Of course Tholdi did. He didn't need or want to hear it again now, but Moritz told it anyway.

'The first edelweiss flowers of the season bloom in the highest reaches of the mountains. If a young man wants to impress his sweetheart, he will risk his neck to pick them for her.'

Tholdi hoped in his heart that Leo could forgive him for what he was about to do.

'How much?' he asked Moritz.

'Make me an offer.'

'Three thousand.'

Moritz whistled through his teeth.

Tholdi stood his ground. 'The gold alone is worth that much.'

'One thousand.'

Tholdi's face flushed with anger. He wanted to grab the ring back and walk away.

'Two and a half.'

'Fifteen hundred. My final offer.'

Moritz held the ring out to Tholdi. Knowing the boy couldn't afford to leave with it. That he was desperate. 'Believe me, you won't get a better price from anyone else.'

Tholdi watched as Moritz counted out the notes. It was all he could do not to embarrass himself with tears.

When the transaction was complete, and Tholdi had repacked his suitcase, Moritz asked: 'So, what now? I expect you will be needing a job.'

Tholdi did not reply. Moritz understood his pain. There had been many others like him. There would be many more.

'Well, if you do I can tell you where to find one.'

6

The town had two weaving mills. The larger one stood close to a bend in the Prut, which carried away the waste that the factories in the area discharged. It was a massive steel structure, an industrial cathedral with a row of lantern windows that ran the length of the roof's spine. Tholdi was not a stranger to the mill, but it had been nearly two years since he'd entered it. He stood now in its giant shadow like an orphan, still gripping the heavy suitcase, deciding how to present himself.

Inside, light fell in glorious sheets across the long, straight rows of mechanised looms. Attending them was a small army of workers, men and women, loading and re-loading the batteries of bobbin shuttles, the pirns, that flew back and forth, weaving the weft threads through the parallel filaments of the warp. Each worker watched closely for any breakages, occasionally stopping a machine to hastily fix the problem. The noise it all made was deafening – the clicking and clacking of the frames, the whizzing sound of the flying pirns, the whirring of machinery, the fork-lifts unloading and stacking the finished rolls of fabric, all of it echoing. The workers seemed immune to it, as if they, too, were tireless machines. More than half of them wore a black armband with the words 'work Jew' in yellow.

'You! I'm talking to you!'

Tholdi realised that a voice was trying to make itself heard over the din, and turned to see one of the mill's overseers, not more than ten metres away. Tholdi went to him.

'Did you want something?' the man asked.

'Work. I'm looking for work.'

The overseer inspected Tholdi, then glanced up to a plat-form high above the factory floor, at the far end of the building. From it were draped two enormous flags that reached halfway to the ground – one bearing Romania's national colours, the other a swastika. Standing behind them, looking down, was a man in a suit and tie. Tholdi knew his face: it was Grigore, one of the two brothers who ran the mill. Before disappearing from sight, Grigore gestured for the boy to be sent up.

'Go on, then,' the overseer prompted.

Still clutching the suitcase, Tholdi wondered how he would manage the narrow, exposed staircase.

'Leave the bag.'

Tholdi hesitated, fearing it would not be there when he returned.

'Do you want work or not?'

Tholdi set down the case, made his way to the far end of the mill floor and began the climb. Reaching the top of the stairs, arriving at the open central space which separated two glassed-in offices, he saw Grigore had withdrawn to the one further from the stairs. On a large desk he was placing rough gold ingots one by one onto a set of scales, and making notes in a ledger.

Grigore closed the ledger and beckoned Tholdi, who stopped at the office's open doorway.

'So, you want a job.'

'Yes, mein Herr.'

'Do you have any experience?'

Tholdi had wondered if Grigore would remember him. Maybe, Tholdi decided, it was for the best that he hadn't.

'I'm a very fast learner.'

'Is that so?'

'Yes, mein Herr.' And Tholdi added: 'In my last year at school I topped my class.'

Grigore laughed. A deep, full-throated laugh. There was cruelty in it. Through the office window he spotted his brother.

'Radu! Come in here!'

Somewhat anxiously, wondering what it was that his brother wanted from him, Radu obeyed.

'Radu, this is . . . What's your name?'

'Berthold.'

'Berthold is a genius.'

That word again.

'Do we have a place on the floor for a genius?'

'Mein Herr, please, I only meant . . .'

Grigore silenced him with a gesture. To his brother he said, 'No experience, but a fast learner. So he claims.'

Radu studied Tholdi. Tholdi studied the floor.

'Don't we know you?' Radu asked.

Tholdi did not reply.

'Is your father not Herr Linker?'

Still no reply from Tholdi. A look between the brothers.

'Answer, boy!' Grigore demanded.

'Yes, mein Herr.'

Radu nodded. 'I thought so.'

Now Grigore studied Tholdi more closely. 'Look at me, boy.'

Tholdi obeyed, raised his eyes.

'Well, well, so it is.'

The situation – the son of the previous owners, begging him for a job – brought a thin smile to Grigore's lips.

'Why didn't you say so?'

'I don't know, mein Herr.'

Grigore turned to his brother. 'The genius doesn't know.'

Radu felt for the boy. It was Tholdi's father who had given Radu his first job in the factory; who had recognised his potential and promoted him, still in his thirties, to the position of senior engineer. When the Russians came, they had nationalised the business, removing the Linkers as owners. Tholdi could no longer work there after school – he was not then of legal age – but

Radu had been able to negotiate a job for Nathan, insisting he was useful to the business, saving him from a Soviet labour camp. Grigore had not been keen to keep Nathan on, but he was new at the time, brought in by his brother to run the business side of things. He'd bowed at first to Radu's experience but now things were very different. In commercial matters the final decisions were his, and sentiment played no part in them. He, like the Germans, was a numbers man.

'So what do you say, Radu? Asset or liability?'

7

Over a soup of beans and potatoes served with thick slices of fresh bread, the heartiest meal they had eaten in months, the two families celebrated their good turn of fortune. Like Grigore, Nathan saw the irony. He had not seen either of the brothers for some time – it was not long after the Russians came that his sight had started to decline dramatically, forcing him to retire from the mill – but he remembered Radu fondly. He was a gentle man. To him he owed his life. Nathan was pleased Tholdi would be working for him.

'He asked me to pass his regards to you,' Tholdi said.

It was a lie, but a harmless one. The more dangerous lies – the secrets and omissions, the betrayals and broken promises – came later. The most dangerous would be the lies Tholdi told to himself.

'Please give him mine.'

'I will, Papa.'

'It was very kind of him to advance you some money,' said Lina.

That was the other lie Tholdi told that night. The one that explained where he'd got the money to pay for their meal. He'd returned with the suitcase still full, and food for the table, as well as enough cash to have their broken front door repaired.

'Could I get work there?' Peppa asked.

'You know the answer to that,' Mira told her daughter. 'You are not yet sixteen.'

'I could pass as sixteen.'

'Peppa!'

'Really, Mama? After all they're doing to us, you're shocked at the thought of me lying about my age?'

'I had to show them my identity card,' Tholdi said. 'They'd discover your lie soon enough.'

'You can change the age on it. I wouldn't be the first,' Peppa said.

'And if you were caught, you wouldn't be the first to be shot,' Tholdi replied.

She scowled. 'All of a sudden you think you're so grown up.'

'Peppa, he's right,' Nathan said, and she conceded defeat. She didn't argue with Nathan.

'Is the other brother still there?' Lina asked. She'd never met him, but she'd heard enough about Grigore to be wary.

'Yes.'

It disturbed Lina to hear that, but Tholdi was lucky to have found paid work, even if Grigore was still there.

'And the wage?' she asked.

'Half.'

Peppa baulked. 'Half what the gentiles get?'

Nathan quoted the old Jewish adage: 'Fifty per cent of something is better than one hundred of nothing.'

The hours were long, too, with only one day off each week. But it meant that Tholdi would now be officially registered as a Jew who was contributing to the war effort; a useful Jew to be spared from random acts of violence or arrest.

'I'm proud of you, my son.'

Tholdi wondered whether his father would have bestowed such praise if he knew how his son had paid for the meal they were eating. Tholdi hoped that if Leo was looking down on him now he too would be proud of the man his grandson had become today – the family's breadwinner, their rock – and forgive him for parting with the ring.

8

Tholdi had never worked the machines. Only swept the floors and tidied the stock. But after school, for countless hours, he'd watched how it was all done, and he did prove to be, as he'd promised, a fast learner. He quickly mastered the required skills. How to swiftly re-load the pirns. How to ensure the yarn fed smoothly from them into the rise and fall of the loom. How to minimise thread breakages and stoppages, and maximise output. He learned, too, how to drive the forklifts. The more useful a worker, the better his chances of keeping his job. And he made a new friend – Karl.

Karl reminded Tholdi of Alex. He was shorter in stature but of similar age and, despite the tragic loss of his parents months earlier, always quick to see the humour in things. Like Alex, his jokes were his armour. His forte was impersonations.

He had found lodgings only a few streets from Tholdi's family and, when their shifts coincided, the two boys walked home together. One afternoon, Karl nudged Tholdi.

'Up ahead.'

Outside one of the buildings the German command now occupied, a soldier in full uniform was standing so rigidly to attention, with such a serious, fixed expression, that he might have been a stone statue. Or, as Karl suggested, someone trying very hard not to fart. As they drew closer, Karl blew a raspberry. The soldier didn't hear it, but he did see Tholdi stop in his tracks and explode with laughter. The statue sprang to life, grabbed Tholdi by the throat and threw him against the wall.

'Damned Jew! Do you think you can get away with that?'

Tholdi was too terrified to speak.

'Please, mein Herr,' Karl pleaded, 'forgive him. He's retarded. A half-wit.'

The soldier looked into Tholdi's eyes and saw dumb terror. The idea that Tholdi had some kind of mental disability was entirely credible.

With a rough shove, the soldier released him. 'Go! Both of you!'

They ran. When they'd turned the next corner, Karl started to laugh, so hard he could barely breathe. Once the shock had passed, Tholdi laughed with him. When he could speak again, when the laughter subsided, he pointed out that they could have been killed.

'Yes, but we weren't,' Karl said. 'Thanks to me *not* being retarded.'

Tholdi punched his arm, but it was true. His friend's quick thinking had saved Tholdi's life. And as reckless as Karl could be, he reminded Tholdi that they were still young – just teenagers after all. If it hadn't been for the rumour that Karl shared with him it might have been possible, despite the war, for Tholdi to lead a relatively carefree existence.

From another worker, Karl had heard that yet more lists of names were being made and submitted to the province's governor – not for Jews who would be spared from the trains but for Jews who would be put on them. And places like the mill were collaborating. Submitting names to be added.

'The trains are going to start again?'

Seeing Tholdi's fear, Karl did his best to play it down. 'Hey, it's just a rumour,' he said.

At home, when asked how the job was going, Tholdi made no mention of what Karl had shared. Lina's heart was unreliable, as her father's had been, and she'd already had one 'turn'. She was lucky to have survived it. Tholdi worried that the truth would be enough to kill her. Besides, so many rumours circulated. Everyone lived day to day, not knowing anything with certainty. But the prospect of the trains starting again would not leave Tholdi's thoughts.

Then one day a miracle occurred, one that would change everything.

Tholdi was at the market in the Ringplatz. There was a commotion, an argument between a farmer and a young woman, just metres from where Tholdi stood. He recognised the woman instantly. The farmer was accusing her of intending to steal an apple. Lyuba accused him of overcharging for inferior-quality fruit. People – mostly other women shopping, but also nearby stallholders – were looking. The farmer called over a gendarme and told him that Lyuba had tried to slip the apple into her bag. When she angrily denied it, he called her a lying Gypsy.

The gendarme appraised the woman before him more closely.

'Do you have papers?'

'I left them at home.'

'A likely story!' the farmer scoffed.

The gendarme turned to him. 'Sir –'

Lyuba ran. The gendarme made to follow her, but the farmer shrugged it off and turned to a waiting customer. The crowd closed around Lyuba and a moment later, without thinking to what end, or what consequences might flow from it, Tholdi also ran through the crowd.

Lyuba walked briskly uphill until she reached the Theaterplatz. Once a fish market, it was now one of the city's more fashionable squares with a formal garden where people strolled and mingled. Lyuba glanced back several times, either sensing she was being followed or fearing it. More than once Tholdi considered giving up the chase.

On Goethegasse, Lyuba approached a building in which visiting musicians and performers had once stayed. These days, since the war had closed down the nearby theatre, many of its rooms were empty. At the front door, as Lyuba was rushing inside, she collided with a man on his way out. Lyuba's shopping bag broke and its contents spilled across the ground. The man was Radu.

Standing by the cart of a street vendor, Tholdi maintained his distance. He couldn't hear what Radu and Lyuba were saying but it was clear that they knew each other, and that he was agitated. When Lyuba stooped to collect her groceries, Radu did not help her. Looking about, he seemed more concerned to see if anyone was watching them. Tholdi took a step back, behind the vendor's cart.

Radu grabbed Lyuba's elbow and hauled her to her feet. Lyuba protested, and tried to retrieve the rest of her groceries but Radu wouldn't allow it. With one last look over his shoulder he bundled Lyuba inside the building.

That night, in his bed, Tholdi thought about what he'd witnessed. It gave him the idea for a proposal. If he was right about the meaning of the exchange he'd observed it might just be a way of keeping them all safe from the rumoured list, from the trains. If he was wrong, or if Radu wasn't open to his proposal, he would surely seal their death warrants.

9

On the mill's wall, looking down on the workers, was a giant clock with hands more like arms. To look at the clock, to take your eyes off your work before the siren sounded the end of your shift, would earn you a reprimand from the overseer. But on this day it was a temptation Tholdi could not resist. Not because he wanted his shift to end, but because he dreaded it. He recalled something his father often said: *Time is your enemy.* Nathan's words made more sense now than ever.

The looms around him clicked and clacked relentlessly. As they locked the threads together, row after row, Tholdi went over and over the words he might use, where he should begin, how he would weave them together. He would need to win over Radu's trust in a matter of moments. He glanced yet again at the clock.

He thought of Alex, what he would do in this situation. Tholdi was sure that he would go through with it. His friend was a born gambler. But what if there was no governor's list? What if the trains were not going to run again? Or, if they were, what if the mill was playing no part in any of it? If it was just a rumour, driven by fear? The probabilities were impossible to calculate.

And yet what were the chances of him having seen Lyuba at the market? Of following her and witnessing what he had? Who could calculate *those* odds? An opportunity like this, he told himself, doesn't come along every day. Then again, there was the risk of Radu's response. If Tholdi was wrong, if Lyuba was not Radu's mistress . . .

The siren let out its long, strangled wail. Everyone made way for the next shift of workers waiting to take over the looms as soon as the overseer had recorded each machine's output. Each worker's output.

'Market?' Karl asked.

He and Tholdi sometimes stopped there on their way home and selected a treat to add to their families' tables. A piece of fresh fruit or a jar of homemade jam.

'Not today.'

Karl sensed his friend's tension.

'I have something to do here,' Tholdi added, without explanation, inferring that Karl shouldn't ask for one.

'How's Peppa doing?' his friend asked instead.

Tholdi had invited Karl to join his family for Shabbat and had noticed the way he looked at Peppa. And why not? To Tholdi, she might still be the little girl he'd grown up with, but Karl saw a young woman, fully formed.

'She's bored. Her days are long.'

Karl sympathised. 'We're lucky we have work.'

'Should I pass anything on to her?'

'Just a hello.' Karl was such a cool customer. Tholdi smiled.

When the next shift was under way, Tholdi approached the overseer.

'Mein Herr?'

'Yes?'

'I need to speak with Herr Radu.'

'About?'

Tholdi had anticipated that the overseer wouldn't easily agree. 'It's personal. A family issue.'

'Which is what?'

'I'd prefer to put it directly. Myself.'

'I wouldn't recommend it,' the overseer warned.

'There's no other way.'

Whatever it was that the boy wished to discuss with Radu, it was clear he had no intention of divulging it. In the end the overseer shrugged. 'It's your life.' He noticed a worker struggling to unload a bolt, twisting the fabric. 'Hey! You!' he shouted.

The worker froze and the overseer strode over to him, leaving Tholdi standing alone. Tholdi looked up at the platform. Felt his heart rate rising. Took a deep breath, made his way to the stairs and began the ascent. It could not have been more dizzying if he were climbing the face of a mountain. At the summit, with his temples throbbing, he looked left and right. Grigore and Radu were in their offices, absorbed in work.

Radu was seated at his desk, poring over a thick pile of papers. Technical reports. He heard a gentle rap and looked over the top of his glasses to see Tholdi standing in the doorway.

He was surprised to see the boy, but not troubled by it. He liked him. 'Berthold,' he said. 'Is there a problem?'

Tholdi felt his throat tighten. His mouth was dry as paper. 'May I come in?'

Closing the door behind him, Tholdi approached the desk and noted the wedding ring on Radu's finger. He felt reassured.

'You need somewhere more discreet,' Tholdi began.

'Excuse me?'

'I saw you both. On the street.'

Now it was Radu's heart that started to race. Was Tholdi really saying what he thought he was saying? Or was Radu's fear of being caught playing tricks on his mind?

'You and . . . your lady friend.'

The blood drained from Radu's face. Tholdi knew it was essential to make his intentions clear quickly. To assure Radu that this was not blackmail.

'I'm here to help you. If *I* could so easily discover your situation . . . You need to meet somewhere less busy.'

Through the glass, Radu saw Grigore step out of his office and stand in the middle of the platform, flipping through papers on a clipboard.

There would be no second chance for Tholdi to put his proposal. His carefully rehearsed words came out in a rush, tumbling over each other.

'Where I live it's quiet. No cafés, no shops,' he said. 'And close to my house is an apartment block. There are six flats in it, most of them vacant. One is furnished. Untouched by the looters. Much nicer than a rooming house, and more private.'

Radu saw that his brother was still on the platform, flipping back and forth between the pages on the clipboard. Something wasn't adding up. *Please God*, Radu prayed, *don't let him come to me with questions now. Not now.*

Tholdi pressed on. 'I can do things for her, too. Cleaning, shopping, whatever is needed. I can –'

'Enough, boy! Be quiet!' Radu snapped.

Tholdi's legs began to shake.

And then Radu asked: 'Does anyone else know?'

Tholdi was elated. A moment before, he was sure that he'd made the biggest mistake of his short life. Now, like a hawker whose wedged foot felt the pressure of the door being released, he felt opportunity opening up to him.

'No. And they never will.'

From his pocket, Tholdi extracted a scrap of paper, and placed it on Radu's desk. 'The owner. His telephone number.'

Radu was about to reach for the paper when he noticed Grigore watching them. He stood quickly and guided Tholdi to the door. As he opened it, he addressed the boy loudly. 'It's an interesting idea. Let me think on it.'

'Thank you, mein Herr.'

Tholdi departed, avoiding Grigore's curious eye. Grigore turned it towards his brother.

'He thinks we could improve our output,' Radu explained. 'By adjusting the pirn speeds.'

'Ah, the genius.'

'Maybe.'

Radu seemed troubled, but Grigore didn't dwell on it. His brother had always been a worrier. Just one of the things that made them so very different.

Radu returned to his desk. When Grigore turned his back, Radu slid the scrap of paper off his desktop and secreted it in a drawer.

10

Unlike his twin brother, who took pride in his physique, Radu loved rich food and had a waistline to prove it. So when he was slow to eat a favourite meal of creamed paprika veal, his wife, Sofia, did not fail to comment.

'It's nothing,' he said. 'Just a few problems at the mill. Nothing we can't resolve.'

'So it won't affect my plans.'

'No.'

'Good.'

The return of the Romanians had been a great relief for Sofia. It had been the Russians who put her husband in charge of the mill, but the new status that arrangement had conferred on him, and on Sofia, had to be very carefully managed. Marches and parades had to be regularly attended, celebrating 'the army of the peasants'. Proletarian slogans and chants endlessly repeated. Homage paid to the icons of the Revolution – Marx and Lenin, as well as Stalin. Mercifully, that had all changed now. And, importantly, Sofia could now visit her younger sister, Nadia, who lived in Paşcani, on the other side of what had been the partition between the Soviet north and the Romanian south of the country, now reunited as they had been in the inter-war years.

'Is she doing well?'

Nadia was two months pregnant. From the outset it had been difficult. Not entirely surprising, the doctors said, for a woman past thirty and whose last pregnancy had been complicated. The absence of her husband, fighting on the Russian front, hadn't made it any easier. Sofia's own husband, meanwhile, had evaded military service. An embarrassment that compounded the years of disappointment in a man who, long before the war began, had shrunk in her eyes. The doctors had been unable to give any conclusive diagnosis, but Sofia was sure it was Radu's fault that she had never conceived.

'Do you really care how my sister's doing?'

Radu didn't bother to reply. It would only lead to another argument that Sofia, as always, would eventually win.

What Sofia did not know was that her regular train trips to visit Nadia had provided the window in which Radu's affair with Lyuba had blossomed. That it had been during one of these absences that he had suggested to Lyuba that she leave the brothel and become his mistress. He had said he would take care of her. Protect her.

When Lyuba told him why he'd been kept waiting, what had happened to her at the market, he regretted having lost his temper with her. But the incident was a wake-up call. Tholdi was right that the rooming house was located in a very public part of the city. And if the boy had been able to put the pieces together, deduce the affair from a distance, what if someone else saw him with Lyuba? If not Sofia herself then one of the mean-spirited women she called her friends, who would undoubtedly feel compelled to share what she'd seen. Losing Lyuba would only be one of the consequences. The other would be the thousand different ways in which Sofia would make Radu pay for her humiliation.

As was Radu's careful, methodical way, he considered the proposal that Tholdi had presented to him from every aspect. The mostly Jewish neighbourhood where Tholdi lived, in a quiet residential street without shops or cafés, would certainly be far more discreet than the present arrangement. The idea of a private and well-appointed apartment also appealed to him. What he needed to feel sure of, what was delaying his decision, was whether the boy could be trusted. Then again, the boy had just as much at stake as he did. More.

'Have you reached a decision?'

Radu was startled by the question. Confused.

It irritated Sofia that there was any need for her to explain. 'What to do about Grigore.'

When the Romanians returned, businesses that the Russians had nationalised were returned to the previous owners. If they were still alive. And if they were gentile. Seizing the opportunity, Grigore had promptly declared his allegiance to their new fascist masters and made a deal that allowed the brothers to retain control of the mill. The government got the lion's share, and the official who brokered the deal, an old friend of Grigore's, pocketed a handsome commission. There was plenty left over and it had made both brothers rich – another aspect of the changed circumstances which Sofia enjoyed – but now Grigore wanted more. A larger share.

'It's extortion!' Sofia declared. 'It's not as if he's short of money. Do *we* own a car?'

Grigore had recently bought himself an Opel Kapitän. A burgundy-coloured two-door coupé cabriolet with white-wall tyres. It was second-hand – civilian production had been suspended by the outbreak of war – but only three years old. It was his pride and joy. Each day at the mill he would select one of the employees to clean and polish it. The employees never objected, realising that this was an opportunity to ingratiate themselves by doing a good job. More often than not it was a girl Grigore chose.

'We don't need a car.'

'That's not the point.'

Perhaps they didn't need one, but they deserved one, she thought. She could easily picture herself being chauffeured in it. Her friends gawking as she sailed past them along the street.

'The point is that you need to stand up to him.'

'We'll see.'

It was Radu's usual way of concluding, inconclusively, any disagreement with his wife that he could not afford to lose. In disgust, Sofia flung down her knife and fork, and rang a small bell they kept on the dining table. Their maid arrived.

'I'm finished,' Sofia declared.

The maid took her plate. As Sofia left the room she muttered to herself, loudly enough for the embarrassed maid to over-hear: 'So weak.'

On his own, and glad of it, Radu finished his meal slowly, continuing to chew over Tholdi's proposal.

11

For Tholdi, waiting for Radu's response was nothing short of torture.

What if Radu decided his best option was to decline Tholdi's proposal and simply dispose of the boy who'd been stupid enough to put it to him? He could easily have him taken away. Arrested and put in a labour camp where he'd receive no pay. Or, worse still, taken to wherever the trains had gone. Tholdi did his best to focus all his energies on his work. He prayed continuously and piously. Made promises to his Maker. Reminded Him that not just his life but those of his family and their close friends were in the balance. As if He needed reminding.

—

Towards the end of the month, the fortnightly pay packets were distributed. Tholdi found a note in his – *Meet me at the warehouse*. Relief washed over him.

Seeing Karl approach, Tholdi slipped the note back into his pay packet.

'My place?' Karl suggested.

'I can't,' Tholdi said. 'I'm meeting someone.'

Karl was intrigued.

'Does she work here?'

'No.' Tholdi let him believe it was a girl. In a way, it was.

'So much mystery,' his friend teased.

It was for the best. For both of them.

Tholdi farewelled Karl on a nearby street corner and, following Radu's instructions, discreetly doubled back towards the mill, to the warehouse that stood down the road. In it were reserves of yarn, thousands of kilometres of filament wrapped around cardboard cones, left behind by the fleeing Russians. Another reason that the mill was so profitable for the brothers.

Tholdi entered the warehouse through a small side door, splashing a slice of light across the floor of its unlit interior. The pungent odour of naphthalene gas, toxic to moths, curled up his nose. If he had known then what he learned later, about the gas chambers disguised as shower blocks, it might have sickened him. Instead it reminded him of Leo, his closet of tailored suits hanging neatly in a row. A memory of finer times.

'Over here.' A voice from the shadows.

Tholdi's eyes adjusted, made out Radu's silhouette. He crossed the floor to join him.

'We will not meet like this again.'

Those few words, tacit confirmation that Radu had decided to accept his proposal and was establishing the rules, were as sweet as any music Tholdi had ever heard. He thanked God for hearing his prayers.

'And you will speak of this arrangement with no-one. None of it. Is that understood?'

'Yes, mein Herr. I swear it. On my parents' lives.'

Radu handed Tholdi a pair of keys. One of three pairs, all the same. One for Tholdi, one for Lyuba, one for himself.

'Her name is Lyuba. When I plan to pay her a visit, I will let you know. A gesture, like so.' Radu used his middle finger to trace the line of his brow. 'You will let Lyuba know to expect me the following night.'

'Yes, mein Herr.'

Radu handed Tholdi an envelope. 'For whatever she needs. That should be more than enough to start. There will be the same amount each fortnight added to your wages.'

Tholdi pocketed it.

'You have two days to make it all ready.' Radu turned to leave.

'Mein Herr?'

Radu turned back. 'Are we not finished?'

Tholdi knew he was taking another gamble. Doubling up, Alex would have called it. Like lying, gambling was fast becoming second nature to Tholdi. The war, for all its terrors, was making him into a man in ways even Alex could not have foreseen. Holding his nerve, Tholdi rolled the dice once more.

'I know someone. Not at the market – somewhere else. He has everything. Wine, smallgoods, delicacies of all kinds.'

'And how much commission will you pocket from that?'

Radu's suspicions were correct, Tholdi did hope to squeeze a little from the arrangement.

'Do not mistake me for a fool, young man. That would be very dangerous.'

'Mein Herr, I'm thinking of you. It will make your, your meetings more pleasurable. But if you don't want me to . . .' Tholdi waited.

'I will think on it.'

'As you wish, mein Herr. And if there's anything else you want –'

'I will find a way to ask for it. Unless I send for you, do not come to my office again. Ever.'

'Yes, mein Herr.'

'Two days.'

Radu turned again and walked away, his footsteps echoing. For the first time in what seemed an eternity, Tholdi's heartbeat slowed and life filled his lungs.

12

In the rooming house, Lyuba sat with Radu on the edge of the bed. In her hand was the address Radu had given her.

'It sounds nice,' he said. 'Much better than here. And anything you need, just ask the boy.'

Lyuba wasn't happy about the boy shopping for her. Despite the argument she'd had with the farmer, she enjoyed going to the market. It reminded her of happier days long ago when she would visit the city with her father.

'Lyuba, it's better this way.'

'If I had my own papers . . .'

'I told you, I'm trying. It's not easy.'

A birth certificate was required. She had none. All she possessed was the prostitute's licence that Madame Denile had acquired for her, back before the Soviets came.

Lyuba apologised for her impatience. 'Who is this boy?' she asked.

'He works for me. At the mill.'

'Well, so long as he can be trusted.'

'He can.'

'How can you be so sure?'

Radu became irritable. 'Lyuba, please, enough questions. I know what I'm doing.'

She knew better than to argue.

Radu softened his tone. 'I'm doing all this for you. To keep you safe.'

That, Lyuba knew, was a half-truth at best. Mainly, Radu was protecting himself.

'Here.' He handed her two hundred-leu notes. 'For a carriage.'

A horse-drawn carriage. Taxi cabs were an extravagance reserved for the rich. He could have afforded one, but she didn't demand it. Pocketing the cash, she thanked Radu.

'Will I know when you're coming?'

'The boy will tell you.'

'Does this boy have a name?'

'Berthold.'

Radu took Lyuba's hand and stroked it. 'I wish it could be different.'

Did he mean he wished there was no war? No persecutions? No suffering? No. He meant he'd developed feelings for her and wished he didn't have to hide them. Wished they could be together, openly. All of which, even if she'd also wanted it, was a romantic fantasy. One which, at the brothel, she would have tactfully extinguished. But these were very different circumstances. Radu was no longer one of Lyuba's clients; he was her only client.

She looked up into his eyes and smiled sadly. 'Me too,' she said.

13

The apartment that Tholdi found for Lyuba had been occupied by a Dr Mandel. Not a medical doctor, but a man of letters. A scholar who lectured at the university. His subjects were philosophy and art history. Tholdi greeted him in passing often – Dr Mandel always tipped his hat politely – but he'd never before been inside his home. Nor had any of Dr Mandel's other neighbours. He was a very private man. Now, turning the lock and opening the front door, Tholdi hoped that it would live up to the promise he'd made to Radu. He was greeted by the musty odour of stale air but, other than a layer of fine dust, everything was in even better order than he'd dared hope. Moving from room to room, imagining Lyuba occupying their spaces, Tholdi opened the windows.

In the sitting room was a generous sofa with plump, brocade-covered cushions and an obviously much-loved armchair that still wore the impression of the last time Dr Mandel had sat in it. The walls were hung with original works of art. One of them, a drawing in charcoal of a naked man, bore Dr Mandel's own signature. On a side table beside the armchair was a stack of books – the last, Tholdi imagined, that Dr Mandel had ever read – and a small vase made of Venetian glass. If there were still flowers in the park, Tholdi would have picked some to fill it.

Dr Mandel was also fond of classical music. There was a piano, and a gramophone too. Tholdi flipped through the records – Brahms, Chopin, Mozart, Beethoven – and considered requisitioning the gramophone for his own enjoyment. He decided against it. It would make Radu's nights with Lyuba more pleasurable. And that, above everything, was what mattered to them all. What their lives now depended upon.

The dining room led to Dr Mandel's study, lined with floor-to-ceiling bookshelves. Tholdi wondered if Lyuba could read. He suspected not, and moved on to the bedroom. With its large mattress and abundance of pillows and cushions it was as luxurious, surely, as any well-appointed bordello. The bed was neatly made up. Had Dr Mandel expected to return, or was this just another expression of his fastidious character? Tholdi decided to strip it anyway. He imagined the pleasure it would give Lyuba to feel crisp, fresh sheets against her skin.

It wasn't only thanks to Dr Mandel that everything was in such good order. His landlord, Herr Pazyuk, had played a part, too. Like everyone else, he had been kept in the dark about the purpose of the ghetto. Dr Mandel had been his tenant for many years, always paying his rent on time and never giving any trouble, and Herr Pazyuk had hoped he might return. And so, in those first few weeks, Herr Pazyuk spent many long hours on Dr Mandel's comfortable sofa, or at his dining table, making sure no-one mistook the place for an abandoned property. At night, when he was not there, he left lights on. Different ones each time. Doina called him 'the scarecrow'. Pazyuk's wife called him a fool, and said it would be better if they forgot all about Dr Mandel and sold his home's contents for whatever they could get. So when Radu turned up, asking to rent the place exactly as it was, sight unseen, Herr Pazyuk gave thanks to the Almighty. Sure, he'd been forced to drop the rent – with so many vacant apartments, he was in no position to haggle – but it gave him considerable pleasure to hear his wife concede that all those hours spent scaring away the looters had not been wasted.

Tholdi returned to the piano. It was an upright, like the one he had grown up with. Dr Mandel's had a veneer of honey-brown maple wood. Tholdi was unable to resist the urge to open its lid, test the keys. It had been months since he'd last played. A lifetime, it seemed. He allowed himself a short, ascending scale. How sweet the sound of it! He ached to sit and bring the instrument to life, but he didn't dare. His being there at all would attract enough attention, enough talk. Once Lyuba arrived, things were only going to get harder. For him and for those close to him. But he was confident that Radu would be pleased with the arrangement and he hoped that Lyuba would be too. That she would find in Dr Mandel's home some kind of comfort, some measure of refuge from the madness of the war.

Before leaving Tholdi closed all the windows, but it wasn't until he stepped outside onto the pavement that he noticed Doina standing at the entrance to their building, some twenty metres away. Hands on hips and feet apart, as if they were bolted into the pavement, she was staring directly at him. And at the bundle of sheets in his arms.

There was no avoiding her, and she did not move aside to let him pass. Manoeuvring through the gap between her and the doorframe, Tholdi wished her a good day. She did not reply.

14

Lina went to the market often. Like Lyuba, she enjoyed it, as did Mira. Not only because they liked to select their own fresh produce, but because it was an outing. A chance to mingle and gossip about other people's lives. Lately, instead of arched eyebrows and titillated laughter, there were sunken eyes in long faces.

From now on, Tholdi would also be stopping by the market regularly – not for his family, but for the woman who was about to move into their street. To help deliver the news of her imminent arrival, Tholdi had stopped by the market that day to get something special for dinner with his family – beef, a choice cut. It sat now, unwrapped, on Lina's kitchen bench. Lina regarded it as if it might be laced with poison. She did not dare touch it.

'Mama, there's nothing wrong with it.'

Lina wanted to believe him, but she couldn't recall the last time she had cooked a meal made with fresh meat.

'Is it kosher?'

He wasn't sure whether or not she was using the word literally. In any case, since when was she so strict? Like most middle-class Jews in Czernowitz, they were Reformists. Liberal Jews.

'You want me to take it back?'

Lina pushed Tholdi away, and with carrots and onions and love turned the meat into goulash. It sat on the stove, waiting to be served. But first, her son had some good news. Everyone came to the dining table.

Tholdi chose his words carefully.

'I . . . we . . . have acquired a benefactor,' he began.

The questions flew from all sides.

'What kind of benefactor?'

'How do you know him?'

'Is he one of us?'

'Do we know him?'

'Why does he want to help?'

Tholdi raised his hands for silence. 'None of that matters. And his identity needs to remain a secret.'

They all knew there had to be more. Waited for it.

'There's a woman. She will be moving into Dr Mandel's.'

As the implications sank in, looks were exchanged around the dining table.

'She's a Gypsy,' Tholdi added.

More looks.

Peppa, as usual, was the one to say it aloud. 'So our new benefactor has a filthy tsigayner nafka.'

Whore.

Blood rushed to Tholdi's cheeks, not with embarrassment but anger. When he spoke, it was with a quiet, steely voice they'd never heard from him before.

'She's no more filthy than we are filthy Jews. And what she is to him is none of our business.'

No-one dared to contradict him.

'What do we tell our neighbours?' Mira asked.

'Nothing.'

'But they will talk.'

'I'm sure they will. And we will be well fed.'

That was something they all wanted. Famine had claimed many lives. And the aroma coming from the kitchen was intoxicating.

The goulash was served. As it was a Friday, Shabbat, Lina lit candles before they ate, and Nathan recited the Kiddush, the blessing. Lina made a silent prayer of her own, that they would be forgiven for accepting the protection of this new 'benefactor' and the meal his patronage had made possible. She feared it would send them all to hell – but it tasted of heaven.

15

Tholdi wasn't the only one who found ways to skim a few lei now and then. Lyuba also looked for opportunities. Not that there were many. Lyuba's lover – that's the word he liked her to use – was a careful man. Unlike his brother, he didn't get about with a fat wallet, didn't care to show off his wealth, worried that doing so could invite danger. And he certainly didn't lavish it upon his mistress. If he did, she might put enough aside to one day disappear. Lyuba suspected that was another reason behind Radu not arranging the identity papers she wanted. It would have given her too much freedom of movement. Radu wasn't wrong to think that way. Not that Lyuba had any idea where she'd disappear to, or how she'd survive, but escape had entered her mind often. At first, hourly. Now just daily. In the mornings, when she woke and was reminded where she was. At night, when she had to block it out so she could sleep.

Under the new arrangements, with this boy doing most of her shopping, putting aside any money for herself was going to be more difficult. The only cash she would see was the meagre allowance she had negotiated, for the personal items which, she had argued, a woman needed to buy for herself.

Radu had told her to take a carriage, a practical solution to the problem, but despite the cold she'd decided to keep the fare for herself and walk. The skies were clear and she only had one bag to carry. Now she stood on the corner of Sturm and Haydngasse, in her hand the address Radu had given her. Thanks to her work at the brothel, she spoke Romanian, German and these days even some basic Russian – but, as Tholdi had suspected, she'd never learned to read or write any of them, and the street signs, in a part of the city she'd never been to before, were useless to her. Though she didn't know it, she was only metres from her destination.

To help with her arrival, Radu had made sure Tholdi had the day off work. All afternoon he'd been waiting for her, leaning out of his bedroom window, looking towards the direction of the Hauptstrasse, from which she would surely come. She didn't appear in the street until late in the afternoon, glancing up at the nearby buildings. Tholdi grabbed the pot he had prepared and left the house as quickly as he could – but not fast enough. Stepping out into the street, seeing what was unfolding a little way down on the other side, he stopped and watched.

'Can I help you?'

Lyuba turned to see Doina. 'I'm looking for this address,' she said, holding out the scrap of paper.

Doina studied the address, then studied the olive-skinned, green-eyed woman. Lyuba knew that look. So very different from the look of appraisal that a man gave.

'It's there.' Doina pointed. 'Other side, the next corner down.'

'Thank you.'

Doina did not tell Lyuba that she was welcome. She wasn't. Lyuba could see that. Tholdi didn't want to explain the pot to Doina and stepped back inside their building's entrance hall, into a corner where she wouldn't see him as she passed. He waited to hear the door of her apartment open and close.

Across the street, on the first-floor landing, Lyuba slid the key into the lock and opened the door to number four. She hadn't expected the sight that greeted her. It was more than just an improvement on the bare room she'd been living in. Even the best of the rooms at Madame Denile's, the ones reserved for the wealthiest clients, didn't match it. She closed the door, put down her bag and moved into the sitting room. She noted the piano. It reminded her of another one, in another house – a place of memories she preferred to forget – but that was easily set aside from her thoughts. Someone, the boy she presumed, had done a thorough job of making the apartment ready. There was not a speck of dust and it smelled fresh. Glad to take the weight off her feet, Lyuba sank into the down-filled cushions of the sofa and luxuriated in their sumptuous comfort.

A sound at the door. Another key in the same lock. She tensed. Heard the door open.

'Hello?' A boy's voice.

Then footsteps. Lyuba stood.

Tholdi appeared in the doorway. He stopped. 'I'm sorry. I should have knocked, but . . . in future I will.' The idea that they were going to share some kind of future sent a ripple of excitement through him.

'You're Berthold?'

'Yes.'

'Lyuba.'

He realised that she was introducing herself – that she had not yet remembered him. 'Call me Tholdi if you like. It's shorter.'

It was the name Alex had used at the brothel. He waited for her reaction, but there was none.

'Is that for me?' she asked.

He remembered the pot he was holding. 'Yes. It's goulash.'

She stepped forward to accept it. With Lyuba so close, Tholdi's pulse quickened.

'There's wood in the stove,' he added. 'I've set the fire, too. And made up the bed.'

'Thank you.' Lyuba wondered what the boy was waiting for. 'Was there something else?'

Tholdi glanced about the room. For a prop. Something to stretch the moment. 'There's a gramophone, too.' He pointed it out to her. 'He might enjoy music.'

They both understood that 'he' meant Radu.

'I've never used one.'

'I can show you.'

She nodded. Still, Tholdi waited.

Lyuba raised the pot in her hands. 'I should put this in the kitchen.'

'Of course. I'll let you get settled.'

Tholdi left, at last. She reflected for a moment on the boy's odd behaviour, then took the pot to the kitchen and lifted its lid. The aroma was good. Without giving Tholdi a further moment's thought, she stoked the stove, heated the goulash and sat down alone to eat it.

Tholdi meanwhile shared his own meal with his family. He was unusually withdrawn.

'Was there a problem?' Lina asked. They all knew by now that Lyuba had arrived.

'No.'

It was Mira who provided a little more information. 'She won't be needing any of Dr Mandel's books. She couldn't even read the street sign. Doina had to help her.'

That night, lying on his bed, Tholdi reviewed it all. Should he have said something? Reminded Lyuba that they'd met before? In the days leading up to her arrival, he'd imagined her surprise at seeing him again. Considered how he would explain it. Wondered how much he should tell her about the circumstances that had led to it. But she hadn't remembered him at all. Then again, he reasoned, why would she? Their first meeting, nearly six months back, had been so brief. He consoled himself with the thought that it was probably for the best. What had begun as an attraction, an impulse, had turned into something else entirely. Something far more important. An opportunity to keep his name off the rumoured list. To be protected. That, surely, outweighed any history between two people who were, in reality, little more than strangers. It was probably better that she hadn't remembered him. That their relationship was purely one of mutual expedience, devoid of any personal complications. That was the first of the lies he told himself.

He stood, moved to the window and looked out into the night. In the street below, the figure of a man was briefly illuminated by the flare of a match. It was Sergio, one of the patrol guards who'd recently been assigned to enforce the curfew in their area, lighting a cigarette. Beyond Sergio, behind drawn drapes, lights were on in the apartment that was once Dr Mandel's. Tholdi was just able to view it if he looked diagonally downwards. One by one, the lights were extinguished – first in the sitting room, then in the bedroom.

In the glass of his own bedroom window, Tholdi became aware of a reflection and turned to see Peppa in the hallway, watching him. Tholdi wondered how long she'd been standing there. Without seeking an answer to his question, he walked to the door and gently closed it.

16

When it had started, Grigore couldn't be sure. Probably from the moment Radu had been born, minutes after Grigore. Grigore had come out with relative ease, but Radu had been more difficult. He'd wanted to enter the world the wrong way around, feet first. And from the moment he had eventually arrived, after a great deal of coaxing, he was very obviously the weaker of the twins, in constant need of their mother's attention.

In Grigore's view, he'd received far too much of it. He'd been coddled and turned into a spoiled, oversensitive child who cried easily. Grigore was constantly blamed for his brother's tears. Of course, he did enjoy teasing little Radu. What older brother doesn't enjoy that sort of pastime? But he resented the punishments he received, which never seemed to fit the crimes. He was often beaten. It was almost as if Radu enjoyed watching. In his own cowardly way, always hiding behind his mother's authority, Radu, not Grigore, was the cruel one. That, in any case, is how Grigore saw it. Little wonder, he thought, that Radu had married Sofia. Another formidable woman to hide behind.

'The boss' Grigore called her. He'd long ago abandoned any pretence of liking her. She was equally fond of him. And she was, he suspected, behind the latest confrontation with his brother.

'Grigore,' Radu said to him, 'it's your interests as well as mine that I'm thinking of.'

'So this isn't Sofia's idea?'

'No.'

'Really? Because it sounds to me like I'm being accused of stealing from you.'

'Grigore, please, don't say something like that.' In truth, Radu would not have been shocked if Grigore had been stealing from him. But that was not what was driving him today. 'Besides,' he continued, 'you're not the one who puts the pay packets together.'

'No, that's Mikael, who *I* hired. Someone you obviously don't trust.'

'Do you trust me?' Radu asked.

Grigore shrugged. 'Sure I do.'

'Good. Then it's settled. I'll take care of the pay packets from now on.'

It was as assertive as Grigore had ever seen his brother. He almost respected him for it. For being so direct for once. If it made him less anxious, fine. Grigore had no doubt that Radu would be honest, down to the last ban. The last Romanian cent.

'Anything to make you happy, Radu.'

The sarcasm wasn't lost on Radu but he was pleased the matter was resolved. And just in time.

'Were you expecting the boss?' Grigore nodded to the mill floor.

Radu looked down from the platform. His wife was approaching, threading her way through the rows of machines.

Tholdi almost collided with her as he unloaded a bolt of fabric. He nearly knocked off the hat that was perched on her head like a bird on its nest.

'Stupid boy! Watch what you're doing!'

Sofia had met Tholdi once before, at his house, but now, a couple of years later and in a different context, she had trouble placing him. He looked vaguely familiar, but she barely gave him a second thought. She re-positioned her hat and continued towards the stairs.

Once she was out of earshot, Karl couldn't resist mimicking her. 'Stupid boy!' He imitated a bird ruffling its feathers, a shim-mying quiver that ran down his body. His performance caught the eye of the overseer.

'Bruckman! Get back to work!'

At the foot of the stairs, Sofia waited for Radu to come down to meet her. She had no intention of exerting herself.

'I need money,' she said, as his foot hit the bottom step. 'For Nadia's.'

'I left some. On your dresser.'

'Not enough.'

'I don't have much with me.'

'Grigore will. Borrow it from him.'

Radu didn't have the will for another fight. Especially not in front of his workers. And the quarrel with Grigore had been enough for one day. Besides, more money meant the possibility of Sofia's visit to her sister lasting longer. More time to himself. More time with Lyuba. He puffed his way back up the stairs.

From his pocket, Grigore produced a wad of notes.

'I'll repay you tomorrow,' Radu promised, putting the cash straight into his pocket.

'Sure you don't want to count them?' More sarcasm from Grigore.

Meanwhile, Sofia waited patiently. Scanning the mill floor, she saw the clumsy boy who'd disturbed her hat watching her, and pursed her lips. He looked away quickly, got on with his work.

Later that day, when the siren sounded and a new army of workers took over the looms, Tholdi lined up to receive his pay packet. He glanced up to the platform, as he'd done each day since the meeting in the warehouse, waiting for the signal. Radu was standing at the platform railing, looking down at him. He ran his middle finger across his brow. When Tholdi was outside the factory he opened his pay packet and found inside it the extra lei that Radu had promised, plus a further amount, and another note: *Do not disappoint me.*

17

The dogs barked ferociously before Moritz came to calm them. He greeted Tholdi with his salesman's affable grin. No matter how many times Tholdi visited, it was the same.

'It's good to see you again, my boy.'

Moritz made it sound like a pleasure. Tholdi wondered if the old man received any small payment for the applicants he sent the mill's way.

'So, what is it I can do for you today?' Moritz asked.

'I'd like a bottle of wine. Something nice.'

'Wine? Such a luxury? I guess this means the job is working out well for you.'

'So far,' Tholdi replied flatly.

Moritz waited for more, but received nothing. 'Well, I have some Burgundy. Would that do?'

'How much?'

He named his price. Tholdi baulked, but Moritz didn't budge. 'Didn't you say something nice? Nice costs.'

Tholdi was in no position to argue. He needed Radu's first night to be memorable. As he waited for Moritz to return with his other purchases, he noted a row of suitcases full, he assumed, of new acquisitions, yet to find room on Moritz's shelves. Tholdi wondered if they'd belonged to people he knew. Or had known.

Moritz returned and the exchange of goods and cash was completed. As Tholdi stood, Moritz asked: 'So, the wine. For a special occasion?'

'Yes.'

Tholdi did not elaborate.

18

Radu had been left shaken by Tholdi's discovery of his affair. Even though Lyuba was in the new apartment now, and the chances of being spotted by someone he or his wife knew had been substantially reduced, Radu had resolved that their future rendezvous would take place under cover of darkness, when the streets were empty. He was also mindful that Tholdi's parents might recognise him. With winter closing in, and the days growing shorter, the timing of this decision was ideal, and for his first visit he couldn't have chosen a better night. The late autumn sun had disappeared hours ago, and shortly after the general curfew the deserted streets were enveloped by a light fog.

Looking down from his bedroom window, Tholdi hoped for a glimpse of Lyuba. His view into her apartment was angled but she'd not yet closed the drapes and through her sitting room window Tholdi could see the glow of the fire he'd set a couple of hours earlier. On the table beside Dr Mandel's favourite armchair was the wine and cheese he'd delivered, waiting for Radu's arrival. A record, he knew, was already on the gramophone's turntable – he'd selected it himself, a piece by Ravel – waiting for the needle to be dropped. Lyuba, he imagined, was now bathing – he'd lit the basement furnace earlier as well, and heated the water in the tank.

Sergio came into view, walking slowly along the street. He stopped to light a cigarette. The flame of the match flared in the fog, illuminating his face. When he inhaled, the ember briefly flickered brightly and then faded.

After Tholdi had shown Lyuba how to use the gramophone, she'd left him alone in the sitting room while she went to the kitchen to retrieve Lina's stew pot. He'd looked into the bedroom and seen the neatly made bed and the emptied suitcase. She must have hung her clothes in the wardrobe. None of that fitted with the idea that Romani people preferred to live in a state of squalor. Did she think of the apartment as her new home? He didn't ask her. In the circumstances, it seemed a tactless question. What mattered was that she made it feel like a home. One that Radu enjoyed visiting. One that would give her keeper pleasure.

Framed by her bedroom window, Lyuba came into Tholdi's view wearing a robe. Opening her wardrobe door, she disappeared from his line of sight. A short time later she reappeared, in a pretty dress. She sat to apply her make-up, affording Tholdi a view of her in partial profile, as if he were looking over her shoulder.

Movement at the street corner caught Tholdi's eye. A man in a heavy overcoat, collar up, and a hat. Radu. He greeted Sergio, who appeared to have been expecting him – no doubt informed by an intermediary and paid in advance to make sure everything ran smoothly. After another moment, Tholdi watched Radu enter Lyuba's building. He reappeared a short time later in her sitting room window. He was no longer wearing his hat, and Lyuba took his coat. She reached for the bottle of wine but Radu pulled her close to him, and impatiently wrapped himself around her. Tholdi's heart beat faster.

Lyuba extricated herself from Radu's embrace, and led him to the bedroom. He embraced her again, unfastening her dress. It fell to the floor before Lyuba closed the drapes, plunging the street into the murky darkness of the night. The only light outside was the ember of Sergio's cigarette. The smoke he exhaled was lost in the fog.

19

Tholdi's presence in Lyuba's life quickly fell into a rhythm. Each day he would knock on her door to ask if there was anything she needed doing or might want from the market. Their exchanges were always brief, and he rarely made eye contact. She thought little of it. Attributed his demeanour to shyness. A lack of confidence.

Then, towards the end of her first week in Dr Mandel's apartment, her first meeting with Tholdi suddenly came back to her. What had triggered the memory she couldn't say, but she found it difficult to believe that he hadn't also recalled it. If she was right, she wondered why he'd not mentioned it. Waiting for Tholdi's arrival, contemplating how she might best deal with the situation, she found herself standing next to the piano. Several times she'd been tempted to open it but had resisted the urge. She lifted the lid. Tapped cautiously, experimentally, at a few of the keys.

Outside, about to knock on the door, Tholdi heard the notes. They were random, isolated, without meaning.

Lyuba closed the piano lid. A moment later she heard the boy's knock. She opened the door to him, and he handed her the bag of groceries.

'Sorry, no apples yet.'

Apples were the one thing she always asked for. The autumn harvest had passed but she'd hoped there might by now be winter apples.

'Is there anything you need me to do for you?'

'Would you mind setting the fire?'

Tholdi was surprised by the request – perhaps because they helped fill the long hours of her day, Lyuba had taken to doing the household chores herself – but he was more than happy to oblige. When he was on his knees, sweeping the ashes into a pan, and she was standing over him, she began her interrogation.

'Moving me here. Was it your idea?'

Tholdi had wondered what she knew. How much Radu had told her.

'I'm thinking it must have been. Since you live so close.'

He replied without looking up. 'The apartment was vacant.'

'How did you know? About us?'

'I guessed.'

'How?'

'I saw you both in the street. You were arguing.'

Lyuba digested the information. This quiet boy was clearly capable of far more than she'd previously imagined.

'Big risk to take,' she said.

You will speak of this arrangement with no-one. None of it. Radu's words echoed in Tholdi's mind.

'It puts meat on our table,' he answered. Tholdi stood and tipped the ashes into a box.

'You know we've met before,' she said.

As intended, the remark caught him off-guard.

'You were with your friend Alex. At Madame Denile's.'

His cheeks began to redden.

'Why didn't you say something?' she asked.

'I didn't want to embarrass you.'

'Why would I be embarrassed? Because we met in a brothel?'

It seemed to her that it was his own embarrassment he was eager to avoid. Was it merely because he was shy, or was there something more to it? Recalling their first meeting, she'd remembered the way his eyes had followed her down the hallway. The way they'd lingered on her. She had no desire to humiliate him, but she needed to make sure he understood that her situation now was very different. Gently, she said, 'You understand that I'm Radu's now. And only his.'

It was a statement of the obvious. Tholdi had never expected anything different. Or had he? The truth was that he hadn't thought through any of his feelings for Lyuba or their potential to complicate the arrangement he'd proposed to Radu.

'Of course,' he said, and then added an apology. 'I didn't intend to deceive you.'

'But you understand what I mean?'

'Yes.'

Lyuba was relieved to hear it.

'So did it all go well for you? At Madame Denile's?'

Tholdi didn't reply. Lyuba understood. Or thought she did.

'It's nothing to be ashamed of. It often happens the first time.'

'It wasn't like that. I just didn't want to.' He confided the truth of it almost in a whisper. 'I wanted my first time to be special.'

Lyuba smiled. A gesture of condolence rather than admiration. 'I see.'

Tholdi's cheeks burned an even deeper shade of red.

From the kitchen came the sound of china shattering. Tholdi and Lyuba exchanged a look, before rushing in to see a cat, all bone and mangy fur, licking traces of gravy from a broken plate. Tholdi stepped forward. The cat abandoned its prize and fled past him. In the sitting room it took cover under the sofa.

Lyuba grabbed a broom and used the handle to prod at it. 'Shoo! Out!' she hissed.

The cat moved further under the sofa and hissed back at her. Tholdi knelt down, looked underneath and saw the cat's terrified eyes, wide open, staring back at him. In his hand was a scrap of meat.

'What are you doing?' Lyuba said.

'Baiting it.'

'If you feed it, it will come back.'

Tholdi looked back at the cat, its eyes now transfixed on the morsel in his fingers.

Lyuba crossed her arms, signalling not only her disapproval but a refusal to accept any responsibility for the consequences of whatever Tholdi chose to do next.

He extended his hand. The cat darted forward and seized its treat, swallowing so quickly that it nearly choked.

The next day, as Lyuba had predicted, it came back for more. Its pitiful appearance and pleading eyes were more than she could resist. Against her own advice, grumbling to herself, she fed it a second time. After that, it didn't come back again. It stayed.

'I told you this would happen,' Lyuba complained the next time Tholdi delivered some groceries.

Tholdi didn't buy her grumbling. 'Admit it. You like the cat.'

'I blame you,' Lyuba replied.

Tholdi shrugged. 'Sure. If that makes it better for you.'

Despite herself, Lyuba laughed.

And her laughter made Tholdi's heart sing.

20

Under the Russians, it had been the citizenry who lived in the greatest fear of spies in their midst – neighbours, employees or friends who might have them arrested as enemies of socialism. Now it was the military that most feared espionage, constantly alert to the possibility that the French or English might broadcast a version of the news from the front that contradicted their own – or, worse, encoded messages directing covert operations. Since a few days ago, when Japan had bombed Pearl Harbor and America had officially entered the war, the authorities were more alert than ever and Nathan's decision to hide the long-wave radio was a constant source of anxiety.

'Nathan, if they catch us . . .'

Lina did not need to finish her sentence, they all understood the consequences, but Nathan refused to reconsider. He was adamant that the dark time they were living through would eventually pass, and that only the radio could tell them when better days were coming.

'And anyway,' he reasoned, 'how would we explain why we didn't surrender it sooner?'

And so it was that at two o'clock each afternoon Nathan camped in the basement with the radio, the wood hatch firmly closed and the volume kept low, to hear the BBC's long-wave German-language broadcasts. When his factory roster permitted, Tholdi joined him. It was not only the latest war news they listened to but entertainment as well. The Austrian actor Martin Miller delivered a parody of Hitler so hilarious that it had them both in tears.

After one of these broadcasts, on a day when Tholdi was not rostered to work at the mill, they discussed Churchill's latest thundering speech – it had been translated into German but was nonetheless rousing – over a game of rummy. Nathan generously let Peppa make up the four, insisting his sight wasn't strong enough to read the cards. It made Peppa feel grown-up, and encouraged her to initiate adult conversation.

'Naturally Churchill says he's going to win. Hitler says the same.'

'But now,' Nathan reminded her, 'we have the Americans as well! I give Hitler another year.'

Lina could not bring herself to share her husband's unbridled optimism. 'Let's hope it's soon enough.'

Tholdi was determined that this day, his one day free from the mill, would not descend into gloom. He offered an even more optimistic assessment than Nathan's.

'If the Brits stopped taking time off for cups of tea, it could be all over by Pesach.'

Passover. The Jewish holiday that celebrated the liberation of the Jews from Egypt. The next one fell in April, only four months away.

'Isn't that right, Papa?' Tholdi said.

It had been Nathan's joke, and he played his part. Everting his palms, just as Leo had done on the night he gave Tholdi the ring, he shrugged and helplessly asked: 'But what can we do?'

Father and son delivered the punchline in unison. 'It's tradition!'

Mira scowled. 'I'm glad you both think it's so funny.'

News about the transports had started trickling back. At the Dniester River, everyone who had made it that far was crammed onto rafts that crossed to Transnistria. There they continued their journey on foot, driven on by guards, to camps dotted all along the narrow valley. Those who fell along the way were shot, their bodies left for birds to feed upon. The rest were herded into barns, pigsties, disused quarries and open fields with little or no food or shelter. In the bitter winter that had set in, thousands were dying of typhus and famine. A schoolfriend of Tholdi's, a pretty blonde girl, had been repeatedly raped and then butchered. Her father was full of shame that he'd been unable to protect her. One night he walked out into the snow, lay down in it, and froze to death. But despite everything they'd heard, Mira refused to give up hope, continuing to tend her little shrine, still lighting the candles. It was heartbreaking to watch.

Tholdi apologised, and Mira was gracious. 'No, I should be sorry,' she said. 'It's good to laugh.'

They concentrated on their cards a moment, then Nathan turned to Peppa with a frown. 'A word of advice to you, my girl . . .'

Peppa braced herself for his reprimand.

'Watch out for my wife. She cheats!'

'How dare you, Nathan!' Lina protested. She looked back at her cards, then asked absently: 'Does anyone know the time?' As Peppa turned to check the clock, Lina snuck a look at one of her cards.

Peppa caught her out. 'Stop that!'

They all laughed, even Mira.

There was, of course, another reason for Tholdi's good spirits. That laughter Lyuba had shared with him the previous day. The song in his heart that had not stopped playing since.

'Rummy!' Peppa lay down a last set, tossed a final card onto the discard pile.

'Mazel tov!' Lina exclaimed.

Mazel. Luck. As Peppa dealt the next round of cards, Tholdi reflected on the mazel that had brought Lyuba back into his life. It brought a quiet smile to his lips.

Peppa noticed. It wasn't the first time lately that she'd seen that smile. She doubted it was because of the hand she'd dealt him, or even because of Nathan's jokes. She placed the undealt cards in the centre of the table and turned the top one over to begin the new game. Without looking up from her own cards, she pretended to ask an innocent question.

'What does she feed it?'

Tholdi tensed. The question could not have been more disingenuous. It was, they all knew, for him. Tholdi kept his focus on the cards in his hand.

'She isn't fussy,' he said.

Rediscovering her sense of humour, Mira looked up. 'Are we still talking about the cat? Not that we've seen this benefactor. Maybe he's a prince.'

The women, it was clear, had been talking. In the circumstances, it was only to be expected.

Tholdi refused to be riled. 'She eats anything. Leftovers.'

'Leftovers? Who these days has leftovers?' Lina asked.

Tholdi calmly played a first card. 'The cat makes her happy.'

Looks between the women. Arched eyebrows.

To hell with them, Tholdi thought. 'The cat's name is Carmen,' he said.

Nathan laughed. 'But of course. What else? Your idea, I'm guessing.'

Tholdi shrugged. 'It fitted.'

A visiting opera company had performed *Carmen* two years earlier, shortly before Britain had declared war. Nathan, whose sight hadn't yet begun its sudden decline, had taken Tholdi to see it.

'You nearly platzed your pants!' Nathan recalled.

Tholdi had been overawed by the whole event, not only the production but also the theatre's lavish Baroque interior and the opulence of the audience – the men in black ties and the bejewelled women in extravagant gowns. He'd felt very inadequate in his modest jacket and tie.

'We'll go back there again one day,' Nathan said.

'Why not? You still have your hearing.'

'And you'll be wearing a smart new dinner suit!'

It was good to let themselves dream a little, to entertain the idea of returning to the life they'd once lived. But Lina found the exchange irritating.

'You know they're calling us collaborators.'

'They?' Nathan asked.

'People. Our friends.'

Tholdi knew exactly who she meant. Doina. Was it a fair accusation? Had they become collaborators? Maybe. But what only Tholdi understood was that their survival and Lyuba's were now inextricably woven together. Even if he'd wanted to, there was no unravelling it. And no revealing it.

'It's not like we're passing secrets to the enemy.' He played another card. 'Besides, if not us, it will only be someone else. Do you want us to go back to living on potato soup?'

It was a surprisingly effective threat. But Peppa, as always, was unable to resist a final word. As she played her card she muttered: 'The cat would be better value in a goulash than being fed some of it.'

Mira and Lina did not disagree.

Tholdi let it go, but her comment wasn't forgotten.

21

Grooming herself on the footpath in the pale winter sunshine, Carmen was blissfully unaware of the politics around her. A delivery man had finished unloading the firewood and, before departing, he spat on the ground near Lyuba's feet. Was it deliberate, Lyuba wondered? She opened the hatch door to her basement and tossed the load of wood down, piece by piece. The man had not offered to help.

Tholdi looked down into the street from his bedroom window and saw Lyuba close the hatch door. She turned back to the street and paused. Tholdi spotted Doina and Mira standing below, looking Lyuba's way. Doina spat at the ground, just as the man had done.

She left Lyuba in no doubt that it was a deliberate gesture. How she would have loved to cross the street and grab Doina by her hair. But it would not have been worth the consequences. And besides, today she had plans. Turning her back on Doina and Mira, Lyuba went inside.

Disgusted by what he'd witnessed, Tholdi decided to pay Lyuba a visit. Coming down the stairs he encountered Doina. He couldn't pass by her without saying something.

'I saw what just happened.'

'What? I don't know what you're talking about.'

They both knew that she did.

Tholdi climbed the stairs to Lyuba's apartment and knocked on her door.

'Come in!' she called from inside.

He'd kept the key. He was pleased she trusted him to use it. Closing the front door, he heard Lyuba's voice again, from the bedroom.

'I'm just dressing.'

Tholdi looked around the sitting room and was again happy to see how neat and homely everything was. It presented a picture of cheerful, settled domesticity, of permanence. Tholdi reflected that it was a strange thing to bring him happiness. After all, they all wanted the war to end, and if it did, so would the arrangement with Radu.

Tholdi's eye fell upon the small Venetian vase, still empty, that had once sat on the armchair's side table. Lyuba had moved it. Tholdi thought of the edelweiss legend, and the dream he'd had months ago.

Lyuba entered the room. Tholdi noticed the silk stockings on her legs, a recent present from Radu. Over her arm was another gift from him, an expensive-looking coat trimmed with fur. She tossed it casually onto the sofa. Lyuba saw that Tholdi's eyes followed it.

'Cashmere,' she said. 'The fur is mink.'

It was obvious that she liked it. Tholdi wished he could shower her with gifts like that, and felt a twinge of jealousy. Lyuba opened her handbag and searched for something in it.

'Was there something you wanted?' she asked him.

'I'm so sorry.'

'About what?'

'I saw. Outside. Just now.'

Lyuba airily dismissed his concern. 'Oh, that. It's nothing.'

Tholdi experienced another twinge – of disappointment. From the bag Lyuba produced a lipstick.

'Are you going somewhere?' Tholdi asked.

'Shopping!' she said brightly, turning to the mirror above the mantelpiece to apply the lipstick.

In the reflection, Lyuba caught Tholdi's flicker of concern.

'Don't worry. Nothing's changed. You're still my favourite houseboy. You'll still get my groceries.'

Houseboy. Is that how she thought of him?

'But,' she continued, 'some things a woman needs to buy for herself.'

'I thought Herr Golescu didn't like you going out.'

'We talked.'

Actually, they'd argued. She'd told Radu that she felt like his prisoner. He'd denied it, but they both knew it was true. By way of apology he'd given her some extra money and told her to buy something nice. There was something else he'd given her, too.

'He finally got it,' Lyuba proudly announced to Tholdi, waving a hand at a document on the side table.

'Have a look,' she said.

Tholdi picked it up. It was an identity card.

'Not cheap to arrange, so Radu told me.'

Lyuba, Tholdi saw, liked that, too.

'Oh and Radu asked if your man has cognac. He'd like a bottle.'

'I'll ask.'

He watched Lyuba finish putting on her lipstick. There was a confidence in her he'd not seen before. The coat, the identity card, the extra freedom she'd negotiated for herself – all of it suggested the arrangement was working out well, and the affair was secure. Tholdi should have been pleased to see it all, and rebuked himself for feeling anything different.

'Was there anything else you need?' he asked her as she put the lipstick back in her bag.

'Actually, yes. An axe.' Lyuba laughed at his surprise. 'For the wood,' she explained. 'It needs to be split.'

'Isn't it already?'

'No.'

Another subtle insult that the wood delivery man had meted out to her.

'Alright, I'll see. If he has one, I can split the wood for you myself.'

'No need for that. I can do it.'

The idea of chopping the wood actually appealed to her. She imagined feeling the axe's weight in her hands, and swinging the blade down. The cracking sound would bounce off her building's courtyard walls, announcing to her neighbours that they had not broken her.

She put on her coat, collected her bag, and ushered Tholdi out with her.

Outside, Doina and Mira were no longer on the street. Lyuba farewelled Tholdi and, passing by Doina's window, catching sight of her, she turned up the mink collar of her new coat.

22

Lyuba had never owned something so extravagant as her new mink-trimmed coat. It was hard not to be a little seduced by it, and she'd made sure the pleasure it gave her was reciprocated. But the coat was also practical. The skies today were clear, but in December the chill air that came from the mountains brought with it the chance of snow. Lyuba loved snow. It made everything look pretty – a respite from the grim horrors of war. She hoped there would be a fresh fall when she returned, in time for her to watch the snowflakes falling outside, from the windows of her warm and comfortable home.

Home. How strange, she reflected, that she'd begun to think of the apartment like that. She no longer thought so often of escape. Partly it was the arrival of winter, a time of hibernation. But there were other reasons, too. Radu's ever-deepening affections, feelings she astutely encouraged and which gave her a fragile but steadily growing sense of security. And, of course, the naïve, romantic boy who wanted his first time to be special.

The coat emboldened her to visit the city's finest street, the Herrengasse. There was a time not long ago, before the war, when policemen were stationed at each end to keep out undesirables. One day, on a visit to the city with her father, who had from time to time found work there repairing roofs, Lyuba had wandered off on her own and reached the street's lower entrance, where it intersected with the Hauptstrasse. When she tried to enter it, a policeman had stood in her way and told her she didn't belong there.

'Why not?' she'd demanded to know.

The policeman had pointed at her feet and told her that being there without proper shoes was against the law. Today she walked the street in shiny leather boots that complemented the stockings, dreaming of how she should spend the extra cash Radu had given her. He'd told her to spend it on herself but it needed to be on something that would please him as much as her. Halfway along the Herrengasse she was drawn to the window display of an expensive perfumery, only recently re-opened for business. It was the kind of shop she'd never have entered before and the woman who greeted her at the counter recognised that almost instantly.

'I'd like some perfume,' Lyuba began.

'Which scent were you after? From which house?'

At the brothel Lyuba had worn the scent that was provided. She had no idea what its name was.

'Something floral.'

The woman smiled – a tight, condescending smile. 'I see. Well this might suit your needs.' She placed a small bottle on the counter. 'Although it's probably not what you're used to.'

More expensive than you're used to, she meant. She told Lyuba the price. Lyuba was shocked but refused to give the woman the satisfaction of seeing it. Refused to retreat.

'May I smell it?'

With obvious reluctance, the woman removed the bottle's lid and sprayed the tiniest possible amount of its contents onto a piece of paper. She handed it to Lyuba at arm's-length. Lyuba inhaled. The scent was exquisite.

'I'll take it.'

Handing Lyuba a bag with the wrapped bottle nestled inside, the woman said knowingly: 'I hope he likes it. I'm sure you're worth it.'

He, they both understood, was neither a husband nor a fiancé – Lyuba wore no ring – but a lover. The one whose money she was spending. Lyuba left the shop without bothering to offer any thanks.

A little further along the Herrengasse, at the Cathedral of the Holy Spirit, Lyuba turned left and headed back uphill to the Austriaplatz, with its little forest of evergreen trees and geometry of connecting paths, diverging and converging. She found a vacant bench in the sun and reflected that if she'd had a sibling, a brother, things might now be very different. He would have been the one to enjoy the occasional city visits, the little adventures her father took her on, and she would never have seen the very different world there, seen the freedoms the gadze women, the non-Romanies, appeared to enjoy. As she approached adulthood she couldn't understand how her mother had been able to give up all that. Of course much later she discovered that, in their own way, gadze women were no freer than any others.

Had the woman in the shop realised she had Romani blood? Is that what had so quickly informed her judgement of Lyuba? Her clear assumption that Lyuba was a kept harlot fitted neatly with the popular fiction of Romani life. That in their forest camps, away from view, Gypsies led lives of shameless debauchery. Nothing could have been further from the truth. In fact Lyuba's people thought much the same of the morals of the gadze. If she had understood that from the start, perhaps she'd have made different choices. Perhaps.

Then again, if her father hadn't found work in the city she would never have been born. It was on one of his work trips that he'd met her mother, then still a teenage girl. Her mother had later claimed she'd had no choice in the matter, that she'd been seduced by the handsome man who toiled for hours in the sun, with his sleeves rolled up, repairing her family's roof. That she'd been powerless to resist him. Now that Lyuba was an adult, she no longer accepted that version of events. Like the pathways of Austriaplatz spread before her, life was a constant series of choices that could lead you further away from the centre of things, or back to it. You never knew in advance what the outcome would be, but the choices were always yours. Lyuba had made ones that were intended to open up her world, to give herself more options. Instead, for now at least, she found herself closed in. Trapped.

Two young children, not more than seven or eight years old, ran past her, screaming and laughing, racing each other to join their friends under a gaily decorated Christmas tree. The other children were playing games – rolling hoops and tossing marbles – watched all the while by a knot of neatly dressed women, some of them tending prams. Now that wealth was again respectable, nannies were back in work and out in public. They reminded Lyuba of the life she'd once lived in a large house, with a large staff. For a time it had felt like being part of a new family, especially at Christmas when everyone received gifts and special treats. That all seemed so long ago now. A chapter of her life she preferred to forget. Touching the small gold cross she still wore around her neck, the one her mother had given her so many years ago, she considered paying a visit to the cathedral, to light a candle. It was a ritual she'd once enjoyed but now it would be an empty gesture. A hypocrisy. Her faith in a God, Christian or otherwise, also belonged somewhere in her past. She left the square and walked downhill towards another part of the city. One fresher in her memory and less crowded these days – a few streets across from the ghetto, on the other side of the Hauptstrasse.

Keeping a safe distance from the brothel's entrance, she watched the customers come and go. Nothing much had changed except the uniforms. Romanian and German instead of Russian. Lyuba wondered how many of the women she'd worked with would still be there. With one, only sixteen, there had been a brief intimacy. Tenderness. She had been such a vulnerable girl, just as Lyuba had been when she first entered Madame Denile's employ at the same age. Lyuba had tried to protect her, school her, but she was too willing to please the men she serviced. What became of her, and the baby she had soon left to give birth to, Lyuba had never found out.

The ghetto was out of sight, and no longer fenced, but when an easterly breeze blew the stench of it wafted over. It had clearly killed business at the nearby smart café, with its outdoor tables. How different it had been only a few months ago, when Madame Denile had spent many hours of her day there smoking gold-tipped Sobranie cigarettes and enjoying only the best of everything. Lyuba recalled the afternoon she'd been invited to join her, and the bottle of French champagne Madame Denile had ordered for them to share. At other tables the patrons spoke in hushed tones, behind raised hands, looking away whenever Madame Denile turned her head in order to blow smoke in their direction. Seeing Lyuba's discomfort, Madame Denile had patted her hand and offered kind, gentle words of advice.

'Fuck them.'

Lyuba regretted that she'd left Madame Denile's employ so abruptly, as had Madame Denile. Lyuba was one of her most popular girls. Allowing herself to be poached, after the years of kindness she'd received, and by a client no less, showed a lack of gratitude. Their parting had not been amicable and going back was not an option.

Seeing a pair of gendarmes come down the street, Lyuba walked on again, towards the industrial area of the town and the strip of forest that lined the river. She walked along its bank to a point from which the freight yards could be seen not more than a hundred metres away. The cattle cars sat idle, with their doors open, waiting to be needed again. Lyuba knew nothing of where they'd been – only the Jews concerned themselves with such tales. But in the countryside the German Einsatzgruppen, the killing squads, had already massacred Roma as well as Jews. Radu had told her about it, and warned that her people in the city could be next. If they were, he said, Madame Denile would not be able to protect her.

Her people. Lyuba no longer had any family, any tribe. Only Radu and, now, the boy. Tholdi. It was obvious that he had a crush on her. She'd made it clear to him that his feelings could never be acted upon, so she saw no harm in it. It might even be useful to her. Power over men wasn't only to be had by giving them what they wanted; sometimes withholding it was even more effective.

As for the contempt of her new neighbours, they could think and say whatever they liked. She owed them no explanations. What did they know of how she'd come to be in their world? What did they know of what she'd had to do to survive?

23

It wasn't until she put out a plate of food and called Carmen's name that Lyuba first noticed the cat wasn't there. She checked everywhere inside – under furniture, inside cupboards, behind curtains – before searching the stairwell. She searched outside as well, in ever-widening circles, calling Carmen's name. Unable to find her, shivering from the icy winter breeze, Lyuba went back inside. The cat had become so attached to her, it seemed inconceivable she'd run away, especially in weather like this. It seemed equally inconceivable that anyone else might have wanted to adopt her. The more she thought about the possibilities, the angrier she became. By sunset, as curfew began, Lyuba was unable to contain her temper any longer. She crossed the street and knocked on Tholdi's door.

It was Peppa who opened it. The two of them had never exchanged a single word.

Lyuba didn't bother to introduce herself. 'Is Tholdi home?'

Peppa blinked.

'I need to see him.' It was a demand, not a request. Lyuba had no intention of leaving without a satisfactory response.

Peppa had no inclination to provide one. 'He's at work,' she said.

Lyuba knew that if Peppa was in some way involved in the cat's disappearance, she would never reveal it. She decided to confront her anyway, to gauge her response.

'It's the cat. I can't find her.'

There was no doubting the accusation behind the question. Peppa thought of the quip she'd made over cards. Mira, she knew, had repeated it to Doina, who had agreed wholeheartedly, observing that it had been a long time since she'd had the luxury of a meal cooked with meat of any kind. Had Doina made good on her threat? The idea appealed to Peppa.

'Sorry. I haven't seen it.'

'What about your friend? The woman I see you talking to sometimes.'

'You'd have to ask her.'

Lyuba had no intention of doing that.

'I'll tell Tholdi you came.' Without waiting for a reply, Peppa closed the door.

Still fuming, Lyuba returned home and prepared for Radu's arrival. That, she reminded herself, was more important. It wasn't until she and Radu were lying together, spent, that Radu noticed the cat's absence and thought to ask about it.

Lyuba did her best to conceal the suspicion and resentment that continued to eat at her. 'It's gone,' she said.

'But you were feeding it. You gave it a home.'

Lyuba shrugged. 'That isn't always enough.'

She regretted the words immediately. Quickly, she added, 'I can't prove it, but I think it was one of the neighbours.'

'But why?'

She saw a chance to reassure Radu that she was content with her world. Content with him. 'Because they're jealous of what I have. With you.'

The thought that Lyuba's neighbours might be so spiteful unsettled Radu. It was something, he unhappily decided, that he should have anticipated.

Lyuba cursed herself for her carelessness. It was ruining Radu's evening. 'Can we not talk about it anymore?' she said. 'It's a cat. Anything could have happened. You are here. That's all that matters to me.' To reinforce the point, she ran her hand up his leg and stroked his thigh, sending a tingle of electricity to his groin.

It wasn't until the following day, at the mill, that Radu recalled their exchange about Carmen, and again felt disturbed.

Down on the mill floor, Tholdi had just completed his shift. The overseer gestured towards the platform. 'You're wanted.' Tholdi looked up and saw Radu there, waiting. Saw him retreat from view.

Tholdi climbed to the platform, and saw Radu behind his desk. He approached cautiously, stopping just inside the office.

'You wanted to see me?'

'The door.'

Tholdi closed it.

'What do you know about this cat?'

'It's missing, mein Herr.'

'That much I know,' Radu snapped. 'Lyuba thinks it was taken. By someone in your street.' He waited for a response. 'Well?'

'It's possible.'

Radu wondered how much Tholdi knew. If he was protecting someone.

'I assume you know by now about the list? The one we provide at the end of each month to the governor?'

So the rumours are all true.

Tholdi was unsure how to respond.

'That's why you came to me in the first place, no?'

Tholdi still held his tongue.

'Answer me!'

'Yes, mein Herr. But I've spoken of it to no-one.'

'Meaning your family.'

'Or anyone else, mein Herr.'

Radu calmed himself. 'I want you to find out what's happened to the cat. You will provide me with a name.'

'And if the cat has merely strayed?' Tholdi asked.

'Then you will find it. Or have your own name added to the list. Your family's names, too. Is that understood?'

'Yes, mein Herr.'

'Good. Go.' Radu put his reading glasses back on, returned to his work.

Tholdi remained. 'There's something else,' he said. 'I'd like to make a suggestion.'

Over the rim of his glasses, Radu looked at him irritably.

'Mein Herr, when you're not there, which is often, Lyuba is all alone. And this business with the cat . . . I think it's made her anxious.'

'So you agree with me. The cat's disappearance isn't a coincidence.'

'It hasn't helped Lyuba feel settled.'

'Are you suggesting there is some kind of threat?'

'I'm suggesting it might help if I could check in on her. Especially at night, after curfew, when you aren't there.'

Radu studied the boy, and again found himself questioning whether he could be trusted.

'Very well,' he said. 'I will arrange it.'

Tholdi was careful to hide it, but he couldn't help feeling a surge of excitement.

Leaving Radu's office, he saw Grigore standing nearby, leaning over a desk, absorbed in yet another wad of reports. Tholdi noticed something else as well. A new piece of jewellery Grigore was wearing. The gold signet ring. Leo's ring.

Grigore looked up from the reports and caught Tholdi staring in his direction. Tholdi looked away quickly and made his way to the stairs. Grigore spotted his brother in his office. He also looked away. What had he had just missed, Grigore wondered. Another discussion about the pirns? He suspected not.

24

To gain access to the apartment above Lyuba's, the looters
had used a lever to prise open the front door, which
remained on its hinges. This was convenient for Tholdi – on
his way back out he left it firmly closed with the aid of a wooden
wedge. He hadn't wanted Carmen to escape, nor did he want
Lyuba to suspect she might be inside. To ensure the cat's mewing
wasn't heard from the stairwell, Tholdi had kept her in the
back bedroom.

Carmen's disappearance was temporary, only three days,
but it upset Lyuba even more than Tholdi had anticipated.
To justify the distress he'd caused, Tholdi had told himself
that he was acting in Lyuba's best interests. She was isolated
and surrounded by hostile strangers, living in a house full of
books she couldn't read a page of. Carmen offered company but

was, after all, only a cat. Tholdi thought Lyuba needed human companionship. Carmen's temporary absence was a small price to pay for it and any gratitude for returning the cat would be a mere bonus. It was another of the lies he told himself.

With Carmen in his arms, complaining loudly, Tholdi knocked on Lyuba's door. At the sight of the cat, spontaneous joy animated Lyuba's face.

'Where did you find her?'

'Outside. Trapped under some rubble.'

Lyuba held out her arms, and Tholdi handed over the cat. They moved inside, where Lyuba found some food scraps. Tholdi had kept Carmen well fed, but she ate hungrily, as if starved, as she always did. Tholdi couldn't have hoped for a more convincing performance.

'I'd given up on her,' Lyuba said. 'I was sure she'd been taken.'

Killed is what Lyuba had actually been thinking.

'In case you hadn't noticed, I'm not very welcome here,' she said.

'Trust me, no harm will come to you. No-one would benefit from that. And I wouldn't allow it.'

Lyuba leaned down and stroked the cat.

Tholdi explained the new arrangements he'd put in place with Radu that would permit him to visit more often, at night. That would permit them to spend more time together.

'We both want you to feel safe,' he said.

Safety, she recalled, was the reason Radu had given for moving her here in the first place. She reflected that her entire adult life, since the moment she'd run away, had been a search for it. Was there anywhere in this world where it could be guaranteed? Would she ever feel safe? Would there ever be an end to the running?

—

Tholdi waited until the following night, when his family were asleep, to test out the new arrangements. Slipping out his front door, closing it behind him without making a sound, he went quietly down the stairs and out into the overcast winter night. Not far away, near the entrance to Lyuba's building, he saw Sergio's solitary figure, ghostly in the dark. As usual, the gendarme was dragging on a cigarette.

'Mein Herr?' Tholdi called.

Sergio turned sharply, his free hand reaching for the gun on his hip. Tholdi raised his own hands, showed Sergio that they were empty.

'I'm Berthold. Tholdi. I believe you've been told about me? By Herr Golescu?'

Sergio relaxed. 'Ah, the boy.'

'Yes.'

'She must be something special, this girl.'

Tholdi's reply was measured. Cautious. 'Not my type. But Herr Golescu likes her.' He gestured at Sergio's cigarette. 'Turkish?'

'Sulima. It's all I can get.'

'What brand do you prefer?'

'I like Lucky Strike but, you know, impossible to buy.'

'American? Not very patriotic.'

'So shoot me.'

'You're the one with the gun.'

Tholdi looked up to Lyuba's apartment, saw her looking down.

'Go on then, kid. Off the street.'

Tholdi moved further along, entered Lyuba's building. On the first-floor landing, she was already waiting for him, with the door open. 'My hero,' she said.

Tholdi blushed. His heart sang, as it had the first time he'd made her laugh.

'Is everything all right?' he asked.

'Yes.'

To prove it, she opened the door a little wider. Tholdi could see the fire burning, Carmen curled up asleep in front of it.

'Good.'

Lyuba couldn't remember when someone had shown her this sort of kindness.

'You should be careful, young man,' she said as Tholdi turned to go.

'Of what?'

'It's well known that Gypsies are thieves. I might steal your heart.'

They were both aware, of course, that she already had.

25

On Grigore's desk was a thick pile of production reports on each of the mill's workers. Next to it was a single sheet of paper. A form. Names, to be forwarded to the governor. When the transportations resumed, those on the list would be rounded up first.

Radu sighed heavily. His signature was required.

'For God's sake, Radu, they're Jews. We're not the only ones doing it.'

He'd never shared his brother's view on The Jewish Problem, nor felt easy about the 'solution' that businesses like theirs had become a part of.

'Do you think they know?' Grigore asked.

'I'm sure of it.'

NIGHT LESSONS IN LITTLE JERUSALEM

'I hope so. The more they fear us, the better.' Grigore leaned back in his chair. 'Actually,' he continued, 'I think we should make an example of one or two. Have them taken.'

He only needed to make a phone call.

Radu wanted none of it. He extended a hand. 'Just give me the pen.'

'Aren't you going to read what you're signing?'

They'd arrived at a formula based on the production reports. Those workers with the lowest output were added automatically. It allowed Radu some sort of justification, telling himself that those slower workers were responsible for their own destiny. But other names were added at the brothers' discretion. The criteria varied.

'Take a look,' Grigore urged, and pushed the form closer to his brother.

Radu knew when Grigore was baiting him. He picked up the sheet of paper warily and read down the list of names. His eyes stopped halfway.

'Linker is one of our best workers,' he said.

'And that makes him feel safe. None of them should feel that.' Grigore studied his brother's reaction. It seemed *he* felt threatened. 'You seem to have taken a shine to Linker.'

'That's nonsense,' Radu responded, doing his best to give away nothing.

'Well maybe, but I don't trust him. He's befriended that other boy. The one who talks too much. Bruckman. Have you not noticed?'

123

Radu had noticed. It bothered him, too, but for reasons he had no intention of revealing. With his brother's pen, Radu drew a line through Tholdi's name and signed the form.

'You look tired,' Grigore observed, as he gathered up the papers.

'I haven't been sleeping well.'

Sofia was to blame. It had been over a week since she'd visited her sister. She was waiting for the holiday they'd planned in the pretty little Carpathian village of Straja. Nadia's husband, Erik, had applied for leave and it was hoped he would join them. Radu was going too. Grigore knew he was dreading it. What he didn't know was that it also meant another week that Radu would spend separated from Lyuba.

'Cheer up, Radu. The break will do you good.'

⸻

The siren sounded. End of shift. Down on the floor, Tholdi and Karl handed the overseer their production reports, grabbed their coats and satchels and headed out into the midwinter gloom. The breeze, sweeping in from the north, had claws.

'My place for a hot chocolate?' Karl asked.

'Where did you get chocolate?'

'Don't ask. If I told you, I'd have to kill you.'

'Sorry, I can't. A family thing.'

'Hanukkah? That's finished already.' Karl had been invited to light the first of the candles. 'Come on,' he pressed. 'It's a girl. It has to be.'

Tholdi was tempted to share a little. If he could trust anyone it was Karl.

'It's nothing serious.'

'I knew it!'

'Look, she's . . .' Tholdi couldn't find the right words. 'It's not like that.' But he knew Karl wasn't going to let it go. Tholdi had to give him something. A crumb, at least. 'She's not a girl. She's . . . older.'

'Ahh, now I understand.' With a twinkle in his eye, Karl painted a fantasy: 'I can see her. Ripe. Sensuous. Experienced. Someone who can teach you how to satisfy a woman's every desire.'

Tholdi laughed but Karl wasn't far from the truth. Or, at least, the truth of Tholdi's own fantasies. The ones he tried not to dwell on. He was excited about the night ahead, but sex would play no part in it. Could never play any part in it. That would be madness.

'Is she married?' Karl persisted.

'I can't say.'

'Oh, you're a dark horse, Linker.'

Tholdi smiled and turned to go. 'See you tomorrow?'

'My day off.'

'Forgot. Enjoy!'

Karl watched Tholdi walk away, wondering about the mysterious woman in his friend's life.

26

'Y ou're becoming one of my best customers!'

Moritz ushered Tholdi inside and settled the dogs. They no longer bared their teeth at Tholdi, greeting him instead with excited affection.

'Have you got it?' Tholdi asked.

'What? No small talk today?'

If he wants small talk, fine, Tholdi thought to himself. 'That ring I sold you – did you get a good price for it? I hope so. Because if my Opa knew where it was now, he'd rise from the earth and reclaim it.'

So the boy had found out Grigore was a customer. Moritz supposed it had been inevitable, but he refused to offer any kind of apology. 'I'm glad you haven't joined your opa,' he said. 'I pray it will stay that way for you.'

Tholdi didn't bother to say so, but Moritz's prayers were worthless to him.

The old man fetched what Tholdi had come for. It was wrapped in heavy cloth.

'It's not new but the blade is sharp,' he said. 'Be careful you're not caught with it.'

It was, they both understood, a potential weapon.

Moritz waited until Tholdi had concealed the axe inside his satchel before he added: 'I have something else for you, too.'

———

That evening, when Lyuba saw what Tholdi had brought, her face lit up. It wasn't the axe that delighted her – though that pleased her, too – but something else. Winter apples.

Lyuba took one and bit into its crisp, golden flesh. Its tart sweetness danced upon her tongue.

'Why always apples?' Tholdi asked.

'We used to eat them straight from the tree. When we didn't get caught.'

'We?'

Lyuba had opened a door. She closed it just as swiftly. 'It was a long time ago.'

'Well, if he gets more, he'll keep them for me.'

'What would I do without you?'

'Eat pears?'

Lyuba laughed, and Tholdi decided to make a confession. One he'd wanted to make before today, several times.

He approached it with a question. 'Do you know what is schicksal?'

The word was foreign to her.

'It means destiny.'

Destiny. That everything happens for a reason. What idea could be more romantic, could appeal more deeply to our need to make order from life's chaos, our desire to make sense of existence? Lyuba had grown up in a world where predicting the future was an arcane art passed down through generations, but also used to empty the pockets of the vulnerable. It was a world Lyuba had rejected.

'Why do you ask?'

'The day I saw you with Herr Golescu in the street? Arguing?'

She remembered it well.

'I'd seen you earlier, at the market with the stallholder. The one who accused you of stealing.'

Lyuba recalled that vividly, too. How she'd fled.

'I followed you. I wasn't planning on anything,' he hastened to assure her. 'It was just an impulse.'

She remembered rushing along the streets. Sensing a follower. Glancing back. Seeing no-one. 'And you're telling me this now because?'

'Friends don't keep secrets from each other.'

'Is that what we are now?'

'I'd like to think so.'

Friend. Like *love*, it was a word Lyuba had learned to be wary of.

'Have you been keeping any other secrets from me?' she asked.

'This isn't really a secret but . . .' He hesitated. 'One time when I came to you, while I was waiting at the door, I heard something.'

'Heard what? Something with Radu?'

'No, nothing like that. It was the piano. You were touching the keys. Playing notes.'

Like a crab withdrawing into its shell, Lyuba's entire being shrank into itself. Tightened. Her stony expression should have warned Tholdi to retreat. He didn't.

'I could teach you to play piano properly,' he said. 'To play music.'

Her response was blunt. 'No.'

'Why not? There's no law against that yet.'

That was true.

'Would it not give you something to fill your days?'

Also true.

'Surely you like music, don't you? It must be in your blood.'

'What do you know of my blood?'

'I always assumed –'

'You know nothing of me. And anyway, the piano isn't a Gypsy instrument.' Lyuba stood. 'I think you should go now.'

Shocked and confused, Tholdi also stood. 'I didn't mean to upset you.'

She didn't reply. Tholdi left.

In bed that night, he thought about the evening he'd spent with Lyuba. It had begun so well yet ended so badly. He wondered what could be behind the way she'd reacted. Was it his offer of the piano lessons? Or was it speaking of her Romani blood? It seemed to him that it had been both. That somehow it was all tied together.

Lyuba, in her own bed, also thought about their evening. Tholdi had stirred up so much in her. Not only silly, superstitious notions that belonged to a past, an idea of herself, she had long ago rejected, but more recent memories as well. Memories of that other piano, the Bösendorfer. Grand and black and so polished you could see your own reflection in it. The master of the house had laughed at her when she'd expressed an interest in it. Had reminded her that she was an illiterate peasant, and a girl. Advised her to confine herself to the tambourine, to dancing. Though not in his house, thank you. Folk music, he insisted, belonged elsewhere. In all her time at Madame Denile's she couldn't remember a moment when she'd felt more humiliated.

In the middle of the night she woke from a dream. Not one set in an alpine meadow sparkling with light, but in a dark place. One where a piano – that same mirror-black piano that reminded her of who and what she was – was consumed by a furious fire. Dampers, bridges and wires flared and twisted in its belly, its lacquered wood and ivory blistering and crackling in the flames. Dancing sparks rose from it and floated away into blackness.

By morning, Lyuba's anger from the previous night had cooled. In its place was a stony resentment. Not towards Tholdi – his intentions had been kind – but towards the man who owned the Bösendorfer. When Tholdi again visited to see if there was anything she needed, she asked if his offer still stood. Tholdi had not forgotten her initial reaction.

'I don't know what I said to –'

'Nothing. You didn't say anything. But if I don't like it . . .'

'We can stop.'

'And no questions.'

'No questions.'

Tholdi was delighted. That evening, after his shift at the mill, he returned and began by sitting at one end of the piano stool. He invited her to join him. She steeled herself, and sat beside him.

'Your shoulders. Let them relax.'

She did as he instructed.

'And don't worry too much about thinking,' he advised her. 'Your mind shouldn't work too hard. Trust yourself to feel the music.'

Tholdi took her hands in his and gently positioned her fingers upon the keys. Showed her how to marry ivory and skin. She was amazed by how quickly and intuitively she became one with the piano – as if it had all this time been patiently waiting for her.

What had been behind Lyuba's initial resistance Tholdi might never know. But what he could see, what was very immediately apparent to him, was that she had a gift.

For Lyuba, it was the start of something profound.

27

The following morning, before going back to the mill, Tholdi asked Nathan if he would teach him how to shave. His facial hair was still little more than fine wisps, but he felt that it was time. After all, he was now the man of the family.

Tholdi's skin was smooth and soft. Not really in need of preparation. But he wanted to know how to do it all properly, just as any fully grown man would, and so Nathan showed him, step by step. First the hot towel, applied to the face. Then, using a strip of leather, the sharpening of the blade. After that, how to use the brush, made of horsehair, to work up and apply a soapy lather. And, finally, how to scrape the blade across the skin without breaking it. The trick, Nathan told his son, was to go with the direction in which the hair grew, not against it.

Nathan made the first few strokes, until Tholdi asked his father if he could do it himself. He didn't like to say so, but his father's poor eyesight made him worry that the sharp blade might slip.

'So . . . our benefactor,' Nathan said, after handing over the razor.

With the blade poised close to his face, Tholdi's hand paused.

'Can you at least tell your father?' Nathan asked.

'Who he is? Sorry, Papa, no.'

Tholdi began shaving. After each stroke, he wiped the blade clean again on a towel.

'But the affair is something you found out. Something you uncovered.'

That much, Tholdi decided, he could safely reveal. 'I saw them both on the street.'

'Ah, so you knew him already.'

Tholdi didn't dare reveal anything further.

'Or was it her you recognised?'

'Please, Papa, no more.'

In the end, not a single drop of blood was shed and Tholdi left home feeling very grown up, as well as a little worried. Karl would be sure to notice the generous splash of Nathan's rationed cologne that his father had used to finish off Tholdi's first shave. There would be more questions, all of them leading to the same mystery. Even if he told Karl his secret, would he understand how his friend felt towards Lyuba? The intense feelings that could never be expressed physically? Or would Karl tease him mercilessly, just as Alex would have done?

When Tholdi arrived at their usual meeting point, Karl wasn't there. Perhaps he had gone on without him. Tholdi waited a few minutes in case, and then walked on alone. There were no excuses for arriving late to a shift. He got to the mill with barely minutes to spare. But where was Karl? With each passing hour Tholdi became more and more anxious, and struggled to keep his eyes from the clock. When finally the siren announced the end of his shift he rushed to get his coat and bag. He was almost out the door when he heard his name spoken. The voice was unmistakeable. He turned to face Grigore.

'Yes, mein Herr?'

'Your friend. Bruckman. You won't be seeing him again.' To make sure Tholdi understood, he added: 'He shouldn't have tried to run.'

Grigore walked away. And Tholdi, once he was outside, did exactly what Karl had done – he ran. Uphill, without stopping, all the way to Karl's apartment block.

The door to the street was open. Tholdi rushed up the stairs two at a time and banged on the front door, repeatedly. No-one responded.

Back on the street, Tholdi looked up at the windows. They were dark and silent. At a neighbouring window he saw a woman looking down, her face desolate. Turning away, she drew the curtain.

That was when Tholdi knew for sure.

28

At the conclusion of their first piano lesson, Tholdi had explained to Lyuba the idea of a scale. The eight notes that were the building blocks of all musical composition. He had said he'd teach her more about it next time, but he had failed to come for the second lesson, the night before. Now he was here and she hurried him in excitedly, not wanting the warmth of the newly lit fire to escape.

'Come in. Come in.'

'I'm sorry,' he said. 'I couldn't come.'

Lyuba didn't ask him to explain. Instead, she ushered him towards the piano.

Tholdi noticed the scent she was wearing.

'Is that the one from the Herrengasse?'

She had told him about the haughty woman who'd sold it to her.

'Yes. I know I should save it for him.' For Radu. 'But it's a special night.'

Not only their next lesson but, she reminded him, New Year's Eve. He'd never seen her like this. Not happy in a defiant way, as she'd been on the day that she'd bought the perfume, but in an innocent way; the way a young girl might be if she were being taken out on a first date.

'Shall we begin?' she asked.

They sat at the piano, side by side, their legs pressed against each other. The effect of it was even more intoxicating than the perfume she was wearing. Despite the previous day's events, it aroused him. He wished it didn't. Thankfully, Lyuba didn't notice. She was entirely focused on her hands, the keys, and the challenge of mastering her first scale. When they finished the lesson, she was eager for his approval.

'What do you think? Am I doing well?'

'Yes, you are.' His voice was flat. Tholdi knew he didn't sound convincing. He added: 'No, honestly. You have a talent. I've already told you so.'

'You wouldn't lie to me?'

'About something like this, no.'

It struck Lyuba as an odd response. What was it that he *would* lie to her about? She suggested they share a glass of wine. There was some left over from Radu's last visit, and it needed to be drunk before it spoiled. They sat on the sofa close to the fire that Carmen was sleeping next to, purring.

Lyuba raised her glass and proposed a toast. 'L'chaim!'

'Where did you learn that?'

'Where do you think?'

At Madame Denile's Alex hadn't been Lyuba's only Jewish customer.

Tholdi raised his glass to hers and echoed the toast with as much cheer as he could. Lyuba saw the effort it took and decided she couldn't ignore his mood any longer.

'Has something happened?' she asked.

He had to give an answer of some kind. 'It's someone from the mill.'

She saw his pain. It had been a long time since someone else's hurt had moved her. She leaned forward to poke at the fire. 'I know why I'm here,' she said. 'The list.'

Tholdi was shocked. He wondered how long she'd known. 'Herr Golescu told you?'

'I asked him.'

'Why?'

Lyuba turned back to him, looked him squarely in the face. 'A little meat on your table? No-one risks their life for that.'

So it was finally out in the open between them. What the affair with Radu meant to them both. How much they needed each other. Tholdi felt he owed her an explanation.

'He asked me not to speak of it with anyone.'

'He said the same to me,' she replied.

They promised each other they would never speak of it again. As if nothing had happened between them, Lyuba casually changed the subject.

'So, reading music. Is it like reading books?'

'No. Very different.'

'Could I learn it?'

'I'm sure you could, if you wanted to.'

'I do.'

There was a new confidence in Lyuba. It pleased Tholdi to see it. She offered to top up his glass and reminded him that they had another five days ahead of them without Radu. The mention of their benefactor's name stirred up questions that had been on Tholdi's mind for some time now. Questions that until this moment he hadn't dare to ask.

'Does he treat you well?'

Lyuba's reply was guarded. It wasn't a topic she was keen to discuss in any detail.

'It's different than Madame Denile's. But nothing you need to worry about.'

Handing back his glass, she again brought them back to the place where they both felt safe.

'Can you play from memory?'

He knew dozens by heart. Could play whole concertos without a single sheet of music to remind him of the notes.

'Some,' he replied.

'Would you play one for me? Something cheerful?'

She was asking this, he knew, not just for herself. What had befallen Karl was a tragedy but it was only one more in a long procession of tragedies, with many more yet to come. They had to keep going, to find ways to avoid descending into despair. Lyuba settled back on the sofa. Carmen jumped up and curled into a ball beside her. Tholdi took his place back on the piano stool and thought about what he might play. The idea of something festive was too much. Instead, the piece he chose was by a Russian composer.

'Nikolai Medtner. He wrote this when he was only eighteen. It's based on a poem about an angel who carries a young soul down to earth in the night. A new life.'

He didn't mention that the young soul of the poem was destined for a world of sorrow and tears.

Outside, in the cold, Sergio shivered and sighed. His request to have New Year's Eve off, to spend with friends, had been refused. As he reached for another cigarette, he was arrested by the first bitter-sweet notes of the Medtner melody, floating through the melancholy winter fog.

When Tholdi had finished playing he saw that Lyuba was sitting completely still. Her eyes glistened.

'Did you like it?' he asked her.

'It was perfect.'

The piece had stirred Lyuba even more deeply than he'd hoped. He was pleased. Only much later would he understand that it wasn't just the music that had moved her.

29

A week later, at a snow-covered chalet in Straja, Radu celebrated Orthodox Christmas. Lavish feasts were served and carols sung with drunken gusto over mulled wine consumed by the jugful. Even Nadia, now past the troubles of her first trimester, partook. What harm could it do? The pile of presents Sofia had so carefully wrapped was descended upon by the children like wolves falling upon prey, tearing the paper away like skin. If it weren't for Erik having arrived in his uniform they all could easily have forgotten there was a war being fought. Erik didn't speak of it in front of the others, didn't wish to spoil the merriment, but when he was alone with Radu he pointedly remarked that Sofia must have spent a small fortune on the presents, and reported that Nadia had told him all about how well the mill was doing. How much money was being made. By the time Radu boarded the train for home with Sofia, over a week later, he was exhausted. All he could think about was seeing Lyuba again.

In his absence, Grigore had made sure the looms never stopped. He'd had to put in extra hours, but Grigore had no family to demand his time these days. Two years ago, after more than ten years of marriage, his wife had left him. Taken the children and gone back to live with her ageing parents. It had been a scandal. He didn't care. She was a cow. After their first child was born, she never got her figure back. Never even tried. Did she care about that? No, all she cared about was having a man who could house and feed her and her children. He was well rid of her. And now that he had wealth and power, there were plenty of other women out there he could have without the noose of marriage. Women whose own husbands were either away or dead. Who were hungry for the warmth of a man's body.

From above he watched Radu enter the mill through the side door near the bottom of the stairs, and climb to the platform.

Grigore lit a cigarette. 'I expected you to look more refreshed.'

As always with Grigore, sarcasm. Radu ignored it. 'Has everything been going smoothly?' he asked.

'Believe it or not, we managed without you.'

Later that day, Radu stood at the platform railing and looked down at the mill's floor. Searched for Tholdi. The boy was by the forklift. He eventually looked up and saw Radu. Radu ran a finger across his brow.

—

At Moritz's, Tholdi purchased two bottles of wine, a wheel of blue cheese, and chocolate.

'So again with the luxuries. It's been a while.'

Tholdi handed over some lei. Moritz waited, expecting more.

'It's all I have,' Tholdi said.

Moritz knew he was lying.

'For such a good customer, it should be enough,' the boy added.

Moritz weighed it up. 'Split the difference.'

Tholdi put his hand back in his pocket and found he had more lei there after all.

—

Lyuba opened her door to Tholdi. She had spent the day cleaning the apartment, making sure everything was ready for Radu's return. She was covered in dirt and sweat.

'You'll have to excuse me looking like this,' she said. 'I need to bathe.'

To Tholdi it made no difference. What mattered to him was that the past two weeks, having Lyuba all to himself, had come to an end.

Lyuba read his thoughts. 'Don't look so sad. It's what we have to do.'

When his expression didn't change, she sighed. She, too, had enjoyed their time together without Radu. Even more, perhaps, than Tholdi. Still, what was a night here and there with the man who made it all possible? Was it such a high price to pay?

30

'But why? You've been at the mill all day.'

'I told you, there have been problems. On the night shifts. Things Grigore needs me to take care of.'

Sofia didn't believe it for a moment. She knew exactly what his real plans for the evening were.

'It's the girl. You were thinking of nothing else the whole time we were away.'

'You're being ridiculous.'

'Do you think I'm stupid?'

'I think you've been talking to Nadia.'

She had. In lowered voices, so the men couldn't hear, Sofia and Nadia had shared everything. Conspired. Plotted. Strategised.

'I know what you've been up to when I go away. For god's sake, be a man for once. Admit it.'

When he failed to deny it, Sofia pressed home her advantage.

'I will not be humiliated anymore. It's enough. Tonight, when you see this girl, you're to tell her it's over. If you don't end it, I'll make your life hell.'

Later that evening, on his way to Lyuba, Radu thought about those words. He had no doubt that Sofia would make good on her threat. He thought of the ways in which she might deliver it. Unlike Grigore's wife, she wouldn't leave him. Unfortunately.

Radu had his own key, but, like Tholdi, he always knocked. Lyuba opened the door to him. She was even more beautiful than Radu remembered, and greeted him with a smile that warmed him like the sun. His heart sank at the thought of Sofia's ultimatum.

Across the road, in the darkness of his bedroom, Tholdi found himself once again wondering what Radu demanded of Lyuba. What she was expected to do in order to satisfy him. These thoughts stirred in him a disturbing mixture of anger and arousal. Both sensations were unwelcome.

When Radu returned home that same night he told Sofia that he'd decided to grant her wish. To be, for once, a man. From now on, he would spend time away from her whenever he wished. Without any more lies. In their spare room, he made up the bed that Sofia had bought in the hope that, once the baby was born, Nadia and Erik might visit them. The mattress was, as Erik liked it, firm. Not at all the kind that Radu preferred. That night it gave Radu the soundest sleep he'd had in his own home for years.

31

After Radu's declaration, Sofia had spent a restless night alone in her soft marital bed. She was forced to admit to herself that she'd overplayed her hand – and, she had to concede, underestimated her husband's whore. Who was she? Where did he keep her? Sofia considered finding and confronting her. Ordering her out of their lives. But what power did she have to do that? What if the girl refused? Laughed in her face? Sofia decided that option, for now at least, was not a wise one. The idea of leaving Radu, as Grigore's wife had left him, crossed her mind, though only briefly. It would have left her penniless. And where would she go? To her pregnant sister's? No, the only course open to her now was to accept the mistress and hope that over time, as most affairs do, it would run out of steam. That the sex, as thrilling as it might be now, would eventually bore Radu.

After discussing the terms of their new marital arrangement over breakfast – Sofia was very keen to at least save some face – Radu made his way to work feeling positively buoyant. He even broke his own rules and paid Lyuba an unexpected daytime visit to proudly reveal what he'd achieved.

'I didn't give her a choice,' he gloated.

'So you'll be living here now?'

'I wish I could. No, for appearances sake I will still live with Sofia. Spend most nights there. I'll be back home before the end of curfew.'

Lyuba breathed a little more easily.

'But I won't have to lie any more. And we'll be able to see each other much more often.'

For once Lyuba struggled to embrace her role.

Radu became concerned. 'You're happy about it, aren't you?'

Lyuba gathered herself, pinned the mask back on. 'Of course I am. It's wonderful news. I just didn't expect it.'

Radu patted his knee. 'Come here.'

She obeyed.

'My beautiful girl,' he said.

He wanted to kiss her. To avoid it, she put her arms around his neck and laid her head on his shoulder. He stroked her hair.

'Have you spoken to the boy?' she asked.

'I'm happy for you to do that.' It was another aspect of the new arrangements that appealed to Radu. 'The less I have to do with him, the better. Grigore has been watching us. The boy can still do things for you but from now on,' he added, 'I'm giving you money each week. An allowance.'

That, she knew, was a real step forward. A change that elevated her status and cemented things more securely. It was a good thing – for Tholdi as well as her.

Later that morning, at the mill, Radu went to Grigore's office and told him that he no longer wished to handle the workers' wages.

'I don't have the time,' he explained.

Grigore raised a skeptical eyebrow. 'So now all of a sudden you trust me to handle it?'

'Grigore, I never distrusted you. It was Mikael I didn't trust.' Radu added, 'I thought you'd be pleased.'

Grigore was. He'd never been comfortable with his brother handling an aspect of the mill's operations that he considered his territory, but once again he suspected there was something Radu wasn't sharing with him. That Radu had a different motive for suggesting this change.

'Very well,' Grigore told him. 'If it's what you want.'

'It is.'

—

That night, Lyuba and Tholdi discussed Radu's new arrangement. Talked through how it would impact them. She knew that if he no longer handled the money Tholdi wouldn't be able to control the commission he made.

'We can share it,' she assured him.

But that wasn't what really troubled Tholdi. 'We'll have less time together,' he said.

'I know.' There was something else that bothered her, too. 'I just hope he doesn't tire of me. Forbidden fruit is always sweeter.'

Later, alone in bed, Tholdi returned over and over again to that idea of forbidden fruit. Would making love to Lyuba diminish the feelings for her that he had been suppressing for months now? He doubted it. And now, despite his best efforts to resist, he found himself fantasising more and more about what it would be like to make love to her.

32

It was little more than ten years since electric lighting had come to the households of Czernowitz. Before then gas was used. In the more elegant homes, ceilings were affixed with ornate vents, plaster roses whose filigree mouldings allowed the fumes to escape up into the space between floors, and from there, through exterior wall vents, to the air outside. In some homes they had been retained. Electric lights now hung from them. Tholdi had calculated that if he returned to the vacant upstairs apartment where he'd briefly kept Carmen hostage, and cut a hole in the floorboards, he'd be able to look down through the plaster lacework into Lyuba's apartment.

He hadn't anticipated running into Peppa, though.

'What's in the bag?' she asked.

'Tools.'

'For?'

'Repairs.'

'What kind of repairs?'

'Who are you? The Gestapo?'

Peppa turned the screws. 'You're lying.'

'Maybe I just don't like being spied on.'

'Maybe you've got something to hide.'

Tholdi rolled his eyes. It seemed to him that they'd been having exchanges like this ever since he could remember. Now, as the man of the family, did he really need to indulge her petulance?

'Why do you always have to have the last word?' he asked.

'You could just tell me the truth.'

Since the piano lessons, which in the stillness of the night could be heard up and down the street, even through the closed windows, it had become obvious that his regular visits were no longer only about Lyuba's domestic needs.

'You know she's outside now.'

That was true. *Thwack!* The sound of wood being violently split in half, muted but nonetheless distinct, came from behind the solid walls of Lyuba's building. Tholdi ignored Peppa's sniping. Walked on.

She shouted at his back, loud enough for the whole street to hear, 'I know what's going on!'

That was certainly not true. How could she? He didn't know himself.

He'd justified what he was about to do next by telling himself that it was, like Carmen's abduction, for Lyuba's benefit. She'd assured him that Radu demanded nothing of her that he needed to worry about, but how could Tholdi be sure? What he might do, if his worst fantasies proved real, was a question he'd not been able to answer. What *could* he do? Charge in? Defend her? Be her hero? It was a scenario he enjoyed picturing, but which could never be played out. It belonged on a stage, in an opera. If he wanted to keep himself and his parents alive, that's where it needed to stay. And the truth of it, if he'd been more honest with himself, was less noble than any of that. He wanted to see. To watch.

Peppa, meanwhile, didn't take her eyes off him until Tholdi turned into the entrance hall of Lyuba's building.

As in most blocks, the internal stairway was the only way up. In the better ones, like Lyuba's, the stairs were made of terrazzo. The soles of his leather shoes echoed on them. Passing the door to Lyuba's apartment, Tholdi made a mental note to be quieter next time. On the next level, he bent down to remove the wedge of wood he'd left to keep the upper apartment's door closed, and entered. He was tempted to look out the window, to see if Peppa was still watching, but didn't dare; he stayed well back, and left the drapes open. Closing them during the day might in any event only draw attention to the fact that someone was inside.

As with the other homes that had been looted, debris was everywhere. When he'd briefly held Carmen hostage there,

Tholdi hadn't bothered to clear it. Now he tidied the sitting room floor, piling the rubbish against a wall. Like the drapes, the sitting room rug, old and worthless to the looters, was still there. To Tholdi it would be very valuable indeed. He peeled it back to reveal the wooden floor. On his knees, he tapped the boards, searching for a hollow sound. When he'd found it, he extracted a handsaw from his bag and cut a rough-edged square hole. A window. He'd only just completed it when he heard Lyuba return home. The sounds he could hear – the door opening and closing, Lyuba's footsteps, the heavy axe being stored in a cupboard – were surprisingly clear. Like a cat, he crouched down silently and peered through the window he'd cut. Looking through the filigree plasterwork was like looking through a heavy lace curtain. It offered up a picture in fragments, leaving the imagination to fill in the masked spaces. Lyuba came into view and then disappeared again, in the direction of her bedroom. Tholdi carefully rolled back the rug, gathered his tools, and left the apartment the way he'd come, stepping lightly on the terrazzo stairway as he passed Lyuba's door.

33

It was several days before Radu's next visit. Tholdi knew he was coming – he'd received the signal and visited Moritz to buy luxuries – and after the sun had set, after dinner had been eaten and everyone had retired to their rooms, he positioned himself at his bedroom window to watch and wait. Looking down on the street he saw Sergio light one cigarette after another. Before Radu's figure turned the corner, he must have gone through at least half a packet.

The two men exchanged their by now ritual greeting and Radu went up to the flat. Tholdi decided he should wait another thirty minutes before he slipped quietly outside into the dark. He only made it to twenty.

'Sergio?' he called, his voice low.

The guard turned around.

'What are you doing out here? She's with him.'

'I know. I've got something for you.'

Tholdi revealed from inside his jacket four packets of Lucky Strikes.

'Where did you get them?'

'Just take them. They're a gift.'

'In exchange for?'

Sergio was not a fool. He knew that Tholdi would want something in return.

'Herr Golescu isn't the only one with a secret girlfriend.'

Sergio smiled. 'I see.'

'And since you've already been told I'm allowed to be outside . . .'

Sergio considered the transaction Tholdi was proposing and, with a small shrug, accepted the cigarettes. Tholdi walked away and turned the corner.

The large front doors of the building around the corner from Lyuba's were locked at night, but Tholdi had made his way into its basement earlier that day, unlocked the hatch door and wedged it ajar. Now, he slid through the opening and down into the darkened storage space. From there he ascended to the street-level entrance hall and went over to the building's back door, sliding the bolt and opening the door a fraction before slipping outside. It gave on to a courtyard shared with Lyuba's building. It, too, had a back entrance which he had left unbolted earlier that day. Inside, he removed his shoes and made his way up the cold terrazzo of the internal stairs.

Approaching Lyuba's door, his pulse quickened. Passing it, he could hear music playing inside on the gramophone. He entered the apartment above hers on tip-toe and crossed the sitting room floor softly. He drew the heavy drapes before he peeled back the floor rug and removed the square of wood that he'd cut from it. Light from Lyuba's apartment gushed up like a fountain of water, throwing a delicate lace pattern onto the ceiling. The music on the gramophone was clear now: a nocturne number by Chopin. Tholdi crept forward. He thought of his mother's insistence that wearing socks inside the house was bad luck. Something you only did when someone died. It was a reminder of just how dangerous a game he was playing.

At first he could see neither Lyuba nor Radu. But by moving around, changing his angle, he eventually located them. He could see the tops of their heads, and their laps. They were seated side by side on the sofa, drinking wine and chatting amiably. With the music playing, Tholdi couldn't make out what they were talking about, but something Radu said made Lyuba throw back her head and laugh. For a moment, he could see her face.

Radu drew her to him and kissed her neck. After another brief exchange, their voices even lower, Lyuba stood and offered Radu her hand. He took it and they left the room. Tholdi shifted in time to glimpse them disappear into the bedroom. It reminded him of that first meeting. The night at the brothel. When Lyuba had disappeared into a room with Alex.

Later that night, back in his own bedroom, Tholdi replayed in his mind the little slice of intimacy he'd witnessed. There was nothing in it, nothing at all, that suggested roughness or mistreatment. Then again, perhaps that came later, in Lyuba's bed. And so, when the opportunity again presented itself, Tholdi returned with the tool bag and created a second spyhole through which he could properly satisfy his curiosity.

———

In Radu's mind, what he enjoyed two nights a week with Lyuba was lovemaking. Lyuba of course encouraged him to believe that it was the same for her too. Simulating orgasm came easily to her. More challenging was the pillow talk that followed.

'How can you love someone,' he asked, 'if you never kiss them?'

'Did I say that I love you?' she teased.

'But you do. Don't you?'

Lyuba stroked his chest. 'Do I make you happy?' she asked.

'You know you do.'

'Isn't that more important than words?'

'If I made you my wife, would you kiss me then?'

'If you were my husband, of course.'

That, she knew, would never happen. Did she actually care about him? Beyond his role in her survival, not at all.

'You know I love you,' he said.

'And I love you too, Radu.'

Her words warmed his heart, and sent a surge of blood to his cock.

For Tholdi, who had nothing to compare it to, the sexual acts he so privately viewed, the peep show, was at first exciting.

He wasn't able to taste the forbidden fruit but through the lace plasterwork, in pieces, it was now tantalisingly revealed.

Radu was, if nothing else, an enthusiastic lover. His ability to reach a climax that left them both apparently spent, was truly impressive. Though not quite as impressive as Lyuba's own performance. With Radu heaving and groaning on top of her, his thinning pate buried in her neck, Tholdi could see Lyuba's upturned face, and the bored, patient expression it wore even as she moaned with pleasure and whispered Radu's name into his ear. Radu never once questioned whether her climaxes, which invariably coincided with his own, were real.

Tholdi's favourite moments, the ones that made him catch his breath and reminded him to stay still and quiet, were those when he almost felt that he, although she didn't know it, was alone with her. The bathroom had also been converted from gas to electric light and there, too, he cut a window. Through it, he watched Lyuba stretched out in the bathtub. The sight of the water exploring the contours of her body as it ran across her glistening olive skin became for Tholdi far more exciting than Radu's repetitive acts of penetration.

Afterwards, alone in his own bed, he would gather those precious moments in his mind and imagine himself making love to Lyuba slowly and sensuously, caressing every curve and fold of her body as fluidly as water. He hoped that Peppa, in the next room, couldn't hear him masturbating.

34

As the weeks went by, Tholdi found the time he spent with Lyuba increasingly uncomfortable. What if she were to somehow find out about the windows he'd cut into the floor, and the excitement it gave him? And even if she didn't, did that make it acceptable? His conscience reminded him of why he'd cut the holes above Lyuba's ceilings in the first place: the supposed need to reassure himself that Radu wasn't in any way harming or abusing her. That she hadn't been hiding from Tholdi any ugly truth. It was by now undeniable that she wasn't. There had been no hint of anything perverse or distressing, anything that would have warranted Tholdi's heroic intervention. Unless, of course, you counted the thick hair on Radu's back. That must have been, Tholdi thought, repulsive to touch. Still, he knew why Lyuba tolerated it. What was at stake. What she stood to lose. A very large part of which, now, was Tholdi himself.

When she'd first become aware of his attraction to her, Lyuba had expected that at some point she might, as with any other man, find a way to exploit it. Instead, Tholdi had become to her the last thing she expected – a trusted friend. She couldn't recall the last time someone like that had been in her life. Long ago. Before her innocence was ripped from her. Before she'd fled. There had been a succession of small steps leading to their friendship, but it was the piano lessons that had cemented it. They had given her a sense of pride she'd never before experienced. Sharing that with Tholdi, revealing herself to him like that, was an extraordinary experience for both of them. One, Tholdi knew, that revealed far more of Lyuba, and was worth so much more to him, than the moments of voyeurism he'd been indulging week after week, unseen.

In the absence of a rabbi, Tholdi consulted his father.

'What is it, my son?'

Nathan didn't need perfect eyesight to see Tholdi was troubled.

Tholdi put the problem obliquely. 'It's a woman.'

'Is it someone we know?'

It was a question Tholdi avoided. He instead offered: 'I've been watching her.'

'Watching?'

'Without her knowing.'

Nathan grasped the gravity of his son's situation.

'What are your intentions towards this woman? Are they honourable?'

When Tholdi answered, it was in a very small voice, with eyes downcast. 'No.'

'Not Peppa, I'm thinking.'

'No.'

Nathan sat back in his chair and sighed. If it was not Peppa there was, he felt sure, only one other possibility. Nathan tried to think what the rabbi would do, and asked: 'What is your own opinion on it? What does your conscience say?'

'That it's wrong. That it should stop.'

'Then there is your answer.'

'Do you think I should say a vidui?'

The Jewish equivalent of confession. Made not to any mortal but directly to God, aloud, on a Tanakh. The Hebrew Bible.

'It can't hurt.'

That night before going to sleep Tholdi said his vidui. It did hurt a little. Like being an alcoholic and emptying bottles of spirit down a drain.

The next time he saw Lyuba, to give her another lesson, Tholdi wondered if she had for even a moment been aware of the presence looking down upon her.

'I made some cider,' she said. 'Would you like some?'

'Please, yes.'

Lyuba went to fetch it. Sitting alone at the piano, Tholdi looked up to the ceiling rose. It revealed nothing. Had her ignorance of it all made any difference? Made it any more acceptable? He knew the answers. Knew that what he had been doing was a betrayal. That if she ever learned of it, it would destroy everything between them. The trust that had become so precious to them both. The light in her eyes would die, and the thought of seeing that happen was more than he could bear.

Lyuba returned with the cider. Made from the winter apples Tholdi had given her, and sweetened with honey, another treat he had been able to bring her, it was delicious. A shared pleasure. After they had finished their glasses, Lyuba was eager to resume the lesson. To learn more. Her eyes shone with the delight it gave her, and Tholdi was glad of his decision. Had no doubt that giving up his secret obsession had been the right thing to do.

35

The neighbourhood gossip about collaborating with the enemy posed some very vexing moral questions. Did helping to sustain Radu's affair with Lyuba really constitute an act of collaboration? Was collaboration ever excusable? Did it make a difference if it didn't jeopardise the life of another? Or if, for the collaborator, the alternative was death? Was it wrong to be pleased that your name was not added to the mill's monthly list when you knew that someone else's would be instead? They were questions that a rabbi's subtle mind might perhaps find a way to resolve. In any event at the root of the tensions between Peppa and Tholdi were far less philosophical questions.

As she stood with her daughter, chopping vegetables, Mira cut directly to the core of the matter.

'All this pecking at him. It isn't going to help.'

Peppa flicked her mother a glance. Pecking at whom? Help what? But she knew the answers.

In case there was any doubt, Mira added, 'At Tholdi.'

'No-one's pecking.'

'You are. Just like a hen.'

'He annoys me,' Peppa conceded.

'And I understand why.'

Peppa frowned. It wasn't a conversation she wanted to have.

'You've always liked him. I know that. And now that you're a woman . . .'

Woman. It was the first time anyone had acknowledged Peppa as such. The word hung in the air, full of so many implications. Mira waited for Peppa's response.

'It's her. The whore. He's with her all the time.'

An exaggeration perhaps, but Tholdi was over there with her often. Beyond the piano lessons, what went on inside Lyuba's apartment neither Peppa nor her mother knew. Mira could understand her daughter's jealousy, the urges she was struggling with. She also understood what Peppa's aspirations were. What she hoped might one day, if they both lived to adulthood, come to be between her and Tholdi.

'Relations outside marriage are not for women like us,' Mira said. 'Not if you want a man to take you seriously as a prospect.'

'Women like us?'

'For all women I won't speak. For a Jewess, yes. That's the way it is.'

'But for the men?'

Mira shrugged. *It is what it is*, her shoulders said.

'Your time will come. Trust me. But for now . . . don't push.'

Later, over dinner, Mira suggested a round of rummy.

'Sorry, I can't,' said Tholdi. 'I promised Lyuba another piano lesson.'

'More night lessons,' Lina observed pointedly.

Peppa couldn't resist adding, 'She's a very keen student. Apparently.'

Mira pursed her lips. So much for her motherly advice.

Nathan attempted to lighten things with a little humour. 'What did one undertaker say to the other?'

'Really, Papa?' Tholdi said. They'd all heard the joke before. More than once.

Nathan was undeterred. 'If the rich could die for the poor . . .' He waited for someone to complete the punchline. No-one did. '. . . they could make for themselves a good living!'

Nathan's was the only laughter. It petered out quickly, in a little sigh of surrender. He'd tried his best.

After dinner, alone in the kitchen, the two mothers reviewed the situation.

'It can't be easy for her,' Lina offered. 'The woman, I mean. Living alone like that. No family.'

'So now you're feeling sorry for the whore?'

'Haven't you heard? Her people are being killed too.'

'Not here.'

'Not yet.'

'It's not the same,' Mira concluded.

Lina wasn't sure why. Because there were fewer of them? Because they were inferior? She chose to avoid the argument, having neither clear answers nor the energy to find them. In any case, it wasn't really Lyuba she'd wanted to defend.

36

Lyuba wasn't the only one with long, empty days to fill. Peppa busied herself as much as she could with domestic duties, but it was a poor substitute for the stimulation and engagement of school and friends. It gave her a lot of time to think. More than was healthy. As she pounded and squeezed wet bed linen, rinsing and wringing the soap from them, making them ready to hang and dry, she mulled over her mother's words of caution.

She was grateful for the way Mira had spoken to her. Not as a child but woman to woman. As an adult. Mira had told the truth, or at least her version of it, directly and honestly. But it was a truth, a view of the world, that Peppa deeply resented. One in which there was one set of rules for women and another very different set for men. One that permitted men the possibility of sex before marriage. Even encouraged it. Not that she knew for sure that Tholdi and Lyuba were having 'relations', as her mother would put it, but she was certain that something was going on. Something other than the shopping Tholdi delivered and the piano lessons he gave. Something that would explain what she had chosen not to share with her mother.

Unlike Tholdi's bedroom, Peppa's did not have a view of the street, but in recent weeks, when she heard Tholdi heading outside, she'd watched him from the sitting room window. She'd seen him speaking with Sergio. She'd seen their mysterious benefactor come and go too, also stopping to speak with Sergio. On some nights, she'd seen both.

What, Peppa wondered, was the meaning of all this? And why on the nights when their benefactor came did Tholdi disappear from view around the corner of the street? Where did he go? Was Tholdi seeing someone she didn't know about? Her instincts told her it had to do with the woman. And where she lived. And she could no longer resist the temptation to investigate.

She chose a day when Tholdi was at the mill and Lyuba was in town. Without too much trouble she found, around the corner, the wood hatch that Tholdi used, and peered through it, down into the dark and dank-smelling basement. Was this the way Tholdi went? Where did it lead to? She worried that if she went through the hatch, she might wind up stranded down there, surrounded by who knew what. She nearly gave up on it all when a much more straight-forward solution occurred to her; to investigate from inside Lyuba's building. Its main door was open.

It was the door on the top floor that attracted her attention. The one which, like the hatch door around the corner, was closed with a wedge of wood. She removed it, crept inside, and in the sitting room saw the debris that Tholdi had pushed against a wall. Looking around the room she noticed that the sunlight streaming in through the window cast small shadows on the rug's surface. It was bumpy, uneven.

Peppa peeled back the rug and saw that a square section cut from the floorboards had been wedged imperfectly back into place. When she removed the block of wood she found herself looking straight down into Lyuba's sitting room. Carmen was there, contentedly grooming herself. Exploring further, Peppa found other holes above the other rooms. Above Lyuba's bed, and above her bath. She had no doubt who had made them. Would her mother be as disgusted as she was? Would she yet again find excuses for Tholdi's behaviour?

As Peppa was leaving the building, stepping out into the street, Lyuba turned the corner, saw her and stopped. For a moment the two women locked eyes. Peppa looked away, and quickly crossed the street. Lyuba hurried up to her front door and found it still locked. Inside, everything was in order, with Carmen purring on the sofa, undisturbed. It gave her some relief that Peppa had not been there but why, she wondered, had she been in the building at all? And what was the meaning of the guilty look on the girl's face?

Peppa meanwhile brought in the washing she'd hung out to dry earlier. Mira offered to help her fold it. Still in shock, still processing what she'd discovered, Peppa was mute.

Her daughter's moods were beginning to wear down Mira's patience.

'What is it now?' she asked.

'It's nothing.'

Peppa ate her meal that evening in silence. She feared that if she looked at Tholdi she might pick up her plate and hurl it at him. Lina questioned Mira with a look, but Mira had no reply.

Nathan was the one who gently probed. 'You're very quiet tonight.'

'It's a woman's thing,' Peppa told him.

'Ah, I see. Well . . .'

Not something for a man to involve himself in.

'Mama, may I be excused?' Peppa asked.

'You haven't finished your meal.'

In these times, a sin.

'I'm not feeling well.'

'Alright, then,' Mira replied, though she knew it was not Peppa's time of the month. It was something else. She glanced Lina's way, but was met with a shrug.

Alone in her bedroom, Peppa kept turning it all over in her mind. If Tholdi was spying on Lyuba, was it only when their benefactor was there with her? Did that make Tholdi a deviant? Did it rule out the possibility that he also had sex with Lyuba? Should she confront Tholdi? God knows she wanted to. But only God, she thought, knew what might fly from her mouth once she revealed what she'd seen.

37

With so much time to spend at the piano, Lyuba's skills had progressed at a rate neither she or Tholdi could have predicted. When he next visited, he presented her with some handwritten sheet music. Medtner's 'The Angel'.

As if she was defending herself, Lyuba folded her arms. 'I can't play a piece like that.'

'I know how much you like it.'

'And how hard it is. I saw that when you played it.'

'This is a simplified version. Would I give it to you if I thought you couldn't learn it?' Tholdi persisted, 'I transcribed it myself, especially for you.'

He left Lyuba little choice. To reject the gesture would have been ungrateful. Unfolding her arms, she took the sheet music from Tholdi. 'If this makes a fool of me I will blame you.'

'As usual,' he retorted.

Their exchange of smiles made Tholdi more glad than ever that he'd put an end to his voyeurism.

Before she sat down at the piano, there was something Lyuba needed to raise. 'The girl who lives with you. Peppa.'

'What about her?'

'I'm sure it's nothing, but . . . I saw her. Two days ago. Coming out of the building.'

'Which building?'

'This one. Mine.'

Tholdi's heart began to race. He did his best not to let Lyuba see his alarm. 'I'll ask her about it,' he said.

Later, before going home, he crept up to the apartment above and checked for any sign that someone had been there. Nothing obvious presented itself to him but Peppa's sullen manner over the past couple of days suggested otherwise.

With a terrible sinking feeling in his stomach, he went home to look for her. Mira told him that she was in her room, reading. He rapped gently on the door, and was ignored. He rapped again.

'Peppa, it's me.'

'Go away. You're sick.'

He knew then that she had been in the apartment above Lyuba's. Tholdi spoke again through the closed door. 'Peppa, please.'

After a moment he heard footsteps and the door opened. Peppa's voice was full of anger and hurt. 'Now we both know what that bag of tools was about.'

'Can I come in?'

Grudgingly, she admitted him and closed the door again. She didn't wait to hear whatever lies he might have prepared for her.

'Are you having . . . relations with her?'

'No!'

'Don't shout,' Peppa cautioned him. 'Unless you want everyone to know what you are.'

'You can't tell anyone.'

'What? That you're fardorben?'

Depraved.

A fresh wave of shame, the shame he thought he'd unburdened himself of, swept across him. Should he offer up to Peppa the same excuse he'd used to justify his actions to himself? The one he'd since admitted to himself was a lie? Would it be any use to tell her he'd given up his spying? That he'd made a vidui? Silent remorse, it seemed to him, was the only response that would not lead to more outrage, more accusations.

Peppa's anger gave way to something else. To pain and confusion. 'Are you in love with her?'

'No. Of course not.'

She wasn't convinced. Nor was Tholdi.

'Then is this what you want?' she asked, undoing the buttons of her blouse.

'Peppa, don't.'

'Because I can give you that.'

'Stop it.'

'Why? You like to look.'

175

'Stop it! Stop it!' Tholdi yelled at her.

The door flew open. Lina saw Peppa's exposed cleavage. 'What's going on here?' she demanded.

Neither of them spoke. As Tholdi left the room, pushing past his mother into the hallway, Peppa silently buttoned up her blouse.

38

In the end Peppa promised Tholdi she wouldn't tell her mother, or his parents, what she'd discovered that day in the apartment above Lyuba's. That it would remain their secret. But Tholdi knew that the argument Lina had walked in on would be shared with Mira, and that it would need an explanation. Knew that there would be no peace until one was offered.

The following night, at the dinner table, he told the story of how Lyuba's situation had come about. Some aspects he omitted. His first meeting with Lyuba at the brothel. The erotic dreams that followed. The infatuation and the voyeurism. They didn't need to know any of that. The abridged version was alarming enough. They all sat in stunned silence.

Nathan spoke first. 'This governor's list. How did you discover it?'

'Karl heard of it.'

Karl. Nearly four months had passed since he'd disappeared from their lives. Tholdi had said he'd moved to the other mill. None of them had wanted to question the lie. There was only so much bad news they could bear to hear.

'So the trains,' Mira asked. 'This list means they will start again?'

Since the first transportations from the ghetto, six months had passed. Long enough for people to believe they were safe.

'That I don't know,' Tholdi replied. 'Maybe not. Who can say?'

Lina asked why Tholdi hadn't told them any of it sooner.

He took her hand. 'Mama, your heart. I didn't want you to worry.'

Tholdi recalled the oath he'd sworn to Radu on his parents' lives. That part of the story he did not share with his mother, who would see bad luck in him having broken his promise. Tholdi prayed that Radu also would never discover he'd broken it.

Mira couldn't believe that he'd negotiated the arrangement with Radu entirely on his own. 'You didn't think to consult your father first?' she said.

As always, Nathan was quick to defend Tholdi. 'It was his decision to make.'

'So Peppa and I, we are part of the arrangement too, yes?'

Tholdi didn't answer.

'I see,' Mira said, folding her arms.

Peppa attempted to interject. It was her actions that had led to this heated, hostile moment, after all. 'Mama, stop.'

'Why? Am I wrong?'

'No,' Tholdi conceded.

'You see. It's sheer luck that we're here at all.'

'That and the last of Papa's American dollars,' Tholdi said. 'How do you think you got out of the ghetto?'

Seeing his father's reaction, Tholdi regretted his words. Nathan had never mentioned the money he paid, and would have preferred it to remain that way.

'Is that true?' Mira asked Nathan.

'Jakob would have done the same,' he replied.

Mira's remorse was visible. It needed no words. A semblance of calm returned to the dinner table. In a conciliatory tone she asked Tholdi, 'So what now?'

He looked at each of them. 'What matters is that we keep my arrangement with Radu to ourselves. We don't tell anyone.'

No-one spoke.

'And also,' he added, 'that we do everything we can to make sure the arrangement continues smoothly.'

That meant, they realised, abandoning the contempt for Lyuba they'd made little effort to conceal up until now.

Peppa spoke for them all. 'We understand.'

Mira noticed the shadow of a smile on Nathan's lips.

'You're amused by all this? You think it's one of your jokes?'

'You've never met Radu's wife. Ask Lina what she thinks of her.'

To celebrate Radu's promotion at the mill, back when Nathan still owned it, Lina had cooked a feast. Sofia turned her nose up at it. At them. Claimed she had allergies. Radu had been mortified.

'She's not a nice woman,' Lina confirmed.

'She's a klafte.' A bitch. Not the sort of word Nathan used often. 'I'm surprised Radu didn't begin an affair sooner,' he said.

39

Tholdi's revelation changed everything. For Peppa it was the hardest. She believed Tholdi had told her the truth, that he hadn't had sex with Lyuba, which was a consolation. But she was still struggling to comprehend everything that had happened. Despite herself, she still loved Tholdi.

She spoke to her mother to reinforce the need for secrecy, stressing that she couldn't share what Tholdi had told them with anyone. To be sure her mother understood what she was saying, she spelled it out.

'That includes Doina.'

Mira resented her daughter's advice. 'You think I'm stupid?'

'Of course not, Mama. But I know what Doina is like. If she smells a secret, she will do anything to uncover it.'

What she actually thought – that her mother was as much of an inveterate gossip as Doina – Peppa didn't dare say.

Lina, meanwhile, thought of her recent exchange with Mira, the one about Lyuba's people. In truth, the reason she hadn't argued the point was that she agreed with Mira. She thought of the old joke: 'What do you do when you see a Gypsy? Close your wallet!'

It was, she now admitted to herself, no better than the sort of things the Nazis said of her own people. But would she have reached this conclusion if her life, and that of her husband and son, were not at stake? That, she also conceded, was very unlikely. Her remorse took the form of a Gugelhupf cake, which she delivered to Lyuba herself, some days after Tholdi's revelations. Climbing the stairs to Lyuba's door, knocking tentatively, she wondered how she would be received. When Lyuba opened the door to her, she made sure that the cake was the first thing the woman saw.

'I made this for you.'

Lyuba had no idea why, or how to respond.

'I would have liked to put in more fruit,' Lina said, 'but you know how it is. Fruit is such a luxury these days. May I come in?'

There was so much humility in Lina's greeting, so much genuine warmth, that Lyuba stepped aside. She closed the door after Lina, boiled water and made a pot of tea. Sliced and served the cake. Then she sat back and waited to hear whatever it was that Lina had come to say.

'My son told us why you're here.'

This was news to Lyuba. She wondered what had prompted Tholdi to explain, and what it had to do with Lina's visit.

'Have you heard of Yom Kippur?' Lina began.

Lyuba hadn't.

'In our faith, it's the holiest day of the year. The day when we atone for our sins. Make amends. With loved ones and friends. And with our neighbours. When we apologise for any hurt we've caused and ask for forgiveness.'

'Sins,' Lyuba repeated flatly.

'Wrongs. Injustices.'

Lyuba waited for more. She felt it was the least she deserved.

'We haven't been kind. And I'm sorry.'

Lyuba wasn't at all sure she was willing to accept the apology. 'This Yom . . .'

'Kippur. Yom Kippur.'

'Is today?'

'No, it's not. But I didn't think it should wait.'

'Because?'

'Because it's the right thing to do.'

'And also because you now understand that without me you might not survive.'

Lina accepted the rebuke. In her shoes, she would probably have felt the same way.

'Is your family safe?' Lina asked.

'I have no idea.'

And, it seemed, no interest. Instead of establishing common ground, Lina had met a wall. She pressed on anyway.

'Well to us, to me, family is everything. Will I live to see the end of this terrible war? I don't know. But I do know this: I will do whatever it takes to make sure that my son does.'

'I see. So this apology you make. This atonement. Does it matter if it's not sincere?'

'Of course it does. It's made in the sight of God.'

'With cake.'

Lyuba hadn't eaten even a mouthful.

'With love.'

Lyuba didn't doubt Lina's sincerity about that. Even if the love wasn't for her, if it was really for Tholdi.

After Lina had gone, Lyuba looked at her untouched slice of cake. Thought of Lina's words. The traditions that were so foreign to her. She broke off a tiny piece and, like a sacrament, placed it on her tongue.

40

Peppa, Mira and Lina stood with Tholdi, all of them looking at the instrument he'd placed in the centre of the dining table. An instrument whose keys could produce not melody, but symbols – symbols that could be woven into an infinite possibility of words. Tholdi had found it in Lyuba's apartment, in a cupboard in the study, and had offered it to Peppa as a gift of thanks for keeping his secret. A peace offering. She wasn't sure she was willing to accept it.

'It would be a useful skill to have,' her mother suggested.

'For a girl,' Peppa replied.

'Was Dr Mandel a girl?' Tholdi asked.

No-one said what they all thought – that he might as well have been, given his inclinations.

'So you see me becoming a typist.'

Tholdi shrugged. 'What you do with it is up to you. It's not like you don't have the time.'

That was the other thing that had prompted Tholdi to give Peppa the typewriter. The long hours of boredom she had to endure. Hours she'd filled thinking of him. Watching him.

'There's a manual as well.'

It explained how to load the inked ribbon. How to insert the paper and wind it around the cylindrical platen. There was also a section, with tutorials, on how to use its keys with all ten fingers.

The typewriter reminded Mira of her niece, Katya. 'She was a secretary. Very fast with the keys.'

'Oh, yes, she was fast all right,' Lina quipped. 'It's how she met her husband.'

It was well known that Katya and her husband had had 'relations' before marriage.

Mira brushed that aside. 'And three beautiful children they now have. In Canada.'

They had been among the lucky ones who'd got out in time.

Peppa picked up the book and flipped to the tutorials. 'Not just for girls?' she said. She read aloud from a page: 'Ich bin ein Fräulein.'

Tholdi resisted the urge to roll his eyes. 'It's a practice phrase. For your fingers. Like a piano scale.'

'We could make a book of our own . . .'

They all looked to Nathan, who as usual had been maintaining a safe distance from the women.

'. . . of my jokes!'

'That, my darling, is your best joke yet,' said Lina drily.

The joke gave Tholdi an idea. Nathan did not see his own life as having been extraordinary. He was after all one of thousands who had lived through a world war only to be engulfed by another. Who had lived in a country that had been won and lost by a succession of aggressors and claimants. Who had made fortunes and been stripped of them. Who had endured all of it with dignity and grace. But to Tholdi it was anything but ordinary. The memoir that Tholdi persuaded his father to dictate to Peppa, slowly and patiently so she could afterwards type it all up, became a work of love. One that reminded Peppa why she had always been so fond of Tholdi, and line by line, page by page, mended the rift between them. Nathan insisted the jokes be kept in.

Tholdi meanwhile went back to the apartment above Lyuba's and ensured the blocks of floorboard were snugly fitted into the boards from which they'd been cut, and that the rugs laid back over them were flat and smooth. Before he left, he prayed that his past transgressions would remain securely entombed there.

41

Radu nearly missed the call. When the phone rang, he was leaving for the day.

'Herr Golescu?' The caller was brusque, with a manner that announced his authority.

Radu answered tentatively. 'Yes?'

'We have a woman here who claims to know you. Lyuba Fieraru.'

The caller identified himself as a Gestapo officer.

With difficulty, Radu kept his voice steady. 'What's she done?'

'That's what we've been trying to determine.'

—

In an elevated part of the city with large freestanding villas and spacious gardens, a residential area reserved for its wealthiest residents, Lyuba had been arrested for suspicious behaviour. She had been reported by a resident of a nearby villa who had observed Lyuba standing in the street without any particular purpose. Lyuba's arrest had led to a lengthy interrogation by a Gestapo officer, in a bare, brightly lit basement room. Yet again, the officer asked her to explain what she had been doing in the wealthy neighbourhood's street.

'I've already told you. I was resting.'

'After going for a stroll.'

'Yes.'

'You were there for almost half an hour.'

Lyuba again repeated her story. 'I was tired. I needed to rest my feet.'

'Why didn't you go to back to the park?'

The neighbourhood overlooked the city's largest park, several hectares in size. Lyuba claimed she had been there before stopping in the street where she'd been observed and arrested.

'I was on my way home.'

Which was not far from the park but in the other direction from it. Another fact the officer pointed out. And for which Lyuba had an answer.

'The park is large. I took the wrong exit.'

Her story was plausible but not convincing.

'And you don't know who that villa belongs to?'

The owner was an industrialist. A man who owned a steel mill. One of the lucky ones who'd escaped Stalin's purges and returned to reclaim his wealth.

'No,' Lyuba replied. Emphatically.

The Gestapo officer again inspected Lyuba's identity card. It didn't look like a forgery but he'd never before seen a Romanian woman who looked like Lyuba. And if she was what he suspected her to be – a spy – her people would have provided her with papers that seemed authentic.

—

Radu assured the caller that he would come to the station immediately. He looked across at Grigore's office and saw that he was still at his desk. Hating that it was necessary, swallowing his pride, Radu went to him.

'I need your help.'

Grigore couldn't recall the last time he'd heard those words from his brother.

'What's it about?'

'A woman.'

'A woman?'

'Yes.'

Grigore was intrigued. He sensed that he was going to enjoy this.

In Grigore's car, the one Sofia was so envious of, they drove the short distance uphill to a hotel on the Ringplatz which in the Austrian era had been the city's grandest. Its opulent rooms, as well as its name – the Hotel zum Schwarzen Adler, the Black Eagle – had made it the logical choice for the Gestapo to set up their headquarters.

Riding in the passenger seat of Grigore's Opel, with his brother beside him at the wheel, Radu now regretted not owning a car of his own. He stared straight ahead. Kept his eyes on the road. Did his best to ignore Grigore's inquisitive sidelong glances.

Whoever this woman was, Grigore thought, Radu's connection to her was intense. Presumably intimate. Why else would Radu put himself on the line this way?

'So, this woman. Are you going to tell me about her?'

Radu didn't reply.

'One of your whores from the brothel?'

'I'd appreciate your discretion.'

'Of course. We can't let the boss know about it, can we?'

The threat was thinly veiled.

'She already knows.'

'Knows what? That you have a curvă?

Slut. A Romanian word for it.

Radu refused to discuss it further.

It wasn't just a ride that Radu needed from Grigore. It was his relationship with the Germans. The relationship that had allowed the brothers to retain control of the mill. The sight of his car, a statement of power and importance, would also be helpful. Radu asked Grigore to park the car in plain sight of anyone looking out from inside the Gestapo offices, and the two brothers went inside together. At the reception desk Radu explained that they were there to see someone. He gave the name of the Gestapo officer who'd telephoned him.

Soon after, the brothers found themselves sitting opposite the officer, on the other side of his expansive desk. Radu explained that they did valuable work for the war effort. Grigore backed him up, and raised the name of the area commander. Made it clear that he knew the man well. Suggested to the officer that a phone call would confirm it. If he felt it necessary.

Instead the officer decided to find out what Grigore knew of the woman.

'She's my brother's mistress.'

A more dignified epithet than the one he'd used earlier.

The officer addressed Radu. 'Is this true?'

'Yes.'

'And it's also true that she's a Gypsy.'

'Part. Her mother is Ukrainian.'

'So a Mischling.' Mixed blood. 'The worst kind,' the officer declared. 'Vermin. In our country we dealt with them first. I don't understand why you are not yet dealing with them here already. All of them.'

'In our country they are still citizens.'

Grigore flicked his brother a warning glance, and stepped in to smooth things over.

'It's the Romanian way,' he mocked. 'One problem at a time. Once we've finished with the Jews . . .'

'Ah, yes. The famous Romanian efficiency.'

The officer returned Grigore's cool, ironic smile, but his attention remained with Radu.

'Can *you* explain her actions today?'

'I intend to ask her about it myself.' Radu could see that the officer was not yet satisfied. 'She trusts me. If there's anything irregular in it, I promise you I'll report it. I understand our priorities.'

Grigore again spoke up on Radu's behalf.

'We're proud to call ourselves your allies. We would never do anything to jeopardise that.'

Or, the officer understood, the wealth it evidently brought them.

'Mein Herr,' Radu pressed, 'I assure you she's not a spy. I am willing to take responsibility for that assurance. Personally.'

With his finger the officer tapped a document on his desk – Lyuba's identity card.

'Did you arrange this?'

'Is there a problem with it?'

'What documents did you present?'

'She had none. She wasn't born in the city.'

'None? She had a prostitute's licence. I checked with your people's records.'

'I meant –'

'I know what you meant. No birth certificate.'

Radu did not argue the point any further.

'May I offer you some advice, Herr Golescu? If I were you I'd consider very carefully whether or not to continue your relationship with this woman. Prostitutes are a danger to public health. When the Gypsy problem is dealt with here, her kind will be a priority.'

The officer slid Lyuba's identity card across the table to Radu.

'For now, she may keep this. But we'll make sure your people's police records are updated. Her occupation will be recorded as before. If there are any further changes in her circumstances, be sure to inform the police. Yourself. Personally.'

⚊

In the hotel lobby, waiting for Lyuba to be brought to him, Radu thanked Grigore for his help. 'We can make our own way back,' he said.

'I don't mind waiting.'

Radu was firm. 'Please just go.' Having Grigore meet Lyuba was the last thing he wanted.

Being dismissed didn't sit well with Grigore. For a moment he considered resisting. 'You owe me for this,' he said.

Radu had expected his brother would say that. With Grigore, nothing was for nothing.

Grigore left. Minutes later, Lyuba was brought in. She held her head high, her shoulders back. Radu thanked the Gestapo officer for his assistance and apologised for his brother's absence, explaining that he had not been able to wait.

In the back seat of the military vehicle that was arranged for them, Radu's silence was ice-cold, furious. Lyuba was the first to speak, repeating the same story she'd given her interrogators.

'I wanted to walk.'

In the rear-vision mirror, Radu saw the driver's eyes upon him.

'Not now,' Radu hissed, but Lyuba was in no mood to be obedient.

'Somewhere nice,' she said. 'I wanted to walk somewhere nice.'

'The park isn't nice?'

'I'm a Gypsy. They stare. They look at how I'm dressed. Wonder who pays for it all. I wanted to be alone. Is that so hard to understand?'

Radu was shocked by her defiance. He'd been expecting shame, remorse, gratitude. It occurred to him that the only other woman who'd ever spoken to him this way was Sofia. How, he wondered, had he let this happen? Either he needed to end it with Lyuba, or he needed to assert himself. To remind her that in this relationship *he* was the boss.

At Lyuba's street, at its intersection with the Hauptstrasse, Radu told the driver to pull over and ordered Lyuba to get out. Without another word to her, Radu drove away in the car. Lyuba stood watching. Wondered if it might be the last time she ever saw him. Thought about the consequences of that. She turned to see Tholdi approaching, on his way home from the mill. Their eyes met briefly before she walked on towards the place she called home.

Inside, glad to be alone, she poured herself a large glass of brandy from the special bottle Tholdi had bought from Moritz. Watched by Carmen, she drained the glass in one swallow. Radu would be sure to notice the level of the bottle had dropped. She didn't care. As she poured herself another generous measure, there was a familiar rap on the door. She knew who it would be and, downing the second glass, feeling the effect of the alcohol flood through her, she tried to ignore it.

On the other side of the door, Tholdi hesitated, then knocked again. The door flew open and Lyuba stood before him.

'Yes? What?'

He could smell the brandy on her breath.

'I'm sorry, just . . . Are you all right?'

'My hero.'

She'd called him that once before, with affection. Not this time.

'What if I'm not all right? What would you do about it?'

'Why? What's happened?'

She considered telling him. Wanted to. Then she told herself she was being weak. He might call himself her friend, but what could he do to help her? Nothing.

'Don't worry. I'll fix it.'

'Fix what?'

'Please. Just be a good little boy and go home to your mother.'

She closed the door. On each side of it, the two of them stood. *Good little boy.* Tholdi felt humiliated, but wanted to knock again. To find out what had turned Lyuba's world upside down.

On her side of the door, Lyuba waited for him to walk away. After a moment she got her wish, but there was no comfort in hearing Tholdi's fading footfall.

42

That evening Radu surprised Sofia by announcing he'd changed his plans and would be spending the night at home. He offered no explanation, but Sofia sensed that the ground had somehow shifted – that it had something to do with the whore. Had she in some way displeased him? Was he finally tiring of the girl? Whatever it was, Sofia decided it was better not to ask, and she should instead seize the small opportunity that seemed to present itself. She told the cook to prepare a meal for two – something nice – and opened a good bottle of wine. Midway through the meal, halfway through the bottle, she gently reminded Radu that their wedding anniversary was approaching.

For a moment he stopped chewing. When he'd resumed, and swallowed his mouthful of food, he asked: 'And you're reminding me of this why?'

Sofia couldn't blame him for wondering.

'Do you remember our first kiss?'

'Sofia, please, don't –'

'Let me finish.'

He didn't really have a choice.

'I wanted my first kiss to be with someone else. A boy you never met. A boy my parents didn't approve of. They were terrified I would marry him. Or worse. That he'd get me pregnant. Life is full of irony.'

Radu understood that their failure to conceive was what, above all else, had turned his wife into a woman so obsessed with appearances. It was why she invested so much time and energy in her sister's family. The role of the benevolent aunt.

'Sofia, we will never know. Maybe it's been me. The doctor told us it might be.'

'The point is, even though I've never been in love with you, I am fond of you. More than I knew.'

Hard as her heart was, Sofia was speaking from it. Directly and honestly. With a respect for her husband that he hadn't felt from her for longer than he could remember. Perhaps ever.

'And,' Sofia continued, 'I regret the way I've treated you. Punished you. You never deserved that.'

This moment was the result of his having taken a stand. After years of being worn down, of avoiding confrontation at any cost, he'd asserted himself. Now that their positions were reversed and he held the power, he was wary of any kind of retreat.

'Isn't it a bit late for all this?'

'Not if we're going to be together for the rest of our lives.'

It was a prospect he'd pushed out of his mind. Something to be dealt with later. If and when the war was over.

'It can't go on forever,' she said.

He didn't know if she was referring to the war, or the affair. Or both.

'Sofia, I don't know what you expect me to say.'

'I don't expect you to say, or do, anything. Not right now. But, when you're ready, I'm asking for your forgiveness.'

In all their years together it was something she'd never sought. Not once. As they finished their meal, Radu considered her question, and what had happened that day. Whether Lyuba had become, as Grigore would describe it, a liability. A chapter of his life that he should perhaps bring to an end.

—

In the apartment, with Carmen at her feet waiting for scraps, Lyuba ate alone, reflecting on her actions, and the lives she'd endangered – not only her own, but Tholdi's as well. She was under no illusion that all he'd done for her was selfless. He was saving his own skin. That of his parents, too. And he was infatuated with her. Or he had been. Probably still was. But he had given her so much. Treated her with respect and dignity. She hoped that the damage she'd done that day – not only with Radu – could be repaired.

43

Peppa opened the door. For a second time she found herself face to face with Lyuba. The first encounter seemed like a lifetime ago. Something from another place and time. The tone of their exchange was entirely different now. Almost amicable.

'Is Tholdi home?'

Lyuba knew the answer to her question. Knew it was Tholdi's day off. From her own window, she'd looked up and seen him in his bedroom.

Lina appeared at Peppa's shoulder. 'What's wrong? What's happened?'

'I just wanted –'

Behind Peppa and Lina, Tholdi arrived.

'Mama, it's okay. It's nothing.'

'He's right,' Lyuba confirmed. 'Nothing has happened.'

Lina breathed easily again. Allowed herself to be led away by Peppa.

Alone with Tholdi, Lyuba was the one to speak first. 'I've been practising that piece you gave me. Do you want to hear it?'

It was an olive branch, but Tholdi was slow to accept it. 'Are you going to tell me what happened yesterday?'

Lyuba understood that she owed him that. 'Not here though.'

They made their way across the street and up to Lyuba's apartment in silence. Inside, they settled themselves on the sofa. Lyuba took a moment to decide how she would begin. She knew that she would need to be more candid than she'd been with the Gestapo officer. But that's where she began her story, with how she'd found herself in an interrogation room.

As with the view from the holes in the floor above them, the picture was presented to Tholdi in disjointed pieces, like the coming together of a puzzle.

'Someone saw me standing on the street and called the police. They thought I might be a spy. I was handed over to the Gestapo.'

That explained the argument with Radu he'd seen from a distance.

'If your mother hadn't given me that cake –'

'Cake?'

'Your mother gave me a cake. She didn't tell you?'

'No.'

'It was a peace offering. After you told her about the list. Why *did* you tell her?' It was the first chance she'd had to ask.

'I told them all.'

'Because?'

'It just came out,' he stammered.

Tholdi tried to recall the last time he'd lied to her. Not since he'd 'found' Carmen. Tholdi was grateful Lyuba didn't question it. How could he explain why he'd told his family? Why he hadn't shared that with her? Lyuba continued her story.

'Well, the cake brought up a lot of things for me. From my past.'

Tholdi had always known, instinctively, not to ask Lyuba about her past, and had never once pushed her to speak of it. She did so now with her eyes downcast, staring into her clasped hands.

'The apples I used to pick? It was at a house on Landwehgasse. That's where they arrested me.'

Tholdi knew the street well. Everyone did. It was where the millionaires lived.

'I worked there once. As a maid. After I ran away.'

'From where?'

'From a wedding. Mine. When I was twelve.'

'How old was the man?'

'Fourteen. It was all arranged when I was eight.'

Tholdi had for a long time wondered why Lyuba never spoke of her family. Now it was very clear to him. But the rest remained a puzzle.

'And the cake brought this all up because . . .'

'Your mother didn't really bake it for me. She baked it for you. Because she loves you.'

Tholdi waited patiently for Lyuba to make the final connection.

'At the house on Landwehgasse there was a baby. I was his nanny. After your mother's visit I had an urge to see him again. An impulse.' Lyuba finally looked once more into Tholdi's eyes. 'It was stupid of me. Radu was right to be angry.'

'Did you get to see him? The child, I mean.'

'No.'

Tholdi thought about everything she'd told him. He had more questions but before he could ask them Lyuba stood. Tholdi thought he was being dismissed.

'Shall I play for you now?'

'Please.'

Lyuba sat at the piano, and positioned her hands on the keys. 'I might make some mistakes,' she cautioned, glancing over to him.

Tholdi knew how much his approval meant to her, and reminded her, 'Just remember . . .'

'To feel the music.'

'Yes.'

Her technique wasn't perfect, but Lyuba played the notes with a touch that was both feather-light and profoundly sad. It captured the intention of Medtner's composition, and the heart-breaking poem on which it was based, in a way that couldn't be taught. Playing like that had to come from the soul. From life.

—

Tholdi dawdled home with his head full of everything he had learnt that evening, all of it swirling in his mind. As he reached for his keys, as he was about to open his front door, thoughts of Lyuba were shattered by the sound of loud laughter – a man's voice inside. He recognised it instantly. It did not belong to his father.

In the drawing room, everyone was drinking vodka and eating chocolates. When Tholdi entered, they turned to him. The man at the centre of them all, a ghost who'd come back to life, beamed.

'Aren't you going to say hello?' Alex asked.

44

As always, Alex saw the funny side. Over a meal that Mira had prepared, he teased Tholdi.

'The look on your face!'

'It's the hair,' Tholdi deadpanned.

'Do you like it? The girls do.'

'My brother, the bottle blond.'

Nathan's head bobbed side to side, equivocally. 'It's not so bad.'

'Not so bad? It's perfect! He's perfect!' Mira hovered over Alex with a full ladle, another helping.

'Mama, it's wonderful, but –'

Before he could finish his sentence, she emptied the ladle onto his plate. 'Eat! Eat!'

'Like he's skin and bone,' Lina quipped.

Travelling with documents that identified him as an employee of a large German construction company, one that had military contracts in various occupied territories, Alex had for the past few months been enjoying the comfort of German barracks, eating and drinking all he wanted. He was, if anything, a little overweight.

'Better people you will never come across,' he said.

He was talking about the group of Polish forgers whom he'd had the extraordinary good fortune to encounter. He'd spotted them in a café in Timişoara, the small town he had escaped to from the train. Over the course of three coffees he observed them closely. It was the subtlest of details – a shoulder shrug, a head equivocating from side to side, a slight everting of palms – that emboldened him to introduce himself, and to tell them he was an escaped Jew. Once they were assured that he was genuine, they quickly realised how well he could suit their plans. They needed someone to do the first runs, to see if the documents would pass inspection. He not only possessed the Aryan looks they needed, and spoke excellent German, but he had the chutzpah the task required. The swagger that Tholdi had always envied.

'So brave!' Mira exclaimed with pride.

Alex brushed off the adulation. 'It's war. You survive.'

Unable to contain herself, Mira dropped the ladle, squeezed Alex's cheeks with a vice-like grip, and launched upon him yet another barrage of kisses.

'Mama, enough already!'

'You see! I told you!' she proclaimed proudly. *That my prayers would be answered*, she meant. *That I wasn't meshugge. Crazy. That I knew my son would come back.*

Nathan placed a consoling hand on Alex's shoulder. 'Your father would be proud of you.'

Alex's escape from the train, the one he'd been on with Jakob, was the part of his tale that had been hardest for him to tell. He understood what Nathan's hand meant. That he should not feel the weight of guilt.

'It all happened so quickly.'

To remove corpses, the train had been forced to stop on its journey to the Dniester River. The heavy door of Alex's car had not been firmly closed and with Jakob's help Alex had managed to open it again, just enough to squeeze through and jump down. An early snowdrift cushioned his fall. He was glad of that, for Jakob. He'd expected, as he sat up, to see his father in the snow beside him. But Jakob was still on the train, looking down at him. Their eyes met. Then, after the briefest of moments, before the train resumed its journey, Jakob used what little strength he had left to heave the door closed again. The memory of that final moment, of his father's face, would never be erased from Alex's memory.

'So what now?' Tholdi asked.

'I missed Mama's cooking but that's not the only reason I came. Now I get you all out of here. To somewhere safe.'

Glancing around the dining table, Alex saw the apprehension on their faces. 'What, you want to stay here? You think the trains won't start again? You think it's over?'

No-one answered him. Alex assumed this was the same kind of resistance he'd encountered many times now. The passive surrender to blind hope. The refusal to fight back. The insane belief that what was happening to everyone else would somehow not happen to them.

'If you think being out of the ghetto means you're safe . . .'

'We don't,' said Tholdi. He told Alex about the governor's list, and the mill's monthly contributions to it.

'Then what's there to think about?'

Lina answered. 'We have an arrangement.'

'A benefactor,' Mira added.

'What kind of arrangement?' Alex asked.

Lina left it to Tholdi to explain. When he was finished, Alex leaned back in his chair and regarded his old friend with new eyes.

'Quite the gambler you've become.'

'I thought of what you would do.'

'And this affair. While it goes on –'

'We are protected.'

It was Lina who finished his sentence, but Alex saw that any one of them might have spoken up. That they'd all come to accept the arrangement. The fact that it involved a collaborator, or that it made them all, by association, collaborators, was of no consequence to him. Nor did he imagine for a moment that his own plan, the escape, would be easy. The only thing that mattered to him was that they all lived long enough to see the war's end. Ever the betting man, Alex asked Tholdi the one question that only he could answer.

'So this affair. Will it last?'

Tholdi shrugged. 'Who can say?'

Yet another lie. Or, at best, a half-truth. Tholdi might have revealed the events of that day. The rift that Lyuba's actions had created. The threat it posed to them all. But he raised none of it. He also hadn't mentioned who their benefactor's mistress was, or his feelings for her. That last omission, Tholdi saw, Peppa had silently noted.

Nathan, meanwhile, wanted to know more about Alex's plan. Alex didn't discount that there were dangers and complications. They would all need new identities and stories, rehearsed, to explain their travel. Lina's heart raced at the thought of it all, but Mira spoke without any hesitation.

'I say we go.'

Her son had returned to save them. It was God's will. She would take her chances with his plan, as would her daughter.

'I don't get a say in this?' Peppa protested.

'No. In this you will do as I say.'

Lina frowned. 'But Mira, if they catch you . . .'

Alex understood Lina's anxiety, and sought to reassure her. They would need to execute his plan in stages, he explained, splitting into two groups rather than escaping together. He could make the trip first with Mira and Peppa – unlike Tholdi, they had no employer who would notice their absence – and if they made it through, he would return to make the journey again, with Tholdi and his parents, once they knew the others were safe. In the end, Lina agreed.

'What about Doina?' Peppa asked. 'She's already been asking me questions.'

She'd been asking about Lyuba, about why there had been a noticeable shift in their feelings towards her. Keeping the arrangement with Radu from her was hard enough, but once Mira and Peppa left the street Doina would have to be included in their plans. Until she was, she would not stop asking questions.

'Can she be trusted?' Alex asked.

'Do we have a choice?' Nathan retorted.

As they discussed the pros and cons of bringing Doina into their confidence, it weighed on Tholdi's conscience that he'd not fully brought his best friend into his. That he'd given an abridged version of the facts, just as he had to everyone else. But what weighed heavier still, what filled Tholdi with shame, was how he'd felt when he learned that Alex was alive. He should have been overjoyed, like everyone else. But the truth of it was that Alex's return changed everything. Of course he was happy to learn that Alex had been spared the horrors of the camps. If only he hadn't come back to them.

45

Tholdi sat with Lyuba, listening to her account of the night she had passed with Radu, the first with him since her arrest and interrogation two days before. She described how at first Radu had been cold towards her, pointing out that her actions had endangered them both. He'd reminded her that she was his property, that he held her life in the palm of his hand and could extinguish it at any moment. Lyuba had apologised repeatedly and sworn that she would never again do something so stupid, never again place Radu in a position like that.

To make sure of it, he'd imposed new restrictions on her: 'From now on you will not go into town. You will not go anywhere without my permission. Whatever needs you have, Berthold will tend to them. Is that understood?'

Tholdi found it difficult to meet Lyuba's eyes. He could think of nothing other than Alex's plan, and the complete secrecy it required. If it succeeded, Tholdi would disappear from Lyuba's life, suddenly and without explanation. For Tholdi, it would be a wrench; for Lyuba, the consequences could be far more severe. Without his involvement the affair, which now seemed to be on fragile ground, might collapse. It was a betrayal that made his voyeurism seem trivial.

'Tholdi, stop worrying. I said I'd fix it and I did. We made love. At least he thinks we did.'

'What about your identity card?'

'Radu couldn't get it back.'

Tholdi wasn't the only one who had lied to Lyuba.

Placing her hand on Tholdi's, Lyuba reassured him. 'I still have you.'

46

'**P**lace of birth?'

Peppa hesitated, tried to steal a look at her new birth certificate.

'Peppa, you need to memorise it!'

'Are they going to ask a question like that?'

Alex had forgotten just how argumentative his sister could be. He took a moment to calm himself, not so much for Peppa's benefit as the others'.

'If they have any suspicions, any at all, there will be all kinds of questions. If you are unsure of an answer, even for a moment . . .'

He didn't need to complete the sentence. They weren't the first to try to get out. They'd all heard the stories of those who'd failed.

Lina knew that Mira's decision was final, but she was unable to shake off the fear she felt for her old family friends.

'I'm sorry, Alex,' she said. 'Tell us again why you all have to say it's a return journey?'

'We'll be saying we've made the journey more than once, both ways. More journeys, more stamps, less scrutiny.'

Nathan saw that Lina wasn't convinced. 'It makes sense,' he said. 'If other officials have accepted your pass, so will the next.'

All the stamps said *verificat*. Verified. Consistent with their story that they had travelled several times in recent months to see an elderly relative, each time catching the train from their home in the provincial city of Buzău, about seventy miles from the capital, Bucharest, further south. The plan was to avoid the railway stations there, the country's most heavily guarded, by travelling the final stretch hidden on the back of a truck. In Bucharest they would wait out the end of the war.

This last part of the plan also troubled Lina. 'Why the capital?'

Alex again offered reassurance. 'Because there we have a network of people who can help us. There are safe houses.'

'And the birth certificates?' Peppa asked. 'We need them because?'

'Insurance. The more papers we can produce, the better.'

'He's thought of everything!' Nathan trumpeted.

Alex sighed. 'Except the photos.'

The photos would be added to both their new identity cards, and then validated with a final, official stamp – one that Alex, risking his own life, had brought with him, secreted in the lining of his bag. He'd hoped to use photos from the family album, or take new ones with his camera, the one he'd hidden. Learning that it had been stolen was a disappointment, but there had to be a way they could obtain a camera somehow.

Tholdi saw an obstacle.

'Even if we had a camera, how would we get the pictures developed?'

Peppa looked to Mira. 'Do you think Doina would help us?'

Alex saw his mother's reluctance and, for now, swept that hurdle aside. 'One thing at a time. First we need a camera.'

'What about that man you see?' Nathan asked Tholdi.

They all knew by now of the role Moritz played in Tholdi's arrangements.

'If he has one,' Tholdi replied, 'it will be expensive.'

Alex grew impatient. 'You know, Tholdi, for someone who's learned to be such a risk-taker, you could be less of a defeatist.'

He was right. Without even being conscious of it, Tholdi was looking for reasons the plan would not succeed.

'What about my stamp collection?' Alex said. 'We could sell it. Or did the bastards take that, too?'

They hadn't. And Mira had kept it safe. She proudly handed Alex a box. He opened it, took out one of the albums and inspected its condition. It was still perfect. Alex couldn't believe the looters had left them.

'They're peasants,' Nathan said. 'What would they know of their worth?'

For Alex, the albums had a worth beyond price. As a yarn agent, his father had imported fibres from all over the world. Cotton, wool and silk came from the Americas, Asia and Australia, and were distributed to weaving mills across Europe. From all those places, letters and parcels came, and Jakob taught Alex how to soak the envelopes in warm water until the glue dissolved and the stamps floated free. Then, after gently drying them on towels, they would arrange the stamps, country by country, row by row, in the albums' cellophane sleeves. Jakob added rare stamps that he purchased from dealers and gave to his son as gifts. Until puberty, when Alex developed more independent interests, the hobby had given them both many hours of shared pleasure. It was Jakob who had continued the hobby, on his own, and Alex now recalled the days when he came home from socialising with his friends to find his father sitting on his own, adding to the collection. Holding back tears, he promised himself that if he survived the war he would travel all the world's continents, taking with him the memory of his father.

'Make sure you get a good deal,' he said to Tholdi.

—

Tholdi made the journey to Moritz's with leaden feet. When Moritz saw what Tholdi had brought him, a stillness came over the old man. He picked up one of the albums. Ran his hand over the fine leather cover. Opened it to peruse the contents slowly, page by page.

'My son used to collect stamps too.'

It was, Tholdi realised, the only time that Moritz had ever revealed anything of himself. He wondered where Moritz's son might be now.

'So tell me again,' Moritz said. 'You want a camera why?'

'To replace the photos the looters destroyed. Who knows what will happen to us? Who will survive? We want the memories, at least. To pass down.'

Moritz sighed. Not with impatience, but compassion.

'My boy, I know what you think of me. Did I give you a fair price for your opa's ring? I think so. In the circumstances, at the time. Did I make some commission from sending you to the mill? Sure. Just like you've made commissions from all your trips to me. From all those luxuries you've bought. And for who? You're not going to tell me, are you, that it was all for your family? That they are so fond of soft cheese and fine wines? But am I going to tell anyone what you are doing? That business I'll leave to others.'

There were people who made money from such things – informants who prowled public places and reported anything or anyone who looked suspicious to the authorities.

Moritz left the room and after a few minutes returned with what Tholdi needed. The camera was a box type, produced in the thousands before the war. It was almost identical to Alex's.

'There's an enlarger here, too,' Moritz said. 'But for what you need . . .'

An enlarger wasn't necessary. Not for small, passport-sized photos.

'How will you get them developed?' he asked Tholdi.

'We have a neighbour who might help us.'

Moritz placed a box between them containing photographic paper, developing trays and chemicals, and several rolls of film. Enough to allow for any mistakes.

'There are instructions. A manual.'

At the front door, Moritz kissed the middle finger of his right hand and touched it to the mezuzah on his doorframe. 'Tefilat Haderech.'

Tholdi knew the meaning of those words. A blessing for someone who was about to make a journey. One that implored their Maker to guide the traveller's footsteps to a destination of joy and peace. Tholdi would have been satisfied with all of them making it there alive.

47

'Now that's more like it!'

On a table in front of Alex, Tholdi had spread out everything he'd bought from Moritz. Alex threw an arm around his old friend's shoulders.

'We can do this! The basement will be perfect!'

For the developing. But first the photos needed to be taken. The following morning when the light was good he seated all of them, one at a time, in front of a blank wall and snapped their image. A white paper background would have been ideal, as in a studio, with a tripod to steady the camera, but Alex was confident no-one would notice the difference. Afterwards, he and Tholdi set up their basement darkroom, laying out the various trays – one for the developer, one for the fixer, another for the rinsing – and then strung out a clothesline and pegs for the drying process.

Next they stuck masking tape over the gaps around the door and covered the wood hatch with newspaper. The result was airless, and the chemicals were pungent, at times nearly overwhelming, but all light was prevented from entering. The space was pitch black. It took their eyes time to adjust. A red light bulb swung from the low ceiling – they'd improvised with coloured cellophane– but it could only be turned on once the images had been fixed. In the darkness they had to be careful not to hit their heads on it. The small processing tank, stainless steel with a spindle inside and a screw-top lid, was placed on a bench, ready to receive the first roll of exposed film.

As they developed the images, Alex shared with Tholdi more of his adventures – details that he had considered it better the others didn't hear.

'My papers say I'm twenty. It fits better with my story.'

With a Polish passport, one that identified him as a Volksdeutscher, an ethnic German, and now bore multiple stamps, he'd visited some of Eastern Europe's finest cities – and enjoyed some of their finest young women.

'In Budapest there's one . . . You should see her.'

'Zaftik?'

'Jawohl, mein Herr!'

They shared a smile. Like old times. Alex had expected there to be more such moments, but he'd found Tholdi distant and withdrawn.

He took the photo images, still in one strip, from the rinsing tray and pegged them to the line. Tholdi turned on the red light.

'They look good,' Alex said.

Tholdi had to agree. He set about cleaning the trays and tidying the equipment.

'Speaking of zaftik,' Alex added, 'I saw your benefactor's woman today.'

Tholdi tensed.

'She was getting dressed. With the curtains wide open. I only saw her from behind, at an angle, but from what I caught . . .' His hands shaped an invisible hourglass in the air.

'Where were you?'

'At the window.'

'What if you'd been seen?'

'I know. Not smart. I was bored.'

'You should be more careful.'

As Tholdi finished cleaning up, Alex studied him – his old friend with whom he shared so much history.

'Tholdi?'

'Yes?'

'Is there something you're not telling me?'

'Like what?'

'Are you worried my plan won't work?'

What actually troubled him, Tholdi was unable to share.

'I want us to all be together,' Alex said. 'That's what you want, too, isn't it?'

'Of course. Why wouldn't it be?' Tholdi turned away and continued cleaning the trays.

———

With everything spread out on the dining table, Alex put together their forged documents. Peppa worked in the same room, at a small writing desk, busily typing the latest chapter of Nathan's memoirs from her handwritten notes. Before she left, she wanted to get as much of it finished as she could. While waiting for the stamps' ink to dry, Alex stood and stretched. Yielding to temptation, he drew the curtain a little and scanned the street. Wood had been delivered across the street. The benefactor's woman was throwing a load of it down into her basement, and this time Alex saw her face.

'Peppa?'

'Yes?'

Clack clack clack, the typing continued.

'What do you know about your benefactor's mistress?'

The typing stopped, and Peppa looked up, her curiosity piqued. 'She's tsigayner. I know that.' She couldn't resist adding something else. 'And she's got Tholdi on a string.'

When Tholdi returned from the mill that evening, Alex took him into the most secluded room of the apartment, the maid's room where his mother slept, and confronted him.

'So it is her?' Alex demanded.

Tholdi couldn't deny it.

'Why didn't you say so?'

'I told you. He's in love with her,' said Peppa.

Tholdi saw that Peppa had followed them. She, too, wanted to hear what Tholdi had to say for himself. Alex would have preferred her not to be with them but he urgently needed to know the truth.

'Have you been sleeping with her?'

'What? Are you crazy?'

'I remember the way you looked at her that night.'

'What night?' Peppa asked. Tholdi ignored her too.

'Well?' Alex said.

'No.'

'So then why didn't you tell me?'

'I thought it would stir things up. For you.'

'What? You thought I'd be jealous? That I'd do something crazy? You're the one who's meshugge.'

Peppa had told Alex about the little holes in the floor that she'd discovered. The spying. The confrontation that had followed.

'Now I understand why you wanted me to stay away from the windows.'

Tholdi did his best to contain the situation. 'Alex, what does it change?'

Alex stared hard at his old friend for several long seconds, and then left the room. If he had answered that question now, in the heat of the moment, it would have been with just one word – *everything* – and he knew the damage to their friendship would have been irreparable.

Peppa turned to Tholdi. 'So you both knew her before the ghetto. Before you got the job at the mill. Where from?'

Tholdi glared at her. 'Why, Peppa? Why did you tell him?'

'You're going to blame me for this? It's your doing. All of it.'

'You promised.'

'I promised not to tell our parents, and I didn't.'

She, too, marched out.

For the next three days, Alex avoided Tholdi, unable to look him in the eye. When Tholdi entered a room, Alex left it. Never in his life had Tholdi felt so alone. When Alex at last came to his bedroom and asked to sit down with him, Tholdi greeted the request with a mix of relief and apprehension.

As he closed the door, Alex said calmly, 'So tell me. Is Peppa right? Are you in love with Lyuba?'

Tholdi owed it to Alex to answer honestly. Or as honestly as he could. To make himself understood. 'I care about her.'

'About a whore. A prostitute.'

'You don't know her. Not like I do.'

Alex didn't ask Tholdi to explain. Whatever had transpired between them, only one thing now mattered to Alex: that all his meticulous planning would not be brought undone. Tholdi assured Alex that he had shared nothing of it with Lyuba, and promised that it would stay that way. Tholdi swore to it, once again, on his parents' lives.

Almost a week after he'd returned, Alex set out for the railway station with Peppa and Mira. He had some parting words for Tholdi.

'Don't do anything I wouldn't do.'

Tholdi laughed. 'Is there anything you wouldn't do?'

Their friendship had been pushed to breaking point, but it had survived. The two – young men, no longer boys – shared a final embrace.

Peppa also wrapped her arms around Tholdi. Held him close and tight. Whispered in his ear. Extracted her own promise from him.

'No more spying. If you got caught . . .'

'No more. I promise.'

'Good. I want to see you again. Alive.'

Mira had to prise her from him. 'Time to leave.'

Peppa didn't want to let him go, but she finally released him. Kissed his cheek. Left tears on his skin.

'Please God,' Lina beseeched the heavens, 'keep them safe.'

And then they were gone.

48

It would be weeks before Alex returned for them. If he returned. The waiting was agony. It made Tholdi's days at the mill seem like a reprieve, an escape from the awful silence that now engulfed his home. From the kitchen there no longer drifted the chatter of Lina and Mira, cooking together. Preparing meals on her own now, in a constant state of anxiety, Lina seemed to do everything as if in a trance. With each passing day the circles under her eyes became a little darker and deeper.

Tholdi also missed the endless little arguments Peppa had stirred up, no matter how many times her mother warned her not to, just as he missed the relentless clacking of the typewriter, which he'd found so annoying. Peppa had managed to complete Nathan's early years, at the end of the last century. The pages were full of precious details of daily life that no history book crammed with names and dates and battles could ever hope to capture.

'We can finish them when we're all together again,' Nathan had said to Peppa before she left.

Peppa had put them in a drawer of the writing desk. Behind them Tholdi hid the papers Alex had forged. The ones awaiting his return, and the second part of the escape plan.

Ever the optimist, Nathan did his best to keep them focused on the future. He listened every day without fail to the BBC news broadcasts, which were now reporting German losses in Russia and Allied victories in Africa. The tide of the war, Nathan declared, was turning.

The three of them spent many hours memorising every detail of their new identities, as well as the story they had invented to explain their need to travel. More than once Lina made mistakes, became anxious and flustered. Each time Nathan reassured his wife.

'Relax, Lina. It will come. Let's try again.'

At least with his parents Tholdi could speak openly about their imminent departure. Knowing he would soon be abandoning her, being in Lyuba's company was now a constant strain. It wasn't hard to explain why Peppa and Mira had so suddenly disappeared – many, like Karl, had been taken – but he hated to lie to her.

'Tholdi, I'm sorry,' Lyuba said, when she first learned that Mira and her daughter were gone.

Her sympathy was genuine. It surprised them both, and made Tholdi feel a new kind of guilt. But he had no choice – he couldn't tell her the truth. Not after swearing on his parents' lives for a second time.

49

W hat Tholdi did next bordered on insanity. If he was caught, in possession of a camera and without his armband, there would be no escaping interrogation, followed by certain death. But taking risks had become a way of life, and now that he'd come this far there was a thrill to them that wouldn't allow him to back out.

With the scent of spring in the air, he thought of the dream he'd had all those months ago, and of the edelweiss legend. There was no doubt that his plan was every bit as daring as climbing any high alpine peak. What he wasn't certain of was how Lyuba might react to the parting gift he was hoping to give her. If his plan succeeded, and if his suspicions proved to be correct, he might not be met with gratitude. His heroic gesture might enrage her, she might see it as an intrusion into her past. But unlike when he'd cut out the spy-holes, when the truth of his motives was less noble than he told himself, now at least he was able to be honest with himself. He had to *know*. Before it was too late.

Finding the house had been easier than he'd expected. It was freestanding, on a generous block of land with an apple orchard. A child, perhaps nine or ten years old, and wearing clothes that weren't much better than rags, was picking fruit from branches that overhung the high cast-iron fence. He passed them to a friend, who collected them in a bag. Through the fence's iron bars Tholdi saw an elderly groundsman approach. He shouted at the young thieves.

'Get away from there! Shoo!'

The children grabbed their bag and ran. Muttering curses, the groundsman shuffled back towards a garden shed. Tholdi scanned the villa's tall, elegant French doors. At one pair of them a maid threw open the heavy brocade drapes and opened the doors to shake dust from a rug. Through the open doors, Tholdi spotted a grand piano, shiny and black, and then a child in school uniform ran out into the yard, chasing a puppy. The boy almost bowled the maid over on his way past. She scolded him, telling him to go back inside and get ready for school.

Yes, Tholdi told himself, *this must be the house*. And the boy was surely the child Lyuba had once nannied.

Tholdi heard the nanny yelling after the boy. 'Nicu! Get your bag! It's time to go!'

Nicu. Could it be short for Nicolae? The Romanian version of Nikolai. Tholdi recalled Lyuba's reaction to the piece about an angel bringing a new soul into the world, the one he'd played for her on New Year's Eve, the one by Nikolai Medtner. No wonder it had resonated so deeply with her.

The puppy ran inside. The boy ran after it.

From a little way along the street, on the other side from the boy's house, Tholdi opened his overcoat just enough to position the little box brownie hanging by a leather strap around his neck. He peered down into the viewfinder, focusing on the villa's front gate through which, he prayed, the boy would emerge at any moment.

Minutes passed. They felt like hours. Tholdi glanced at the windows of the houses nearby. He knew the neighbour who had reported Lyuba must live in one of them. Despite the spring breeze, he shivered. Two more minutes, he told himself. Then he would give up. Then he would leave. Without a wristwatch to time it, Tholdi put one hand to his chest and used his own heartbeat to count the seconds. The two minutes passed. To remain any longer was beyond insanity, it was suicide.

And then the front door opened.

'Hurry! We're late!' the nanny called.

Through the camera's viewfinder Tholdi framed his moment of opportunity. There wouldn't be another. A split second before he pressed the shutter button, the boy looked his way, and saw him. Their eyes never met directly, only through the lens of the camera. An instant later, controlling the urge to run, Tholdi walked away, rounding a corner. The nanny had seen none of it. She gripped the boy's hand firmly, and dragged him in the other direction.

50

Just one photograph, that's all Tholdi had had the time to take. In the darkened basement he laid out the developing trays, mixed the chemicals, processed the roll of film and waited for the single exposed frame to reveal itself.

There was the image Tholdi had risked his life to capture. It was small – Tholdi wished now that he'd bought the enlarger from Moritz – but perfectly clear. He placed it inside an envelope and thought again about how Lyuba might react. It was done now. He'd risked his life for it.

On his way out, coming down the stairs, he passed Lina. She asked if he was giving Lyuba a piano lesson.

'Maybe,' he said, as he hurried on outside and up to Lyuba's front door. He took a moment to catch his breath, then knocked and waited with a mixture of excitement and apprehension.

Opening the door, Lyuba immediately sensed this was no ordinary visit.

'May I come in?'

She stepped aside, and closed the door after him. From a pocket, he revealed the envelope. She wondered if it was something official. It made her anxious. 'Is that for me?'

'Yes.'

'What is it?'

'It's a photograph. Of the boy you wanted to see. At least I think it is.'

After a very long moment, she took the envelope from Tholdi and slid out its contents. Lyuba had no doubt whose face was in the photograph. Without taking her eyes from it, she went to the sofa and sat down.

Tholdi kept a respectful distance. 'Is it him?' he asked.

She didn't reply. A single tear spilled down her cheek. Then more. A cascade of tears that came from years of grieving, of regret and guilt, shook her whole body. When at last the tears subsided, and Lyuba stopped shaking, Tholdi had to ask.

'Is he yours?'

When the reply eventually came, it was in a barely audible whisper.

'They wanted a baby so badly. When I told them I was pregnant . . . they promised me I'd be allowed to stay. If it came out a boy.'

'And the father, I assume . . .'

'Yes.'

Tholdi wondered if her employer had forced himself upon her. Whether there had been any seduction. At the time, Lyuba would have been still not much more than a child. By Tholdi's calculations, not more than fourteen.

With the back of her hand, Lyuba wiped away her tears, and her eyes at last met Tholdi's. 'How did you get this?'

'I took the picture myself.'

'If you'd been caught . . .' She shook her head in disbelief. Not for the first time Lyuba wondered what she had done to earn Tholdi's devotion. She felt unworthy of it.

Tholdi was relieved that she wasn't angry, wasn't offended, but he nevertheless suddenly felt like an intruder.

'I should go.'

'No. Don't.'

She slid the photograph back inside the envelope, and stood, moving close to Tholdi. Close enough for him to feel her breath. Her hands reached for the top button of his shirt.

Tholdi flinched, and gripped her wrist. 'What are you doing?'

'You wanted it to be special.'

'Yes, but . . .'

She pressed a finger to his lips. 'I want to. But it will only be this once. Yes?'

His mind raced. He'd fantasised about this so many times. Had ached for it. But if she knew that he was about to abandon her, that the photograph was a parting gift, how might she look back on this moment? How would she remember him?

Tholdi slowly released his grip.

One button at a time, Lyuba opened his shirt. With each button, she paused to press her lips to his smooth skin, descending kiss by tender kiss from his chest down to his taut, young belly. With each one she could feel Tholdi's heart beat faster. When she reached the fine, soft line of dark hair that disappeared down into his trousers, she stood again to look into his eyes and kissed him once more, her lips to his. And then led him by the hand to her bed.

51

When Tholdi woke the next morning, he wondered at first if the previous night had been another dream, like the one he'd had all those months ago. He was afraid to open his eyes. It wasn't until he did, and saw her lying next to him, still asleep, that he knew it was real. He didn't wake her, but slipped away so that he would be back in his own bed before his parents awoke.

Now that summer was approaching, the days were lengthening. The first rays of sun were already colouring the horizon. Crossing the street, he was spotted by Sergio. Luckily he'd come from around the next corner and hadn't seen Tholdi emerging from Lyuba's building. He assumed that Tholdi had spent the night with his girlfriend – the fictional one. He shot Tholdi a wink.

Back in his room, Tholdi climbed into his own bed and lay there, awake, until Lina knocked on his door. Over breakfast, his mother seemed to notice something strange in her son, she fussed over him and asked if he was feverish. Nathan voiced concern, too. Tholdi assured them both that all was well with him.

At the mill, he passed his shift in a kind of reverie. The racket of the looms, usually an assault on his ears, seemed to recede and fade. He replayed how Lyuba had taken control of him. Guided him. Made love to him. The second time she'd let him take the lead. Let him be not a boy, but a man. Could it have been, Tholdi wondered, any more special if his first time had been with a woman he would be spending the rest of his life with? Or even with a woman he could make love with again? He doubted it. Every nerve ending in his body had danced like light upon water. The two of them lying together, both of them spent and entwined, had been a kind of bliss that had touched him as deeply as any piece of music he'd ever heard. The temptation to break his promise to Alex had been almost overwhelming. Keeping it was breaking his heart.

'If Radu ended it,' he'd asked as they lay together, 'what would you do?'

'I try not to think about that,' she'd replied.

'You know you'd survive. You're strong. And you're smart.'

'I can't even read.'

'You can read music.'

'Thanks to you.'

She had smiled, then, and rested her head on his chest. It was the most beautiful smile Tholdi had ever seen.

A voice rudely interrupted Tholdi's reveries. 'Linker! Pirns!'

They were empty. Tholdi re-loaded them, wondering what Lyuba might be doing at that moment. Was she still lying in the rumpled bed where they had made love?

In fact Lyuba was washing the sheets. Radu had only ever visited her during the day once, and still always left very early in the morning while it was dark, but what if today he turned up at her door? There was no point in taking unnecessary chances. Sleeping with Tholdi, even just the one time, had been dangerous enough.

It had taken her by surprise, as much as it had Tholdi, but he'd given her so much and the photograph, on top of everything else, was such an extraordinary gift. So precious to her. *My hero.* When she'd first said it, on the day he found Carmen, she'd been half-joking. Not anymore.

She wondered yet again how it was that she'd cast such a spell over him – what he'd seen in her that first night at Madame Denile's that had so entranced him. Perhaps he was right. Perhaps it was destiny – schicksal – that had brought them together. She only hoped that the gift she'd given him in return wouldn't somehow be their undoing. She'd smoothed things over with Radu and Tholdi had reported to her that the Germans were in retreat. They just had to ride out the rest of the war with nothing else going wrong.

When she'd hung the sheets out to dry in the courtyard, she sat at the piano and looked again at the photograph she had propped up there, imagining what it would be like to have her child back in her life. Not long ago she wouldn't have dared to think of it but now, thanks to Tholdi, anything seemed possible. Granting Tholdi's wish, making his first time special, was the least she could do to thank him. In the end, in its way, it had been special for her, too. Fleetingly, she contemplated a future with Tholdi. It made her laugh. Had he cast a spell over *her*?

—

At Tholdi's, Doina was helping Lina roll up the rugs, ready to take outside to beat the dust from them. Piano notes drifted in through the windows they'd opened to let in the sweet spring air.

'Not so bad,' Doina remarked.

'She's a Gypsy. They're musical,' Lina responded.

'Any word of Alex?'

'Mail is too dangerous. We just have to wait.'

Doina nodded, and was about to gather up the corners of another rug when she paused. 'Look who's here.'

Lina looked out the window just in time. She caught the back of the man entering Lyuba's building.

Absorbed in the music, Lyuba didn't immediately hear the knocking. He had to knock again, more loudly. Lyuba wondered who it might be – Tholdi was at the mill, and it wasn't Radu's familiar knock. She opened the door cautiously, to a man she'd never seen before.

'Can I help you?'

With an oily smile, the man Doina called the scarecrow introduced himself. 'Vladyslav Pazyuk. I'm your landlord. May I come inside?'

Lyuba didn't want to cause any trouble. After closing the door behind him, she asked, 'Is there a problem?'

'No,' he assured her. 'I just wanted to make sure that you're happy here.' He looked about, saw the vase of cut flowers, the open piano, and Carmen grooming herself contentedly. 'And from the look of things, I'd say you are.'

He smiled again. The same oily smile.

'Was that you playing before?' he asked. 'The piano?'

'Yes.'

'Beautiful *and* talented. Herr Golescu is a lucky man.'

It was no compliment. He was making it clear he understood her role. What she was to Radu. To the man who paid her rent.

Lyuba gestured to the rest of the apartment. 'Do you wish to inspect?'

'I've seen enough.'

'Well, if there's nothing else . . .' She opened the door again. 'I'll tell Herr Golescu you called.'

'Not necessary. But thank you.'

On his way out he tipped his hat to her – more mocking than gallant. She was glad when he was gone.

———

Later that day, in the early afternoon, Herr Pazyuk made another visit. This time to the mill. It was Radu he'd come in search of, but Grigore intercepted him on the mill floor. He informed him that his brother was not there, but that he would happily pass on a message. Pazyuk decided that discretion was in order, and would reveal only that his matter had to do with a rental property.

Grigore was intrigued. It could only be about one thing, he thought. He lowered his voice and confided, 'I assume it's to do with his girlfriend.'

Pazyuk's eyebrows levitated. 'I wasn't sure if you knew about her.'

'But of course,' he assured Pazyuk. 'Twins don't have secrets.'

'Now that you mention it, I did notice the similarity.'

They were, in fact, as dissimilar as twins could be. Grigore grinned, as if complimenting the other man's acuity.

'It's the one on Strada Odobescu. Number thirty-two, yes?'

Pazyuk's eyes widened. 'Your brother has more than one girlfriend?'

Grigore made a show of glancing about, to make sure no-one was within earshot. 'He has three.'

Pazyuk's mouth fell open.

'I know. Who would have guessed?'

'Mine is the one on Strada Gheorge Tofan.'

'Number?'

'Twenty-two.'

Grigore grinned again. 'Well I'll be sure to tell him you came by.'

Pazyuk understood that he had been dismissed. That was when it dawned on him that he may have just been lured into a trap. Keen to avoid any further blunders, he thanked Grigore for his time, and left.

As soon as Pazyuk had left, Grigore climbed the stairs to the platform and opened a drawer of the large filing cabinet that lived between the two offices. He combed through the register in which they kept records of the mill's employees, including their home addresses. Among them he found one who lived on Strada Gheorge Tofan. At number seventeen. It took him a little while to identify. Tholdi had given his address by its German name, Sturmgasse. Feeling very clever, Grigore put away the register, and thought about how he could best exploit the information that had just come his way. Over the platform railing he looked down to the mill's floor, where Tholdi was among the workers arriving for a new shift. Then the side door opened, and Radu entered, back from lunch. In Grigore's mind a scenario began to take shape; one that would be both advantageous and enjoyable. He waited for his brother to reach the top of the stairs, wheezing.

'Everything all right?' Radu asked.

Grigore took a moment to decide how he would approach it all.

'How is the boss these days? It's a while since we've seen her here.'

After Radu had asserted himself with her, Sofia had avoided the mill. But until now Grigore had not commented on it. *Why now?* Radu wondered.

'Her sister. The baby,' Radu replied vaguely.

'Not because you're still seeing your whore.'

'I told you, that's ended.'

After the visit to the Gestapo, Grigore had probed his brother about the woman they'd gone to rescue, but without any success. Radu told him he'd taken the Gestapo officer's advice.

'So you'll be having dinner with Sofia tonight?'

As it happened, Radu did plan to.

'Well, give her my regards.' Grigore grinned cryptically and left Radu alone on the platform.

—

Sergio was tapping a cigarette from its pack when the shiny Opel coupé rolled to a stop and parked. The driver got out and approached him.

'I'm Herr Golescu's brother.'

'Sergio, mein Herr.'

Exactly as Grigore expected, he knew Radu.

'What can I do for you, mein Herr?'

'Nothing you don't already do for him.'

From his jacket pocket, Grigore extracted a fat wallet, handed Sergio a large leu note, and then asked: 'Which one is number twenty-two?'

'That one, mein Herr.'

Sergio pointed. Grigore looked up and saw Lyuba passing by the open sitting room window of her first-floor apartment. He thanked Sergio, who watched Grigore enter the foyer of Lyuba's building. Wondering what it all meant.

Lyuba was putting firewood into the stove when she heard the knocking on her door. Hoping it wasn't the landlord again, she opened the door even more cautiously than she had earlier that day.

Grigore grinned. 'Hello. I'm Radu's brother.'

Lyuba instantly sensed danger. She tried to conceal it behind a façade of formality. 'Herr Golescu isn't here. Would you like me to give him a message?'

'I know he's not here.'

'Then what is it I can do for you?'

'What's mine is his, and what's his is mine. We share everything.'

Without any further words, Grigore entered. Lyuba did not dare to bar his way.

52

It was another two nights before Lyuba next saw Radu. She thought about saying something to Tholdi, asking him to pass on a message for Radu to come sooner, but decided that might only inflame the situation. She had no idea if Grigore planned to pay her a second visit and if he didn't intend to come again then perhaps it was best not to mention it. On the other hand, if she didn't say anything to Radu, and he later found out . . . More lies. More omissions. Radu might even see it as a betrayal.

In the end, she decided she would tell him but when she did, his reaction – distress and anger, but not surprise – left her feeling even more disturbed.

'You knew he was coming here?' she asked.

'No, but he said some strange things to me a couple of days ago.'

'Could this have anything to do with Herr Pazyuk?'

'How do you know his name?'

'He came. Three days ago.'

'For what?'

'He didn't say.'

Radu joined the dots. 'That man is an idiot,' he said. He was reluctant to ask more, but felt he had to. 'What did he do? My brother?'

She was just as reluctant to answer – she didn't see how sharing the details would benefit either of them.

'Tell me,' Radu insisted.

'I pleasured him,' she said irritably. 'On my knees.'

Radu looked away in disgust, as if he was the one who'd been used.

Lyuba was not so upset about the act itself. In her years at Madame Denile's she'd done things she'd found far more degrading. What concerned her was whether this signalled a shift in their arrangements. A shift that might be a threat to her survival.

'Will it happen again?' she asked.

Radu couldn't give her an answer. He knew that he would need to confront Grigore. That Grigore would be expecting it, and would, no doubt, enjoy it. Just as he'd enjoyed teasing and torturing Radu when they'd both been children. At least in part that was, Radu suspected, what this was about. What his brother wanted.

When Radu arrived for work the following day, his brother was already there, in his office. Through its glass window they exchanged a look. Radu's face was ashen, Grigore's cheerful. Grigore waited for Radu to come to him.

'Quite a woman, your Lyuba. She obviously knows how to keep a man happy.'

Merely hearing his brother speak her name made Radu's blood run cold.

Grigore turned the knife. 'You know, brother, you really shouldn't lie to me. We're partners.'

It suddenly hit Radu. 'Is that what this is about?'

'Let's be honest with each other, Radu. I'm the one who runs this business. And who knows the people that matter. In the party. You're just a technician. You're doing well to get any share of the profits at all. We've both known that for quite some time now.'

Radu considered his position. What leverage he had. Very little, he concluded.

'How much?'

Grigore had been looking forward to this moment. 'For you? Ten per cent. Plus your usual wage, of course.'

Radu wasn't a violent man, but fury rose up in him.

'Sofia won't like this. How will I explain it to her?'

'That's your problem.'

'And if I refuse?'

'Did you know it's begun now for the Gypsies?'

In the forests, the nomadic Roma – those who'd survived the Einsatzgruppen commandoes – were all being rounded up and made to haul their horse-drawn wagons to Transnistria. The cities would be next. All across the country Romania's police force was putting together yet another list – a national register. On it were the names of Roma who were to be targeted first – anyone who'd ever been arrested or suspected for the most minor of offences, or who was considered a threat to public health. Prostitutes were at the top.

'You were lucky the Gestapo let your whore go the first time,' Grigore reminded him. 'I'd only have to pick it up,' he added, nodding towards the telephone on his desk. He leaned back in his chair, stretched out his legs, lit a cigarette and exhaled. 'I'll give you some time to think about it.'

Radu turned to leave.

'We're not finished.'

Radu forced himself to turn back.

'Two more things. Linker. He's your houseboy. Am I right?'

The question was rhetorical. And Grigore didn't need to know the extent of Tholdi's involvement, the role he'd played in setting up the arrangement Radu had so enjoyed.

'All those little looks between you two. You know I saw them.'

'He's useful.'

'Which is why, for now at least, we'll keep him.'

'What's the other thing?'

'Your landlord.'

Radu had been planning to go and see him that morning.

'What about him?'

'Not the brightest star in the sky, is he? Anyway, there's a letter from him on your desk.'

It informed Radu that the rent had been raised. Radu crushed the letter into a tight ball and threw it across the room. A moment later he left the mill, and headed for the apartment. It was only the second time that he'd dared to go there during the day.

Lyuba was relieved to see him – until she heard about the ultimatum that Grigore had delivered.

'So what now?' she asked.

'If we end it, he'll back off. But you'll be on your own. If we don't . . .' Radu explained Grigore's threat.

'And you'll have your wife to deal with.'

'Yes.'

Over their months together, Radu had on several occasions opened up to Lyuba about his marriage. Unburdened himself to her sympathetic ear. Sofia might tolerate her husband taking a mistress but Lyuba knew that she'd never accept him being demoted to the status of a modestly paid employee.

Lyuba considered the alternatives. She saw that if she didn't take charge of the situation, her world would collapse.

'I say we do nothing.'

Radu was shocked by her suggestion.

'It will buy you some time to negotiate with him. Something he and your wife can both accept.'

'He'll come back. And keep coming back. He's enjoying this.'

More even than Radu had imagined.

'My brother is a sadist,' he declared.

Lyuba considered it all and replied, 'If you don't react to the pain,' she said, 'a sadist soon grows bored.'

53

The idea of intercourse with Lyuba disgusted Grigore as much as if she were a Jew, but on each visit he found new ways to humiliate her. The problem, he came to realise, was that she passed none of it on to his brother, choosing to shield him from it. Grigore was forced to give Radu his own detailed accounts. Radu did his best to seem unmoved by any of it, but Grigore wasn't deceived for a moment. He could see that Radu struggled to contain his emotions, and was sure he would soon enough succumb to his demands.

Lyuba held Radu together as best she could. 'Your brother is a bully,' she told him. 'He'll soon tire of this game. We just need to outlast him.'

Privately, though, she was alarmed. Not by Grigore, but by Radu. Before, even when they'd argued, she'd always been able to put things right between them by stoking the fires of his libido.

Now even her most skilful attentions left him unmoved. She pointed out to him that this was exactly what Grigore wanted, and that this, too, would pass. But more and more often, even on the nights when Grigore was at the mill, Radu chose to stay at home. He told her it was because of back pain, induced by the hard bed he slept on at home. Sofia, he revealed, had urged him to return to the comfort of their soft marital bed. He assured Lyuba that he'd resisted the idea, but she couldn't help seeing it as another ominous signal.

She hid her suffering from Tholdi, too, or tried to, but by now he knew her too well. He could see the tension in her body when she sat at the piano to play for him, and knew she was lying when she told him that all was well with her.

'Please don't tell me I'm imagining it,' he said. 'Is it because of Nicolae?'

The boy was now in her thoughts almost constantly. She kept his photograph on the piano's music stand.

'In a way,' she conceded. 'It's Carmen.'

'What? The cat?'

'She's pregnant.'

Tholdi looked over at the cosy corner of the room that Carmen had recently claimed as her own. She was licking her belly, which was, he now saw, much larger than when she had first arrived, all skin and bone.

Tholdi crouched down beside Carmen and touched a hand to her belly. She hissed and swiped at him with her paw. Rubbing at the scratches on his wrist, where droplets of blood appeared, he looked back at Lyuba and saw her distress. In happier times, homes might have been found for the kittens. But who would want to take them now? Who would want to sacrifice food from their own table to raise a litter of stray cats?

Later, alone, Tholdi went over what Lyuba had said. She had become very attached to Carmen, and he could see how the prospect of having to deal with her unwanted kittens might, for Lyuba, resonate with her own past. But it seemed to him that she was at breaking point. His instincts told him that something else was behind Lyuba's anguish. He considered asking her again what was wrong, but if she'd concealed the truth a first time . . . Lyuba's claws might swipe at him just as Carmen's had.

———

It was Doina who solved the mystery, when she asked Lina who the new man was.

'New man?'

'You haven't seen him? He comes to her every week. One, maybe two times. He has a car.'

On Grigore's next visit, Lina was looking down onto the street and saw him arrive. She'd only once before seen him. One day at the mill, when Nathan's eyesight had caused an accident, and she'd gone to take him home. Worried by what it all meant, she raised it with Tholdi. Asked him if it was possible that Radu's brother was now in some way involved in the affair that they all needed to continue. It was her description of the car that confirmed it to Tholdi.

When Tholdi revealed to Lyuba what he'd learned, and asked her why she'd kept it from him, she did indeed show her claws. 'Because there's nothing we can do about it!' she said, angrily.

Tholdi couldn't understand how Radu had allowed it. Or why. Lyuba explained the demand Grigore had made, and told him that Radu was hoping to negotiate some kind of compromise. She omitted any mention of the humiliation Grigore inflicted upon her, but Tholdi was already appalled.

'Do you know how much money that mill makes?' he said. 'So what if he gives away some of it? He can afford to.'

'We just need to wait,' she said, and refused to discuss it any further.

Seeing his torment, she felt a little remorseful, and softened her tone. 'It's not so bad,' she assured him. 'For a while I'll have two men to make happy. There was a time when there were many.'

Tholdi had quite forgotten that Lyuba had not long ago been a prostitute, servicing many men each week. A nafka, as Peppa had called her. It was not how he thought of her. But what mattered was what kind of client Grigore was. He had every reason to doubt that he treated her with respect.

'Does he hurt you?'

'No.'

He felt sure she was hiding the truth.

'Please, Tholdi, just leave it be.'

What choice did he have?

54

Over six months had now passed since Lyuba had moved into Tholdi's street. In that time, Tholdi's relationship with Sergio had become a cordial one. When, after curfew one night, Tholdi passed him on his way to Lyuba and slipped a pack of cigarettes into Sergio's palm, they greeted each other almost like social acquaintances.

'Bet you're enjoying the warmer weather,' Tholdi remarked.

'That's for sure,' Sergio replied. 'If I had a new boss, my life would be perfect.'

'Maybe the sky will fall on him,' Tholdi suggested.

'Not this week.'

The focus of the Allies' bombing raids was still to the south, around the oilfields. Sergio lit a cigarette and gestured towards Grigore's parked car. 'You know she's not alone.'

'It's the brother.'

Sergio exhaled. 'What's the story there? He's screwing her too now?'

Tholdi shrugged.

'That's sick. Don't you think?'

'None of my business.'

Sergio pulled out a Lucky Strike.

'So you're seeing her again,' he said.

The remark caught Tholdi off-guard.

'Your girlfriend,' Sergio said. 'Or is it a new one?'

Tholdi recalled the dawn wink. 'No. Same.' After the vidui, he'd told Sergio that he and his girl were over. 'We're back on,' he added.

'You don't look very happy about it.'

'It's . . . complicated.'

Sergio didn't press for details. 'Well, good luck.'

Sergio lit his cigarette and watched Tholdi head down the street and around the corner, out of view, as he'd done many times before.

As Tholdi opened the basement hatch and slipped through once again, he thought about the answer he'd given Sergio. Complicated. It didn't even begin to describe the twisting path that had led him to this moment. The obsession he couldn't shake, and the irresistible compulsion he now felt. It meant breaking his promise to Peppa, but he had to see with his own eyes.

Inside the upper-storey apartment, muffled voices drifted up from Lyuba's sitting room. Tholdi closed the drapes, peeled back the rug and carefully prised the block of wood from its slot. The fountain of light gushed up, and the voices became clearer. Kneeling down, Tholdi saw Lyuba from behind. Her naked body partially obscured his view of Grigore, who sat in the chair that he'd seen Radu occupy so many times.

In Grigore's hand was a burning cigarette.

'I'm sorry,' he was saying. 'It was an accident. I was trying to ash it.'

Tholdi shifted, trying for a better view. He saw Lyuba's naked shoulder, and the fresh burn mark.

'Fetch me my coat,' Grigore said, and Lyuba obeyed him. From an inside pocket, he produced a handgun. He stroked the length of its steel shaft.

'Luger semiautomatic. Wehrmacht issue. A gift. In thanks for the good work Radu and I are doing.'

Grigore gripped the gun, his forefinger curled loosely around the trigger. 'On your knees.'

Lyuba hesitated. Grigore met her thigh with the tip of his still burning cigarette. At the touch of it, Lyuba flinched, and complied.

'Now open your mouth.'

She did as he commanded.

'Wider.'

He leant forward and slid the gun into her mouth. Rested the weight of it upon her tongue.

'I'm guessing your road hasn't been an easy one. And it's not about to get any easier. Maybe I should end it for you right now.'

Ever so slightly, he squeezed.

'Shall I do that? End it all? Put you out of your misery?'

Lyuba didn't believe Grigore would fire the gun, but she wasn't about to call his bluff.

'Answer me.'

Almost imperceptibly, so as not to brush Grigore's hand, Lyuba shook her head. He let go of the trigger, slid the gun's shaft from her mouth and put the weapon aside. Then, closing his eyes, he leaned back, relaxed again.

'Finish what you started.'

Lyuba looked at the pistol. It was within her reach. She could easily grab it.

Without opening his eyes again, Grigore grinned. 'Not a good idea.'

She knew he was right.

From above, Tholdi watched the back of Lyuba's head fall and rise again, slowly and repeatedly, until she had brought Grigore to a climax. When it was done, Grigore stood, zipped his trousers and retrieved the Luger. Oblivious to it all, Carmen was in her corner, licking her belly. Grigore saw that it was swollen.

'Is that cat pregnant?'

'Yes.'

'What will you do with the kittens?'

'I don't know.'

'You can't possibly feed them all,' Grigore said, considering the gun in his hand. He looked back to Carmen.

Tholdi wondered if he would he really use it. Sergio would be sure to hear the explosion and come knocking on the door.

'Draw a bath,' Grigore ordered.

Lyuba understood his intention. 'Please, no,' she begged.

'Do it. Now.'

Lyuba left the room and Grigore followed, as did Tholdi, across the floor above them both. Very carefully, in the bathroom above Lyuba's, he removed the wood block from its hole and looked down. The bathwater rose rapidly.

'That should be enough,' Grigore said.

He went back to the sitting room. Tholdi heard Carmen protesting loudly, and a moment later Grigore returned holding her by the scruff of her neck. He dangled her above the water. The cat thrashed and struggled, lashing out desperately with her claws, swiping at the air.

'It's for the best,' Grigore announced.

Lyuba turned to leave.

'Where do you think you're going?'

She turned back. Watching, she understood, was the whole point. Grigore slowly lowered Carmen into the water, still thrashing and mewling. The mewling was silenced but the thrashing continued, roiling the bathwater. After a couple of long minutes, the water calmed and settled.

'Problem solved.'

Grigore lifted Carmen from the water and dropped her lifeless, dripping body onto the bathroom floor.

'I can see myself out,' he said, leaving the bathroom. 'Until next time . . .'

The front door opened and shut. Tholdi watched as Lyuba stood there, completely still. She made no move to collect Carmen, now nothing more than a bundle of wet fur, from the floor. After a few minutes, she turned off the bathroom light, the one in the sitting room as well, and went to bed.

Now in complete darkness, Tholdi slumped against the bathroom wall and sat, motionless, for a full half-hour. When he was finally able to get back on his feet, he replaced the blocks of wood, rolled the rug flat again, and looked outside to make sure Sergio was out of sight. When he was sure that he was, he re-opened the drapes and crept away.

55

When Tholdi next visited Lyuba, he asked after the cat. It would have been strange, he decided, if he didn't. She told him that Carmen had vanished – perhaps, she suggested, to give birth to her litter somewhere more private. Tholdi said nothing. What could he say? That he knew she was lying? That he'd seen?

Instead he asked, 'Does Radu know what's going on?'

'What do you mean?'

He worded his reply carefully. 'I know what he's like. The brother. I know what he's capable of.'

'Tholdi, please, I told you to leave it,' she said, but she saw how hard it was for him to let it go. 'Do you want to wind up on the list?' she asked. 'Think of your parents.'

Again Tholdi was tempted to break his promise to Alex, and again he resisted, praying that the BBC broadcasts Nathan listened to every day were true, and that the tide was turning against Germany and her allies. Tholdi didn't like to say so to his father, but he did not share Nathan's confidence.

At the mill, Tholdi began another shift. The looms were ceaseless, producing more fabric for more uniforms for more men, some of them now barely teenagers, conscripted to replace the fallen bodies. It sickened Tholdi to think that he was playing a part in it all – that Doina had been right, and he was, willingly or not, a collaborator. But what disgusted Tholdi more than anything was Radu's failure to stand up to Grigore.

Towards the end of his shift, Tholdi noticed Grigore leave for the day. When the whistle blew, he looked up to the platform and saw that Radu was still there. Overcome suddenly by a rage he could contain not a minute longer, Tholdi climbed the stairs.

Radu was not pleased to see him. 'What are you doing up here?'

'I need to speak with you.' It was a demand, not a request.

Radu tried to assert his authority. 'I told you never to –'

'You have to stop it.'

Radu was shocked. Never before had Tholdi addressed him with anything other than the most servile deference.

'If you knew what your brother does to her –'

'What has she said to you?' Radu wondered what Tholdi knew, and how he knew it.

'That you love her. That you told her that.'

Radu wondered why Lyuba had shared something so intimate with Tholdi.

'If it's true, you'd give your brother what he wants.'

Radu's own rage began to build. Just how much had Lyuba confided in Tholdi? That she had developed a relationship with the boy, a kind of friendship, had been evident to Radu for some time. In the circumstances, it was inevitable. But more than once he'd wondered if it had gone too far. If it was healthy. If he should discourage it. Now he was regretting that he hadn't.

'Do you know how many times I've removed your name from our lists? How I've protected you?'

'What? Like you protected Bruckman?'

Radu's mouth tightened. 'I can arrange the same for you.'

Tholdi opened his mouth to say something more.

'Your parents too.'

Tholdi's mouth closed.

'Good,' Radu said. 'And from now on you will only see Lyuba when necessary. For her daily needs. No more visits after curfew. And,' he added, 'no more piano lessons.'

Tholdi berated himself. What had he been thinking? What had he hoped to achieve by coming to Radu?

A tinkling came from behind Tholdi's back, and he turned to see Grigore standing in the doorway, dangling a set of keys.

'I forgot them,' Grigore told Radu.

The light caught Leo's signet ring, bouncing off the gold as Grigore pocketed his keys.

'So what's this little gathering about? More suggestions on how to improve our output?'

Grigore had been addressing his brother, but Radu was mute. His questioning gaze shifted to Tholdi, also struck dumb.

'I didn't think so,' Grigore said.

As an afterthought, he asked Tholdi if he had any plans for the evening. 'Because my Opel needs washing.'

On the factory floor Tholdi found a bucket, filled it with water, and met Grigore outside by the car. He soaked a sponge while Grigore lit a cigarette.

'Don't forget the tyres,' Grigore said. He liked their white-walls to be spotless.

Tholdi crouched low. He made sure every inch of the vehicle, including the underside of the running board, received his atten-tion. On the ground was a small, sharp-edged pebble. How he would have loved to pick it up and run it along the length of the Opel's gleaming wine-coloured duco.

⸺

That night, Tholdi visited Lyuba and confessed to her what had happened.

'But I told you to leave it,' she said.

'I know. I should have. I'm sorry.'

Lyuba calmed herself.

'Maybe,' she said, 'he will change his mind. Let's give it a little time and see.'

Time. The enemy.

56

From his bedroom, where he was dressing for work, Tholdi heard his mother cry out in excitement.

'Gott sei Dank! We've been so worried! Sit down! Tell us everything! How are the others? Are they both safe?'

Alex had finally made it back.

Nathan's voice could also be heard. 'Lina, give him a chance to catch his breath. Sit down, my boy, sit down.'

Tholdi didn't move. It shamed him to admit it to himself, but Alex's return once again unleashed a sudden rush of conflicting, unwelcome emotions. He feared he wouldn't be able to hide them from his lifelong friend.

Lina's voice grew louder. 'Tholdi! It's Alex!'

'Coming!' Tholdi called back.

Pulling himself together, he joined them all in the sitting room, where Lina was preparing coffee. Seeing Tholdi, Alex sprang back to his feet. As if Tholdi were the one returning, Alex crossed the room to meet and embrace his old friend. Holding him close, Alex spoke into his ear.

'It's so good to see you again.'

'You too,' Tholdi replied. 'You too.'

His words were sincere, Tholdi *was* glad to see Alex again, alive. But the reunion was overshadowed by a secret unspoken dread. It meant that his days with Lyuba were numbered.

'Coffee?' Lina asked Tholdi.

'I have to get to the mill. I can't be late.'

'Don't you want to hear the news?' Lina asked.

'Mama, I can't be late,' he repeated, then turned back to Alex. 'Did you all get through?'

'There were complications, but yes.'

'Are they safe?'

'In Bucharest, yes. But look, you have to go now. I can tell you all about it tonight.'

'I'm so pleased to see you again,' Tholdi reiterated.

Alex laughed. 'I heard that the first time. Now go.'

Tholdi was grateful for the excuse to remove himself. To process emotions which were, more than ever, at war with each other.

That night, Lina served up a feast: goose soup and fresh bread. No-one noticed Tholdi's poor appetite; they were all too absorbed in Alex's retelling of the journey he'd made with

Mira and Peppa. Now that it was a story with a happy ending, a daring adventure tale that was already assuming the status of a legend, Lina and Nathan were happy to hear it all again, for Tholdi's benefit, and to contribute.

'Tell Tholdi what Peppa did with the guard.'

At one point in their journey, guards had come through their carriage and asked to see their papers – again. Mira had fallen asleep, and being woken abruptly had unbalanced her.

'She forgot her own name!' Lina exclaimed.

Not that Tholdi needed it, but Nathan clarified. 'The one on her documents.'

'Peppa saved us all with her tsitskes,' Alex laughed.

Choosing more polite language, Lina elaborated. 'She caught the guard looking at her blouse, and, well . . .'

Alex finished the retelling. 'She leaned back and pushed her chest out. Then a button popped and her blouse was open. The guard got more than an eyeful.'

Lina laughed at the thought of it. 'Talk about chutzpah!'

Tholdi thought of the day he'd argued so bitterly with Peppa. Over Lyuba.

'Your father would be proud of you both,' Nathan said.

'Was this the complication you mentioned?' Tholdi asked.

'One of them. The worst was right at the start. It was chaos. We nearly didn't get on the train.'

Since the escalation of Allied bombing, security at all the major railways stations had been heightened. The experience prompted Alex to suggest that for the next journey, the one with Tholdi and his parents, they should choose a different embarkation point, a smaller station further along the line. Tholdi, Alex saw, was uneasy. He thought he knew the reason – Lina.

'It's only a minor change to our stories,' he assured his friend.

'And the documents?'

'I can adjust them.'

Tholdi looked to Lina. 'If Mira managed it all, so will I,' she declared. 'Dessert?'

After they'd eaten, Lina cleared the table and left the men to search for the station where they might begin their journey south. Alex spread out a map and railway timetable. Tholdi was meant to be helping him. Nathan's eyesight meant he couldn't be of much use but he sat with them, listening keenly.

'When's your next day off?' Alex asked. 'Tholdi?'

It wasn't the first time that night that Alex had to get Tholdi's attention. Like a hypnotist waking his subject, Alex held his fingers in front of Tholdi and snapped them impatiently.

'Sorry, were you speaking to me?'

'Unless your father is now working at the mill too, yes.' Alex repeated his question. 'Next day off. When?'

'This week? Friday.'

'Perfect!'

'You've found us a station?' Nathan asked.

'Dorneşti. A train stops there once a week. Fridays.'

'But –' Tholdi blurted, and then stopped himself.

'But what, Tholdi?' Alex's patience was nearing its end.

'Is that enough time? For Mama?'

'Three days should be enough. What do you think, Nathan?'

'My wife should never be underestimated.'

'Good,' Alex concluded. 'It's settled.'

57

The following morning, Alex rose to find Tholdi already dressed, and slouched over a cup of coffee at the dining table. It was obvious that Tholdi had not slept well.

'You look like yesterday's porridge.'

'Thanks.'

Alex sat down opposite. 'We have to leave on a day you're not expected at the mill. So you won't be missed.'

'I know.' It wasn't being missed by one of the overseers that was consuming Tholdi's thoughts.

'And,' Alex continued, 'it's better we do it quickly. If Lina has too much time to think about it all she'll only get herself worked up.'

Tholdi stood, finished his coffee. 'See you after work.'

'Aren't you early?'

'I need to stop by Lyuba's.'

Since Alex's return, it was the first time either of them had mentioned her name.

'It's our routine. Don't want her thinking anything's changed.'

Alex was reassured. 'I'll stay out of sight this time.'

⸺

He usually came by a little later. Lyuba opened the door in her dressing gown, apologising for the way she looked. 'I was still in bed.'

To Tholdi, she looked more beautiful than ever.

'Are you coming in?'

'No. The overseer asked me to start early today.' Yet another lie.

'Do you need anything?'

'Nothing that can't wait.'

Lyuba sensed his strange mood. 'Is everything all right?'

'Yes.'

Since Alex had walked back into their lives, the lies were piling up like bodies.

Lyuba sensed Tholdi was holding something back from her but didn't press him. If there was something he didn't want to share, that was his business.

Tholdi's route to the mill took him by the western length of the ghetto. When he had time to do so, as he did today, he usually detoured to avoid it. Today he felt the need to see it. To stop and remind himself of what Alex had returned to save him and his parents from.

Now emptied of nearly all its residents, it was a place of ghosts. Those who remained shuffled around aimlessly, or sat outside their cottages, motionless. Tholdi reflected once more on the mazel that had spared him and his family from those first terrible days. Destiny, schicksal, had been extraordinarily kind to him. Alex's plan to save him and his parents was yet another gift. The idea of rejecting it, as he wanted to, felt like insulting some higher being.

On the mill's floor, Tholdi's day passed in a daze. Only a short time ago, the day after his night with Lyuba had felt like a dream; this day was a nightmare. The noise of the looms closed in around until he wanted to scream. If he had, would anyone have stopped to ask him about his anguish? Each of them there was surviving their own hell.

Tholdi glanced quickly up at the clock. The hands were moving even more slowly than on the day he'd screwed up the courage to put his proposal to Radu. And yet, despite it all, Tholdi didn't want the day to end. Friday. Two more days, and then he'd be gone.

The side door opened and Tholdi watched Radu enter and ascend the stairs. At the platform he met Grigore, and the two men had a brief exchange. It seemed amicable enough. Perhaps Radu had, after all, been able to negotiate some sort of deal with his brother. Tholdi prayed it might be so. It was Lyuba's only chance of survival. The sunlight streaming in through the lantern windows bounced off Leo's gold signet ring, making it sparkle like a tiny, distant star. Tholdi recalled the night that he had stood in the ghetto street with Alex beneath a clear, starry sky, both of them wondering what lay ahead.

——

While Tholdi had been at the mill, Alex had spent the day coaching Lina and Nathan, rehearsing their revised stories. That night, after dinner, they continued. Tholdi joined them – he, too, had to memorise it all. As anticipated, it was Lina who had the greatest difficulty getting it straight.

'I still don't understand why we can't go via Ploieşti.'

Alex ploughed on calmly. 'It's a military hub.'

'But this other way will take us so much longer. Probably a whole day. Maybe even more.'

Tholdi interjected tersely. 'Mama, Ploieşti is right in the middle of the oilfields. It's been bombed. There will be soldiers and officials and . . . Only a fool would go that way.'

Lina crossed her arms. 'So now you think your mama is a fool.'

Alex suggested they all take a break. Nathan concurred, and offered to make them all a pot of Russian tea.

'Ha!' Lina scoffed. 'Your memory might be good, but you can't read a label! God knows what you'd put in the pot.'

She went to do it herself. Nathan followed, not so much to help her with the tea-making as to comfort and reassure her. To shore up her self-confidence.

Alex lowered his voice. 'You need to be more patient with her.'

Tholdi sighed heavily. 'I know.'

'What's going on, Tholdi? You need to talk to me. Now.'

Tholdi stammered. 'It's . . .'

'Is this to do with *her*?'

Tholdi couldn't keep it in any longer. Even if he wanted to, Alex wasn't going to let him. 'While you've been away . . .'

The sentence hung in the air, unfinished.

'What?'

Tholdi hesitated.

'Speak!' Alex demanded.

Tholdi decided to reveal only what was essential. What Alex might be able to understand. 'Radu and Grigore . . . the two brothers who run the mill . . . they're at war with each other. Grigore found out about the affair and is using Lyuba as a kind of bargaining chip. He wants to take over the business.'

'Using her how?'

'Grigore does things to her. Terrible things. I don't know how much more she can take.'

'Have you been spying on her again?'

Tholdi considered lying but he couldn't. Not anymore. 'It's different now.'

'You promised Peppa you wouldn't.'

'She told you that?'

'On our way to Bucharest. We had a lot of time together. She told me everything. Not just the spying, but the other things, too. How much time you spend with her. The piano lessons at night . . .'

'She has a gift.'

Alex couldn't believe what he was hearing. 'Mazel tov! Wonderful! You've discovered a musical prodigy!'

Tholdi fired back ferociously. 'Lyuba needs me. If I go she might not live.'

Alex had never seen his friend like this before. This argument was worse than the one they'd had last time. Alex felt certain something else had changed. Something other than the business between the brothers.

'Have you screwed her yet?'

'You would ask that.'

'Well, have you?'

Tholdi's face said it all.

Alex let out something like a laugh, bitter and devoid of mirth. 'With all your brains and all your talent, everything that my father wished I had even a fraction of, you always envied me.'

'That has nothing to do with it.'

Alex didn't believe a word of it. 'Can't you see what she's done? She's used you. Manipulated you.'

'That's not true.'

'It's what women do, Tholdi. Women like her especially.'

There was no point in arguing. How could Tholdi even begin to explain to Alex that it was he, not Lyuba, who'd been the one to dismantle, piece by piece, the other's defences?

Alex decided he'd heard enough. 'You know what? I don't care what your feelings for Lyuba are. This isn't one of your silly operas. This is real life. And from what you're telling me, the affair, the thing that has been protecting you all, isn't going to last. In which case, the sooner we leave here the better.'

The logic was undeniable. And yet, Alex saw, Tholdi resisted. Logic alone was not enough.

'Tholdi, please, think about what matters here. Think about the people who love you. Not only your parents, but Peppa. And me. My mother, too. We are your family. Can you honestly believe that Lyuba cares about you as we do?'

It was a form of blackmail, naked and without apology, but before Tholdi could respond a loud crash came from the kitchen. He and Alex rushed in to find Nathan supporting Lina. They were surrounded by tins and broken jars from a high shelf that had collapsed.

'If you'd let me get it for you,' Nathan was saying. He turned to Tholdi and Alex. 'She had one of her turns. Her heart.'

'Nonsense,' Lina scoffed. 'My heart is fine. He got in my way!'

'You were in pain! You grabbed at me so hard you tore my shirt!' Nathan showed Tholdi and Alex the rip in his sleeve. 'See!'

Tholdi felt responsible for the tensions he'd provoked, and tried to help his mother to a chair, but she was still smarting from the way he'd spoken to her.

'Leave me be.'

She shooed him away irritably and began to tidy up her kitchen.

'Out! All of you!'

Everyone did as they were commanded.

Tholdi couldn't recall either of his parents being so agitated. They barely ever raised their voices at him, and never at each other. It was clear everyone's nerves were wearing thin. Alex suggested they all get some rest. It would be another long day tomorrow.

He bade the three of them a good night's sleep.

Alex was the first to rise. He was alone at the dining table, reviewing their travel plans when Tholdi entered, and sat down beside him. Alex pretended that the previous night's confrontation had never happened.

'To get to Dornești we're going to need a car,' he said. 'You need to go into town and find a taxi driver who's willing. One who can keep his mouth shut. It will cost a small fortune but I have enough to cover it.'

Tholdi said nothing.

'What? You think your parents can travel all the way to Dornești on a horse and cart?'

'Alex . . .' There was no better way for Tholdi to say it. 'After you went to bed, Papa and I talked. We don't think Mama is up to it. We're staying.'

Fury welled up inside Alex. 'Who started this talk?'

'Alex, her heart –'

'This isn't about your mother. It's about you.'

Tholdi didn't reply. He didn't need to. Nathan walked in and stood behind him. Answered for them both.

'We made the decision together.'

Alex exploded. 'She's a prostitute! He met her at a brothel! With me! The night of his birthday! Did you know that?'

Finally, an answer to the questions Nathan had asked Tholdi months back, but these things no longer mattered to him. 'The war will end,' he said. 'We're winning now.'

'Tell Hitler that. Even if he loses, he's going to kill us all first. He's a madman.'

Nathan looked at Tholdi, silently asking the question: should we reconsider before it's too late? But Tholdi had no answer.

'I'm sorry, Alex,' Nathan said. 'It's been decided.'

To emphasise the point, he placed a reassuring hand on his son's shoulder, just as he'd done when Alex had shared his story about being separated from Jakob. When he was the one wrestling with guilt. Now what Alex felt was disgust.

Alex left the following day. Into Nathan's hand he pressed the money he'd brought with him, as well as the address of the safe house in Bucharest where Mira and Peppa were waiting to be reunited with them. For Lina, who had been his second mother, Alex had a final close embrace. He could not bring himself to embrace Tholdi. Not this time. For him he had only words.

'I wish you well. I pray we will all see each other again.'

Alex held very little hope that his prayer would be answered, and Tholdi knew it.

58

'Tholdi, my boy! Come in, come in!'

As always, Moritz's girls barked loudly. Had they actually missed him? Perhaps. Moritz certainly had. In their way, he and Tholdi had become fond business acquaintances. Ones who hadn't seen each other for some time.

'I thought you must have left already,' Moritz said.

In recent weeks, Radu had lost interest in the little luxuries that had once enhanced his pleasure in Lyuba's company, and Grigore's pleasure relied on other forms of enhancement, not found on Moritz's shelves.

'So, what will it be today? I have some very fine beluga caviar.'

From his pocket, Tholdi extracted a small photograph and handed it to Moritz. He studied the face in it.

'Unusual.' Moritz said. 'Who is she?'

'She needs a new identity card.'

Moritz studied the photograph more closely.

'Is she Jewish? She doesn't look it.'

'She's Gypsy.'

Moritz's eyebrows rose. His eyes followed, meeting with Tholdi's. They were full of unvoiced questions that neither of them had the time to address.

'Can you arrange it?' Tholdi asked.

'Yes, I know someone. But don't you also? Can't he do it?'

'He's gone.'

'It won't be cheap,' Moritz warned. 'Good ones cost. If you get caught, bad ones cost even more.'

'But you can do it?' Tholdi pressed.

'I can ask. How soon does she need it?'

'How soon can you do it?

'Were you always so pushy?'

Tholdi had no patience for humour. Not now.

'Moritz, please.' If Radu ended the affair with Lyuba, the identity card would be Lyuba's only chance to survive.

Moritz held up his hands. 'Alright, okay. Two weeks. Maybe less, but let's say two.'

Tholdi had taken the photograph of Lyuba following Alex's example, sitting her against a plain white wall. While he'd loaded the fresh roll of film into the camera, Lyuba had asked questions, awkward for Tholdi to answer. Tholdi was glad he didn't have to look Lyuba in the eye. That his was fixed upon the camera's viewfinder.

'Are you getting one too?' she asked.

'U-huh. My parents as well.'

'Also with false identities?'

'Of course.'

'Hopefully we won't need them.'

'Can you lift your chin a bit?'

She did.

'And a little more.'

'Like that?'

'Yes.'

With a click, he pressed the camera's shutter button. He took one last shot, and finally straightened.

'That should do.'

Afterwards, when he'd developed the images, Tholdi sat looking at them. In one, there was something about the look in Lyuba's eyes that reminded him of the night she'd rested her head on his chest. He made an extra print of it and placed it in his wallet. The same wallet from which he now extracted Reichsmark, for Moritz. A deposit.

'If it can't be done, I will refund you,' Moritz told him.

By now Tholdi had no doubt he could be trusted. He handed Moritz a sheet of paper. He'd created a whole new identity for Lyuba, and then, using Dr Mandel's typewriter, typed up all the details neatly.

Moritz was impressed. 'Very thorough.' He folded the paper and concealed it with the photograph inside the pages of a book.

When Tholdi next delivered Lyuba's groceries, she asked him how soon her new papers would be ready.

'He says a couple of weeks.'

She nodded. They would both feel better when it was done.

'I asked Radu if we could start the lessons again.'

'And?'

'He refused. I've been practising though. Sometimes at night, too. Have you heard me?'

He had. Through his open bedroom window.

'I miss our lessons,' she said.

'Me too. Going to him was . . . meshugge. That means –'

'I can guess.'

'I'm sorry.'

'Don't be. You were defending me.'

And that, as it turned out, had not been futile after all. Reflecting on Tholdi's words, Radu had decided to meet Grigore's demands in full. In return, Grigore agreed not to tell Sofia. From Lyuba, Radu had also extracted a promise: not to discuss any of it with Tholdi. He'd also returned Lyuba's identity card. His excuse for keeping it was, as always, his desire to protect her.

Lyuba's promise to Radu she promptly broke. How could she not? The news was as much a relief to Tholdi as it was to her. It meant the affair was back on more solid ground. God willing, it would outlast the war, and the false papers would merely be a form of insurance.

'Do you really think your father is right? That Hitler will be defeated?'

'Yes. I do.'

His confidence lifted her spirits. Restored hope. Tholdi thought the timing of it auspicious.

'The night we first met? It was exactly one year ago.'

'Wasn't it your birthday?'

He nodded. She smiled at the memory of that first meeting.

'You were just a boy then.'

It remained unspoken but Lyuba had also changed.

She felt they should celebrate. 'Stay for a bit. Play something for me?'

'I can't. No more lessons, remember?'

'Yes, no more lessons, not no more *playing*. Besides, how would he know? Is someone going to inform on us?'

Sergio might pose a problem, might mention it to Radu, but before curfew fell he was absent. Radu would be none the wiser.

Madame Denile entered her thoughts.

'You know what I say?' Lyuba said, leading Tholdi to the piano. 'Fuck him!'

Tholdi was shocked. He'd never heard Lyuba swear before. But then a broad smile spread across his face. 'Fuck them all!' he said.

It was liberating, as if they were shouting from the rooftop. As if they were both free.

Tholdi sat at the piano as Lyuba settled on the sofa. He considered what to play. He thought of happier days before the nightmare of the war had begun. Before the family's piano had been smashed to pieces on the stairs. When Alex and Peppa and their circle of friends had gathered round and demanded he play something popular. Something they could all sing along to.

'Have you heard of New York?' he asked.

'In America? Of course I have,' she said. 'Even an ignorant Gypsy knows of that.'

'Have you heard of Broadway?'

That she hadn't.

'It's the theatre district. Where people go to see musicals. And without Jews it would be nothing.'

'Musicals. Like operas?'

Tholdi laughed. 'You'll see.' He flexed his fingers, cracked the joints. Cleared his throat. 'This one's a comedy. In it there's a woman with an amorous suitor and . . . Well, it's feferdik.'

Lyuba didn't need to speak Yiddish to understand he meant risqué.

With a Vaudevillian flourish, Tholdi flew his fingers along the keyboard, paused to widen his eyes, and began to sing.

He tried to get in
She told him get out
She tried to resist
He chased her about
Lyuba laughed. She knew what that game was like.

Walking up the street in the bright sunshine and passing beneath Lyuba's opened window, Lina and Doina heard the song. They stopped to listen. They knew it well. When the film of the musical had been released, Lina had seen it three times. As Tholdi reached the chorus, the two women sang, full throated.

So then in the end

What did they do?

For comic suspense, Tholdi drew breath, held back a few beats, then launched into the chorus's punchline with gusto. Lina and Doina too.

They ended the riddle

And met in the middle!

It was the best laugh the two women had shared in a very long time.

59

'The brother visited her again. Last night.'

Tholdi had barely sat down to breakfast when Lina told him.

'Are you sure?'

'Do we know anyone else who owns a car like that?'

Tholdi had been at the mill the night before – he'd been on night shifts all week. As Grigore left for the day he'd passed Tholdi on his way in and wished him a good night. Tholdi had thought it odd. Now he understood.

'I thought you said he wouldn't be coming again,' Lina fretted. 'What does he still want with her? Can't he find another woman to satisfy his needs? Why his brother's?'

That's what Tholdi wanted to know. He went immediately to see Lyuba and hammered impatiently on her door. When she opened it, he could see instantly that his mother had been right. Grigore had returned. It was written on Lyuba's face.

He followed her to the kitchen, where she carried on peeling potatoes.

'He said he missed me,' she reported.

Tholdi imagined Grigore delivering those words with his sadist's grin, thinking himself so very clever.

Sadist. When Radu had used that word to describe his brother, he'd meant it figuratively. As it turned out, though, Grigore's cruelty to Lyuba had awakened in him a kind of excitement he'd never before experienced – an excitement he was unwilling to forgo.

'Is it worse than before? The thing with the gun?'

Lyuba put down the paring knife and looked at him. 'How do you know about that?'

Tholdi hesitated.

'Well?'

'I saw through the window. From my house. You left the curtain open.'

She tried to recall – had she? She dismissed the question from her mind, and continued peeling.

Tholdi could see how deeply his revelation disturbed her. It made him wonder how she'd have reacted if he'd told her the truth – if she knew that the 'window' was a hole he'd cut into the floor above her sitting room several months ago.

'What are we going to do?' Tholdi asked.

'Nothing.'

'But this can't go on.'

'It can. I can. And so can you.'

'Does Radu know?'

'I think so.'

'You haven't seen him?'

Reluctantly, she admitted that it had been more than a week. Since the time when Radu refused Sofia's demand to give up his mistress, he'd never gone more than a few days without visiting Lyuba.

Without saying it, Tholdi and Lyuba were now asking themselves the same question: Is the affair over?

'You are not to go to him again,' Lyuba said.

'But they had a deal. If Grigore has broken his word –'

'What can Radu do about it? Nothing. You shouldn't have gone to him in the first place.'

Her words hurt.

A few days ago, when they both thought Grigore would not be coming anymore, they'd been celebrating. Now, Lyuba worried that she was damaged goods – an asset Radu had over-paid for, and which he wished to be rid of – while Tholdi's thoughts were consumed by the cruelty he knew Grigore was capable of.

—

At the mill and now back on day shifts, the sight of Grigore made Tholdi feel physically ill. Grigore knew it. Enjoyed it. And again asked Tholdi to wash his car.

Again, Grigore watched. 'You've got balls, I'll give you that,' he said, lighting a cigarette. 'My brother told me all about it. How you came to him. Your proposal.'

Tholdi turned his back to Grigore and crouched low to clean the car's grille.

'Has she told you about the fun we have?'

Tholdi kept working.

'Answer me, boy.'

'No.'

'You like her, don't you?'

Tholdi knew Grigore was trying to bait him. 'She's tsigayner,' Tholdi answered.

'Is that some fucking Yid word?'

'Gypsy. We don't mix with them.'

'You Jews don't mix with anyone. That's how you've wound up in the mess you're in. Wealth is like manure. It should be spread around, not controlled and kept by one little tribe. Don't you think?'

'Yes, mein Herr.'

Tholdi found a clean rag to polish the windows. When he'd finished, he went to empty the bucket of filthy water. Floating in it were Grigore's discarded cigarette butts. Grigore kicked it over. The water splashed across Tholdi's shoes and spread out across the ground.

'Lick it up,' Grigore said.

Tholdi hesitated.

'Do it!'

Tholdi got down on his knees.

'That's it. Just like a dog.'

Tholdi licked at the wet ground. With the heel of his shoe, Grigore pushed him over onto his side.

'That's enough. Now get up and get back to work. You have lost time to make up.'

Grigore got into the Opel, started the engine and addressed Tholdi through the window. 'I'm seeing her tonight. I'll tell her you said hello.'

———

Tholdi had been back on the floor of the mill less than an hour before he went to find the overseer. 'I need to go home,' he said. 'I'm not well.'

The overseer wasn't stupid. He'd seen the way Grigore was treating the boy and ordered him to return to work. Without warning, Tholdi vomited, bile splashing into the cuffs of the overseer's trousers.

Lina and Nathan greeted Tholdi's early return with dismay. As always, his mother reached for his forehead to check if he had a fever. He pushed her hand away and went to his room. She brought him some soup, but he didn't eat it. He could think of only one thing.

60

A little before ten o'clock, not long after darkness enveloped the city, the headlights of Grigore's Opel swept the street below Tholdi's bedroom window. Tholdi watched Grigore park and get out. He approached Sergio, and the two men shared a joke before Grigore disappeared inside the entry hall that led to Lyuba's front door. A few moments later, no longer able to contain himself, but without any real plan, Tholdi slipped out into the night.

'Sergio!' he called.

As usual, the gendarme was lighting a cigarette. Tholdi's cheerful voice, from behind, took him by surprise. 'What are you doing out here?'

'What do you think?'

'You can't. Herr Golescu told me not to let you break curfew anymore.'

'But he's not here. And,' Tholdi added with a wink, 'her parents are away at the moment.'

Sergio had always assumed that Tholdi's secret girlfriend was Jewish – but if she was, how could her parents be away? Away where? On holidays? It didn't make sense.

Tholdi tried to sway Sergio. 'Come on. No-one will know.'

'I'm sorry, Tholdi. No.'

Tholdi saw that Sergio's mind was made up.

'Okay. Wouldn't want to get you into any trouble.'

Tholdi headed for home, but when Sergio's back was again turned, he walked further down the street, passing his building. He stopped opposite another a few doors along. In recent months most of the apartments had been occupied by new tenants, but this building remained vacant. Tholdi spotted an unbroken window, found a rock in the gutter and, from the shadows of a doorway across the road, he hurled it. The sound of breaking glass shattered the stillness of the night, and drew Sergio's attention. Gun drawn, he went to investigate.

Behind Sergio's back, Tholdi ran back to Lyuba's building and entered through the front door. Adrenaline pumping through his veins, he removed his shoes and ascended the stairs, two at a time. Once he was safely inside the apartment above Lyuba's, and had closed the door, he paused to catch his breath, and to decide what he would do next. He reminded himself that Grigore was not Radu, and that he carried a gun. But Tholdi had to see. He had to know.

He peeled back the rug above Lyuba's sitting room. He took out the square of floorboard. Light gushed up, but no sound. No voices. Crouching, he peered through the lacework of the ceiling rose. There was no-one to be seen, but then he heard the unmistakable slap of a hand on flesh and a woman's short, sharp, involuntary shriek. The sounds echoed. They were coming from the bathroom.

Outside, in the street, Sergio had failed to discover what had shattered the peace. Perhaps, he thought, it was a cat. They were everywhere, starved and desperate. He was about to dismiss the disturbance, resigning himself to yet another tedious, uneventful night, when he glimpsed a figure, a silhouette, pass one of the broken windows above the Gypsy woman's apartment. The light inside seemed strange.

In the bathroom, Tholdi knelt beside the hole he'd cut in the floor – the one from which, before Carmen's drowning, he'd watched Lyuba bathe. She was again stretched out in the tub below him, naked, but there was no water this time and Grigore stood by the side of the bath, looming over her, his broad back allowing Tholdi only a partial view. His voice could be heard clearly, as if Tholdi were in the room with them.

'You're lucky it's not winter.'

Grigore unzipped the fly of his trousers. A splashing sound followed. 'Do you like that?' he asked Lyuba.

When he'd finished relieving himself on her, his arm and shoulder began to move rhythmically. Tholdi heard his breath grow heavier, excited.

'Hello? Who's there?' Sergio's voice came bouncing off the walls of the stairwell.

Much too late, Tholdi remembered the sitting room drapes he'd forgotten to close. His mind raced. Should he stay still and quiet? Try to hide?

'Who's there?' Sergio called again, his voice closer now, outside the front door.

Tholdi made a dash for the less confined space of the sitting room. He heard the front door opening and Sergio's voice again, louder and more assertive now. 'Gendarme! Show yourself!'

Desperately, Tholdi looked about for something, anything, with which to defend himself. In the shadows, among the debris he'd piled against the wall, was a shard of broken glass.

'Show yourself!' Sergio called again. Gun in hand, he cautiously pushed open the sitting room door. Tholdi leapt at him, swinging the shard wildly. There was a sudden flash of reflected light and both of Sergio's hands flew to his face.

'Oh, Jesus! Oh, Christ!'

Blood seeped through his fingers. It came from his eyes. Tholdi gasped, shocked by his own actions. Then he heard Grigore's voice, calling from the foot of the stairwell.

'Who's up there?' he shouted. 'Come out!'

'In here!' Sergio screamed.

Luger in hand, Grigore bounded up the stairs, his steps echoing. At the front door he was nearly bowled over by Sergio, who stumbled blindly past him. At the top of the stairs, the guard lost his footing and tumbled to the bottom, where he lay, unmoving. Grigore left him there and advanced towards the sitting room – more cautiously now, holding his gun out in front of him.

From the room's shadows, Tholdi took a single step forward. Before Grigore had a chance to comprehend the danger in front of him, the gun in the boy's hand, Tholdi fired a single bullet. Grigore hit the floor with a heavy thud and a blood-curdling cry of pain. In disbelief, he looked from his bloody leg to Tholdi and saw that his whole body was trembling. The boy was in even more shock than he was. The gun in his hand was still raised, pointed now at the space where a moment before Grigore had been standing. Despite the wrenching pain, it made Grigore laugh.

'It's you. The genius.'

Tholdi's bullet had hit an artery in Grigore's left thigh. He gripped it with both hands, trying to staunch the blood pouring from his wound. 'Do you realise what you've just done?'

Tholdi didn't answer.

'You should put that gun down,' Grigore said, 'and beg me for mercy.'

In his state of shock, Tholdi had forgotten he was holding the gun. Grigore looked for his own and saw that it had been sent spinning across the floor. He began to drag himself towards it. The pain was excruciating.

Tholdi knew what he needed to do. He once again aimed the gun at Grigore, but he couldn't bring himself to fire it a second time.

'Do you hear me, boy? You need to put that gun down. Because if you don't, you're as good as dead.'

Footsteps echoed on the stairs. Entering the room, Lyuba stopped to take it all in. Tholdi holding the gun. Grigore trying to reach his. The strange beam of light coming up through the floor.

Grigore desperately tried to drag himself closer to his gun, but Lyuba got there first, easily, and picked it up. He braced for a second bullet. A lethal one.

Instead she walked past him, over to the source of the light. Looking down into the hole, through the lacework, she saw the view that it afforded. Suddenly it all made sense to her. How Tholdi had known so much. How he had seen her fellating Grigore's gun, the gun she now held. She looked over at him.

I wanted to protect you. Those were the words he considered. The defence he thought to offer up. But it was only part of the story. There could be no more omissions. No more lies.

Lyuba wondered how long the hole in the floor had been there. What else Tholdi had seen. 'Are there more?' she asked.

Still Tholdi could not find the words. His silence was affirmation enough.

Grigore saw a chance to save himself. 'Looks like your houseboy is a pervert,' he said.

Gun in hand, Lyuba looked into the other rooms, checked under the rugs and found the other holes. The one above her bathroom. Above her bed.

By the time she returned, Grigore had managed to prop himself up against a wall. A trail of blood marked the short journey he'd made. 'This is all the boy's fault,' he said. 'You've done nothing.'

She walked over to him.

'You can still save yourself,' he said.

Lyuba took aim and began to squeeze the trigger slowly, as he had done.

Grigore began to shake and plead. 'Lyuba, think about this. You will be hunted down. You will be –'

She fired twice. Grigore convulsed as if he'd been electrocuted, his blood spraying her dress. After a moment, his lifeless body slumped forward.

For what seemed a very long time, neither Lyuba nor Tholdi moved or spoke. It was Tholdi who broke their silence. 'We have to go,' he whispered.

He pushed Grigore's body over onto its side and took his wallet from the back pocket of his trousers. As always, it was fat with German Reichsmark. From Grigore's wrist he removed a gold watch. From his dead hand he wrenched free Leo's gold signet ring and slid it onto his own finger.

61

Within hours, Grigore's prediction would be confirmed – at the latest, when Sergio failed to report back at the end of his watch and someone was sent to investigate.

To ensure it didn't happen any sooner than necessary, Lyuba pumped two more bullets from Grigore's Luger into Sergio's still-breathing body, sprawled unconscious at the foot of the stairs. Tholdi was horrified, but Lyuba showed no remorse. They couldn't afford to leave him alive to report what had happened, and who was responsible.

'Can you drive a car?' she asked.

Tholdi was still in shock. Lyuba yelled at him, urgently.

'Tholdi, can you drive?'

Tholdi finally managed to nod. 'Yes. I do sometimes. At the mill.'

'Get your parents. I'll meet you outside.'

Tholdi found Lina in such a state she could barely breathe. Nathan was with her, holding his wife tight in his arms. They'd both heard the gunshots, and then discovered Tholdi's empty bed. His return, unharmed, was at first a blessed relief – until he told them that they needed to leave immediately. They'd use Alex's escape plan, and Lyuba would be leaving with them.

Alarmed and terrified, Lina demanded to know what had happened.

'I'll explain on the way. Pack. Hurry!'

'Explain what?'

Tholdi turned his back on her. The shock had passed, and adrenaline had replaced it. He opened the drawer of the small writing desk, and retrieved the folder containing their forged travel documents. He threw aside the typed pages of the unfinished memoir. They scattered across the floor.

'Tholdi! Tell us!' Lina shouted.

'Mama, please!'

Nathan's voice remained calm and steady. 'Lina, not now,' he said, steering her towards their bedroom. 'Let's just do what he says.'

Tholdi found a pen and quickly filled out the final details on their papers. Alex had applied the stamps, but dates were required – ones that indicated when they'd made their last journey, ones that would fit with their stories of having spent the past few days in Dorneşti.

Back in her own apartment, Lyuba changed into a different dress and fetched her old suitcase. The mink-trimmed coat hung in the wardrobe. Take it or not? The nights were no longer cold, but she might be able to sell it. From behind a book in Dr Mandel's library, she collected the lei she'd managed to save. Over the months, the small sums had added up. She placed the notes in her handbag, alongside the Luger. There were still three bullets in it.

Looking out the window, she saw Nathan and Lina standing beside Grigore's car. Tholdi was loading their bags into the trunk, and she hurried out to join them. Although the women had met before, no words were exchanged. This was not the time for small talk. But since they were all about to travel together in the close confines of the two-door car, their fates irreversibly entwined, Nathan felt some sort of introduction was appropriate.

'Nathan,' he said, without offering his hand.

'Yes, I know,' Lyuba replied.

She gave Tholdi her bag to add to the trunk. Also the coat. Tholdi asked if she'd remembered her papers. Her identity card.

'Only so I can destroy it.'

'But if you get stopped somewhere –'

She completed his sentence. 'Having it will prove I'm the woman they're looking for.'

'You think Radu will give them your name? He'll want to stay out of it.'

'They'll make him talk. And they'll get his name from the landlord.'

Tholdi considered going to Moritz – maybe her false identity card was ready to collect – but Lyuba dismissed the idea. Moritz's house was north, towards the river; they were heading south. To leave the city without being stopped would be dangerous enough; to traverse it first was out of the question.

Tholdi opened the coupé's passenger door and flipped the front seat forward so that his parents could clamber into the back.

'Lina!' a voice called out.

Doina was on the doorstep, in her nightclothes. She saw the panic that had Lina in its grip. She went to her and took her hand.

'Where are you all going?' she cried.

Nathan answered for his wife. Quickly. Before too much was said. 'Best you don't know.'

'You're taking the car?' Doina asked.

'He won't miss it,' Tholdi assured her.

Doina understood his meaning, and did not ask to hear the details. She hugged Lina, who begged her forgiveness. In a few hours, there would be banging on her door, accompanied by ferocious dogs. Doina did not deserve any of it.

'Just be safe,' Doina told her.

The two women did not want to let go of each other.

'Mama, please, get in the car,' Tholdi begged.

Doina released her friend's hand, and watched Nathan help her clamber into the cramped rear seat before he also got in. Tholdi reached for the seat, to flip it back for Lyuba.

'I can do it. Get behind the wheel.'

Tholdi did as Lyuba instructed, and finally they were all inside. As Tholdi turned the key and revved the engine, Lina looked up to the windows of the building that had for half a lifetime been her home.

Doina watched them drive away. She was not the only one. From inside their homes, other neighbours, unseen, lights off, were watching too. By daybreak, when the curfew ended and Sergio's absence was noted, it would begin. They, too, would be woken by the loud barking of dogs and armed Gestapo officers demanding answers.

—

They limped along at first, the car hopping and jerking as Tholdi struggled with the unfamiliar gears. Grigore's fancy car was a very different beast to the forklift he'd driven at the mill.

Lina was waiting for Tholdi's answers, the explanation he'd promised her, but all he would say was: 'It was an accident.'

Lina felt they deserved more but Nathan urged her to let their son concentrate on his driving. His gear changes were becoming smoother, but it was a challenge.

Fearing that a fast-moving vehicle would arouse suspicion, Tholdi proceeded slowly along the city's residential streets. More than once they passed by men in uniforms that matched Sergio's. The men paused to watch the Opel glide by but made no attempt to stop it, no doubt reasoning that it belonged to someone important. Someone who should not be troubled.

It was just as well. On Tholdi's seat, between his legs, was Sergio's gun. Now that shock had given way to action, he was prepared to use it again.

Changing gears, his right hand went from the wheel to the gearstick and back again.

'Is that Opa's ring?' Lina asked.

In all the haste and confusion, she hadn't noticed it until now.

'Yes,' Tholdi said, but he didn't explain it.

Only when the buildings thinned, and they were beyond the city's edge, on the main road that linked Czernowitz with Dorneşti to the south, did Tholdi dare accelerate a little. There were no streetlights, and no moon either. The sky was overcast and starless.

In the front seat, Lyuba sat still and silent, staring at the passing night. She had no idea what she would do next. Taking the train with Tholdi and his parents was out of the question. They would have to separate. How would she survive the next few days, let alone the rest of the war? Would she have stood a better chance if Grigore hadn't been killed? If she hadn't trusted Tholdi, with whom she'd been more intimate than with anyone else in her life? Again, Lyuba wondered when Tholdi had made the holes in the floorboards. Wondered what else he had chosen to keep from her. Wondered if she really knew him at all. And whether any of it now mattered. She needed a plan. That was what she had to focus her mind on.

Lina wanted to go over the travel stories they had rehearsed, and started running through the details – names, dates, addresses – out loud. Tholdi was relieved that she remembered it all so clearly, but he was also acutely aware Lyuba was hearing it, too. For the first time. And that she would understand what it meant.

He glanced across at her. 'I wanted to tell you. I couldn't.'

She stared out the window, into the darkness.

'Alex swore him to secrecy,' Nathan confirmed.

She turned to Tholdi. 'Alex? Your friend?'

'Yes. He's alive. So are Peppa and Mira. He got them out.'

Yet more secrets he'd kept from her.

'And when were you planning to leave?'

'We decided not to.'

She wondered why. Tholdi was reluctant to explain it. Nathan did for him.

'He didn't want to leave you.'

Tholdi was surprised to hear Nathan say it. As was Lina.

'So it wasn't just because of me,' Lina said.

'No, Mama, not just you.'

This news prompted Lyuba to think of everything she *did* know about Tholdi, and all that he'd done for her. All that he'd given her. The risks he'd taken for her. She hadn't asked him to do any of it, but had she not been complicit? Had she not encouraged his infatuation? Cultivated it, even? She asked herself if she regretted Grigore's death. If it would be better if he were still alive. If she were back there with him. Anger and blame began to fade, giving way to acceptance and forgiveness, and she was able to think more clearly about what she might do next.

'What time is your train?' she asked Tholdi.

'Not until after eight.'

Tholdi wished it were earlier. He glanced at Grigore's watch. It was not yet midnight. He was amazed by how much had happened in such a short time.

'Where will you wait for it?' Lyuba asked.

That was something Tholdi hadn't thought of. They would all need to stay out of sight, and the car would have to be abandoned well before they arrived at the station.

'Up ahead on the right,' Lyuba said. 'There's a road. Take it.'

Tholdi didn't question her instruction, and they drove west, towards the heavily forested Carpathian foothills. Another twenty minutes further on Lyuba instructed Tholdi to turn again, onto a winding dirt road that was made for horses and carts rather than cars. They were all thrown about by the constant bumps, forcing Tholdi to slow down.

Lyuba urged him to drive even slower. 'There are deer,' she said.

'Not only deer,' Lina reminded them. Wolves and bears lived in the forest too.

'Where are we going?' Lina asked anxiously after some time.

'The past,' Lyuba said. 'Keep going.'

She wound down her window and through it, into the car's slipstream, she tossed the identity card that she'd torn into tiny pieces.

62

They drove on, in silence, for what seemed like forever. After what had in fact been less than an hour, a light beckoned through the darkness. The road took one last turn and a clearing appeared before them. Up ahead was a small wooden farmhouse. There was life inside. Not electric light, but the glow of a fire. Smoke rose from the chimney. It had all the charm of something from a children's book – and all the foreboding, too. While they were still some distance from it, Lyuba instructed Tholdi to stop the car and dim its headlights.

'You know the people who live here?' he asked.

'I knew them a long time ago.'

She retrieved her coat from the trunk, walked to the house and knocked on its door. It opened, and, after an exchange of unheard words, a figure – man or woman, Tholdi could not make out – allowed Lyuba inside and closed the door again.

Time seemed to stand still. Tholdi cut the engine and removed Leo's ring. Slipped it into his deep trouser pocket.

'Are we supposed to just wait?' Lina said.

'Yes, Mama, we wait.'

From all around, the sounds of the forest closed in on them. The night was warm, but Lina shivered as if it were still the depths of winter. Nathan wrapped a protective arm around her, and she nestled into his chest. Tholdi tried to resist looking at Grigore's watch.

After some time, the front door opened again, and Lyuba came out and beckoned them. Tholdi restarted the engine and drove to her.

As he pulled up, she came to his window. 'They have a cart. When it's time, they'll take you to the station.'

'They remembered you?'

'They remembered my father. He used to do work for them. With the horses.'

The interior of the house was one room, very basically furnished. The occupants, a farmer and his wife, were kind. They shared their food. It was simple but filling. Meat roasted on an open fire. What animal the meat came from wasn't explained, and no-one asked.

In their native Ruthenian, a Slavic dialect few Jews could speak, the farmer and his wife told Lyuba that they hadn't seen any of her people since the previous month when caravans of brightly-coloured wagons, driven on by armed Romanian soldiers, had passed through the area heading east in the direction of the Dniester River. Lyuba's parents were not among them. They hadn't been seen since the previous year, when the German commandoes had swept through the forest. Hearing it all translated by Lyuba, Lina shed tears. Lyuba's own eyes were dry – she had mourned the loss of her parents many years ago.

A couple of hours before dawn, they prepared to set out. It had been decided that Lina and Nathan would travel with the farmer in his cart and wait for Tholdi halfway back to the main road, where the dirt track connected with another. Tholdi would drive Grigore's car, following the same route, then turn down the second track and abandon the car further along before walking back to meet them. In exchange for their help, Lyuba gave the farmer and his wife her coat, and some money too. Tholdi parted with Grigore's wristwatch.

Before Tholdi got back in the Opel, he took care to reassure his mother, lovingly. He felt he had not been the most thoughtful son lately.

'Mama, I'm going to get rid of the car now. But these are good people. I think we can trust them.'

She nodded.

'I love you,' he added, and hugged her.

His words meant the world to Lina. She hadn't heard him say that to her in a long time. A whistle pierced the night air. It was the farmer, with his horse and cart, waiting. Lina wished Lyuba good luck. Lyuba wished Lina the same. Nathan took Lina's arm, and they went to the farmer.

Lyuba walked with Tholdi to the car. They knew that the odds of ever meeting again were incalculably small. Even smaller than the odds of them both surviving. Tholdi wished there was some way he could unwind it all. If only he'd kept his promise to Peppa, and stayed away from the upstairs apartment.

Lyuba had no regrets. 'It was never going to last,' she said. 'But without you, it might have ended sooner.'

'Will you stay with these people?' he asked.

'I don't know yet. But I'm strong and I'm smart. Isn't that what you said?'

From his pocket, Tholdi retrieved Leo's ring. 'I want you to have it,' he said.

'But –'

He pressed a finger to her lips. As she had once done to him.

'I want you to have it,' he said again.

He took her hand, placed the ring in her palm and wrapped her fingers around it.

'If you need to sell it, promise me you will.'

She shook her head.

'Promise me.'

'If you tell me something.'

Tholdi could not imagine what there was left to say.

'Why me?' Lyuba asked.

He'd asked himself the same question so many times. His answer seemed like an evasion but it was honest, and the only one he had to give.

'Schicksal.'

This time Lyuba did not reject the notion. How else could they explain everything that had happened since that first moment they'd met? How their paths had diverged and converged, bringing them to this single moment?

Tholdi got into the car and drove away. Lyuba stood watching until its lights were swallowed up by the forest.

63

The moon had revealed itself. By its light, Tholdi found the spot where the farmer and his wife had suggested he leave the car – not far off the dirt road that connected to the main one. It fell away into a natural hollow about four metres deep. Tholdi put the car into neutral, jumped out quickly and let it roll. It landed with a crashing of branches. He threw more branches in after it, more leaves, until the car could no longer be seen. He hoped it would never be found, for all their sakes.

He still had Sergio's gun, and wondered now if he should keep it. If their travel documents in any way aroused suspicion, and he was searched, it would be a liability. It too he threw into the hollow.

Back at the dirt road, the farmer was waiting. Nathan and Lina were already concealed in the cart, beneath a layer of cabbages. Tholdi climbed in with them. The farmer let out another sharp whistle, and the horse plodded forward. It was a long and bumpy ride.

At a deserted street corner on the outskirts of Doneşti, Tholdi jumped down first and helped his parents to climb out. They thanked the farmer and walked the rest of the way to the station. In the dim pre-dawn light, it was Nathan rather than Lina who needed support, and he rested a hand on his son's shoulder. In his other hand Nathan carried one of the bags. They had considered bringing just the one but thought it might look suspicious, so they'd taken anything heavy out of Nathan's case and put it in the other, for Tholdi to carry. They reached the station just as the sun was rising. About now, Tholdi calculated, it would be noticed that Sergio had failed to report back to his command.

The station was mercifully quiet, absent of any military and attended only by the stationmaster, who was seated, snoring. No doubt he was exhausted. Together in the basement with Nathan, listening to the BBC, Tholdi had heard of the terrible losses the Axis forces were suffering on Russian soil. He presumed the stationmaster must have experienced the consequences, the carriages full of wounded soldiers returning from the front lines, first-hand. Like the mill, the wall behind the counter of the station's little office bore the twin flags of the Romanian government and Nazi Germany. Their country's leader was not Hitler, but Antonescu. Still, Tholdi thought it best to take no chances.

'Heil Hitler!' Tholdi declared loudly.

The stationmaster woke with a start, and jumped to his feet. 'Heil Hitler!' he responded. He was somewhat surprised to see that he was being addressed by a civilian rather than a German soldier.

Tholdi handed him their three identity cards while Nathan and Lina stood back a few paces.

Rubbing the sleep from his eyes, the stationmaster found his glasses and examined the photos, making sure they matched. 'Purpose of journey?' he asked.

'Going home,' Tholdi announced brightly. 'Again,' he added.

The stationmaster took a closer look at the stamps and saw that they had all travelled this route before, more than once. He took another look at the faces in front of him. None of them seemed familiar but his memory these days was not what it used to be.

'Purpose of your visit here?'

'Grandmother's birthday.'

The stationmaster scrutinised Tholdi.

'Father's side or mother's?'

'Mother's.'

The stationmaster's eyes turned to Lina. 'Step forward, please.'

Lina approached.

'Do you have any supporting documents?'

Lina produced the birth certificate that was in her handbag.

The stationmaster studied it closely. 'This grandmother. Surname?'

Tholdi held his breath. He didn't dare glance at his mother.

'Iliescu.'

The stationmaster saw that it matched her maiden name.

'We'll be needing first class seats, of course,' Tholdi declared. Not only because it would be more comfortable for his parents but because an air of entitlement signalled that they should not be questioned further.

'I can try, but you'll be lucky to get seats at all.'

The stationmaster opened his ink pad, and was about to apply the fresh stamps they so vitally needed, when a junior employee approached with urgent information.

'Mein Herr, we have just received news by wire.'

Tholdi swallowed hard.

'There will be an extra service today.'

With more casualties, Tholdi suspected.

'Looks like you're in luck,' the stationmaster said. He issued them tickets and stamped and dated their travel papers.

Tholdi looked at the clock on the stationmaster's wall. The train would be nearly an hour. It was a quiet station, but the less time they spent there, the better.

'Is there anywhere nearby we can get some decent coffee?' Tholdi asked.

'I thought you said you came here often.'

Tholdi's heart beat a little faster. 'We usually take a later service.'

The stationmaster accepted Tholdi's explanation. He had too much else to deal with now. He waved them on.

'There's a café on the next corner. That way.'

'Thank you.' Tholdi took back their travel documents, and then gave the expected farewell, as did Nathan and Lina. 'Heil Hitler!'

In the café they sat in a corner, sipping their coffees. When they spoke, their voices were hushed and earnest. Their smiles, and even the occasional burst of laughter, were for effect.

'You did really well,' Tholdi commended his mother.

'We're smarter than everyone else,' joked Nathan. 'It's why we run the world.'

Tholdi didn't laugh. Nor did Lina.

'Papa, please, not now,' Tholdi said.

Nathan sighed and everted his palms in mock surrender. 'All right. Okay.'

'And stop with the hands,' Tholdi said.

Nathan glanced about discreetly to make sure no-one had seen, and placed his hands firmly back on the table.

Tholdi noticed the waitress, who was clearing plates from a nearby table, looking their way. Before she moved off, he offered her a small smile. She did not return it.

On the wall behind the counter was a clock. Its second hand moved forward with painful precision.

64

R adu had endured another restless night on the hard mattress in the guest bedroom. Towards dawn, he had abandoned it. In the kitchen he found Sofia pouring herself a cup of hot, fresh coffee.

'Would you like some?' she asked.

The coffee smelled good. 'Sure,' he said.

While Sofia fetched a cup, Radu sat at the kitchen table. In front of him was an open bag full of toys and infant's clothes.

'You've been shopping again.'

'Gifts,' she said. 'For Nadia.'

Of course. She'd had the baby. A little boy.

'You'd be very welcome to come,' Sofia said.

To the christening, she meant. It was later that week, but she was leaving today to help her sister prepare.

'I can't. Work.'

They both knew that if Radu wanted to he could make the time, but recent events had encouraged her to hope her marriage might yet be salvaged. A confrontation was the last thing it needed.

A sudden twinge of pain shot through Radu's back. He tried to relieve it by stretching.

Very gently, Sofia again suggested he return to their soft marital bed. 'You could use it while I'm away,' she said.

She would be gone for a week at least. She imagined Radu spending his nights alone. Peacefully. Without the whore, who – for reasons Sofia had shrewdly chosen not to interrogate – Radu was seeing less and less lately.

'We'll see,' he said.

In the past Sofia would have found that reply irritating. Now she responded very differently.

'Whatever you think is best.'

Radu's stomach rumbled audibly.

'Shall I make you some breakfast?'

'You don't want to wait?'

For the maid, he meant, who would be arriving soon. It had been a very long time now since Sofia had lifted a finger, especially for him.

'I still know how to cook.'

'Very well, then.'

Sofia set about cracking and scrambling eggs. With cream. The way Radu liked them.

In the hallway, the telephone rang. Radu answered it. It was the mill's night manager. He was due to go home and wondered if Radu might know his brother's whereabouts. At the start of his shift, Grigore had told the manager that he wanted to discuss something with him before he left, but Grigore had failed to arrive, and was not answering his telephone at home.

Radu was unsettled by the call, wondering if it had anything to do with Lyuba, but he told the night manager not to worry about it – to go home and leave it with him to look into.

As he hung up Sofia called, 'Breakfast is ready.'

65

At last, the train pulled into the platform. The sight of so many military personnel on board, pressed against the carriage windows, did not help Lina's anxiety. Fortunately, they all looked far too exhausted to be threatening. Many were wounded as well, and they were all travelling separately from the civilian passengers.

In the carriage, Nathan helped Lina get comfortable while Tholdi stored their bags in the overhead rack. The conductor came through, checking that everyone had a ticket, but there was no need to present their travel papers again. Nathan folded his hands in his lap, and Lina concentrated on her breathing, doing her best to keep it regular. When the whistle finally blew, and they began to pull away from the platform, she reminded herself not to exhale too loudly. Not to let others see the relief she felt.

Tholdi did his best to engage his parents in small talk. 'I thought she looked really well,' he said.

For a moment, neither of them understood, looking at him blankly.

'She was really pleased we came.'

Nathan and Lina caught on then, and played along.

'She looked lovely in that dress.'

'To think next year she'll be ninety.'

Nathan's mouth opened. A single syllable escaped.

'Ma –'

They all knew what he'd almost blurted out. *Mazel tov!*

Nathan tried to think of another, less Jewish phrase, instead.

'Excuse me.' A middle-aged man seated nearby leaned across the aisle. 'I couldn't help hearing.'

Lina held her breath.

'Did you say ninety?' he asked.

'Yes, next year,' Tholdi confirmed. 'It was my grandmother's eighty-ninth birthday yesterday.'

'My mother,' Lina added.

'Congratulations. That's wonderful.'

'Yes! Wonderful!' Nathan exclaimed, glad that the man across the aisle had provided the word they needed.

A fellow passenger responded to his enthusiasm with an irritable glance. She, like several others at this early hour, was dozing. Or trying to. Tholdi suggested to his parents that they do the same. Without newspapers to hide behind – he wished he'd thought to buy one – it was the easiest way to travel without drawing unwanted attention. They all closed their eyes. Not that they were able to sleep.

The events of the night before ran over and over in Tholdi's head like scenes from a film. He knew that as long as he lived, if he lived, he would never forget them. And he would never forget Lyuba. He offered up a prayer for her safety, as well as theirs. After all that had happened, after the outpouring of hatred and violence that had been allowed to rain down upon the world, did he still believe? He wasn't sure. But he did still believe in hope. And why not? Against the odds, they'd all made it this far. Within hours they'd be safe, reunited with their friends.

'I purchased a first-class ticket! I want a first-class seat!'

A woman's voice. Tholdi resisted the urge to open his eyes and see who it belonged to. With a clatter, something hit the floor.

'Now look what you've done! If it's damaged . . .'

'I'm sorry, madam. I'll fetch it.' That must have been the conductor. 'Sir? Excuse me?'

Tholdi felt the tap of a hand on his shoulder and opened his eyes as if he'd been roused from sleep.

'Under your feet.'

Tholdi saw an infant's rattle on the floor beneath his seat. Picking it up, he turned back to the conductor, and then, for the briefest of moments, he froze. The woman was Sofia. Tholdi quickly handed over the rattle and turned away, closing his eyes again.

The conductor handed the undamaged rattle back to Sofia. 'There we go,' he said. 'And in the next carriage, madam, I think I can find you a seat.'

He went to move along, but Sofia didn't follow. Standing next to Tholdi, she asked: 'Don't I know you?'

Tholdi pretended not to hear.

'You.'

Again he felt his shoulder tapped, this time less courteously, and he was forced to open his eyes. 'I'm sorry?' he said.

'I know you. I'm sure I do.'

'I think you're mistaken.'

The woman who'd been trying to sleep opened her eyes again. 'Now what?' she demanded. The other sleeping passengers started to wake and look around them too. The conductor, now several seats along the aisle, looked back. Only Nathan and Lina, seated opposite Tholdi, pretended to be undisturbed.

'You two!' she said. 'Open your eyes!'

Tholdi stood and placed himself between Sofia and his parents. 'Madam, I don't know what –'

'Jews!' She turned to the conductor. 'These are Jews!'

A murmur ran through the carriage. 'What's going on?'

'Fetch a guard!' Sofia bellowed at the conductor.

'Madam,' Tholdi persisted, 'you are making a mistake.'

The conductor wasn't sure what to do.

'The guard!' Sofia shouted. 'Now!'

The conductor finally obeyed, squeezing by Sofia to go the way he'd come. She stood her ground. She had no intention of going anywhere until this situation was resolved.

The emergency brake was within Nathan's reach. He stood and pulled it. There was the sound of grinding metal, and the train lurched violently. Sofia fell backwards and the rattle flew from her hand as the train came to a stop.

'Run!' Nathan yelled at Tholdi. 'Run! That way!' He gestured urgently towards the door at the far end of the carriage.

'But Papa –'

'Now!'

Tholdi looked back along the aisle. Beyond Sofia, now struggling to get onto her feet again, a guard was pushing towards them. He held a gun.

'Bubala, go!' Lina begged him.

Nathan stood and pushed his son along the aisle, blocking the advancing guard. 'Go!' he shouted.

None of the other passengers, shocked and terrified, made any attempt to stop Tholdi. At the end of the carriage, he looked back and saw the guard push past Sofia, shouting at Nathan to stand aside.

'Run!' Lina screamed.

Tholdi turned as a shot rang out. He opened the carriage door and leapt from the train, landing hard, on his shoulder.

Through the carriage window he saw the guard pushing past Nathan, limp in Lina's arms. Tholdi knew that it was the last time he would ever see his mother and father. He picked himself up and ran towards the forest. More gunshots rang out. Tholdi kept running.

Epilogue

Outside, it was humid and heavy. I opened our hotel window to let in the warm breeze and to soak up the excitement of the city in the street twenty floors below – the tooting of horns and screaming of sirens that in a place like New York never ceases.

'Nathan, step away from there! It's dangerous!'

'Mum, I'm not about to fall.'

My Australian accent bore not a trace of my European ancestry.

'Tholdi, please, tell him.'

Just as it had once been with his father, the man whose name I had been given, my father was the final arbiter.

'Nathan,' he said gently, 'do what your mother tells you.'

I stepped away from the window. In any case, it was time for me to get ready.

'I'll see you in the lobby,' I said.

———

Peppa read the look on her husband's face. The one that rebuked her for speaking to her son like a child.

She shrugged, and everted her palms. 'I'm a mother. Yours was just the same.'

And Tholdi understood that on this night it was his wife, not her famous husband, whose nerves needed calming.

On the coffee table was a copy of *The Times*. Peppa picked it up.

'Have you seen this?'

Tholdi had. The headline – 'Holocaust Survivor to Conduct at Lincoln Center' – did not sit easily with him. Yes, he'd survived that terrible time, but he'd been spared the hell of the camps. Only a week after they'd all fled, the transportations resumed. Six thousand more Jews were herded into the cattle cars, the names all drawn from the list that the mill contributed to each month.

Yours was just the same. Tholdi's parents were never far from his thoughts. Would they have survived if things had been different? If he'd never met Lyuba?

'Do you think she'll be coming tonight?' Peppa asked.

'How could I know?'

So many years had gone by since he'd last heard from her.

In the mirror, Nicolae adjusted his bow tie. He wanted to look his best. For her. He joined his mother just as her student, a young girl, was leaving.

'Thank you, Miss Ziko,' the girl said.

Lyuba closed the door behind her and inspected her son's appearance. 'A tux looks good on you, Nicu.'

'Thank you, *Miss Ziko*,' he joked.

Her real surname. The one she'd been born with.

'You may call me Lyuba,' she smiled, disappearing down the hall to get changed for the evening.

Nicolae remained hopeful that one day she would be comfortable being called Mother. That she would no longer feel the guilt of having abandoned him. He certainly never blamed her for it. What choice had she had? How could she have raised him herself? And when he was old enough to understand it all, she came back for him. Not to take him away but to let him know she existed, and that, if he wanted it, she would be a part of his life.

With her she had brought the photograph of her son that Tholdi had taken so many years before. Before leaving the farmer and his wife she'd buried it in a box, at the base of a tree. It now sat framed alongside many more photos of her son, taken in more recent times, much happier times, with her. Since Nicolae had accepted his new position in Paris, he saw less of Lyuba, but he was still able to visit regularly. It gave him great pride to see the modest but comfortable life his mother had made for herself, and the elegant uptown apartment in which she lived. It had given him great pleasure to help her buy it. To know that at last she had a home that was truly her own. That there would be no more running.

Lyuba had not been able to stay with the farmer and his wife. In September, three months after she'd fled the city with Tholdi, the Romanian Porrajmos – the Romani word for the Holocaust – began. It had become too dangerous to remain with the farmer and his wife, for her as well as them. Further into the forest, at another farm, she had secured shelter and food in return for her labour. The arrangement was a good one until the farmer demanded sex, and his wife became jealous. Lyuba was arrested and taken to a Transnistrian camp. The conditions she survived there were unimaginable but without identity papers she was never connected with Grigore's death, or with Sergio's.

'Lyuba! We'll be late!'

She emerged from her bedroom wearing a simple black dress. She turned her back to Nicolae so he could fasten the clasp of the string of pearls he'd given to her a few years back for her fiftieth birthday. The matching earrings she put on herself, and then turned to face her son.

'Do I look all right?'

'No.'

'No?'

'You look radiant.'

She had only one photograph of herself as a young woman – the one Tholdi had kept. He'd had a copy of it printed and had sent it to her. It might have been the biased view of an only son, but to Nicolae she seemed more beautiful now than then. More self-assured and poised. She could have married if she'd wanted to. Over the years there had been proposals. She'd resisted them all, remained single. She preferred that too.

'Did you read the piece in the *Times*?' he asked.

'Of course.'

Since moving to America, she'd taught herself to read. Another achievement she was proud of. She'd read every bit of the extensive advance publicity Tholdi's visit had generated.

The Times article was accompanied by a picture.

'His wife is with him.'

'I saw,' she said.

The end of the war had brought a new kind of chaos. A world of displaced people and holding camps. When it was all over, Tholdi resettled in Australia, as far from the past as he could get. It was through a Jewish welfare agency that Lyuba found him. When he received her first letter, in Nicolae's handwriting, he wept, overcome with the joy of knowing, after years of wondering, that Lyuba had lived. He replied immediately and for a time the letters flowed back and forth regularly, both of them sharing the hope that one day they might see each other again.

For Peppa, none of it was easy to accommodate. The correspondence prompted questions that she'd never dared to ask her husband directly. She would never know what had happened in that brief window of time between when she left Czernowitz and Tholdi joined her in Bucharest. She told herself not to be jealous of the letters. Not to pry. She, after all, had married Tholdi and given him a son. But Tholdi understood his wife's feelings. Out of respect to her, his letters to Lyuba became gradually less frequent, and shorter. Lyuba understood why. Understood that she needed to let him move on. In her last letter to him, she told him she was moving to America. She did not write again. Did not send her new address.

—

In the backstage green room, a telegram arrived for Tholdi. It was from Alex, who'd kept his long-ago promise to himself and was now on a safari in Africa, the only continent he hadn't yet travelled to. When he'd visited Tholdi in Australia, Alex had admired the local vernacular, enjoying its sense of self-mockery.

Peppa read his telegram aloud: 'Don't stuff it up.'

It broke the tension, as Alex usually managed to do.

'Five minutes!' the stage manager called. 'Five minutes everyone!'

In the auditorium, the assembled players were tuning their instruments as Lyuba and Nicolae took their seats. The lights dimmed, and a hush of expectation descended before Tholdi, in black tails and white tie, entered with the guest pianist, an

Israeli woman. To excited applause, she sat at the piano and Tholdi stepped up onto the conductor's podium. He raised his baton, saw that his orchestra was ready, and the dramatic opening bars of Rachmaninoff's Piano Concerto Number Two electrified the crowd. The second part of the programme was 'The Moldau', by Smetana – his nineteenth-century anthem of hope for the Jewish people of the world. For the many Jews in the audience it could not have been more stirring. Tears flowed. But it was the encore that moved Lyuba in a way that nothing before it had, or could have done.

On any other night Tholdi would have brought the full orchestra back on stage to play a crowd-pleaser – Mozart's Piano Concerto Number Twenty-one always left the audience satisfied, he found. But tonight he returned to the stage alone, without the orchestra, and sat at the piano himself. Lyuba held her breath. Her hands came together in front of her face. And then the first bitter-sweet notes of 'The Angel' floated through the air just as they had on that icy New Year's night in Czernowitz almost thirty years before. For Lyuba it was as if they were alone again, just the two of them.

At the end she and Nicolae joined the rest of the audience in a raucous standing ovation. In their tuxedos and gowns, the New Yorkers clapped and whistled as if a football game had just ended.

Afterwards, in the foyer, Lyuba asked Nicolae to wait for her.

'I won't be long,' she promised.

—

Back in the green room, celebrating the performance, I was allowed a glass of champagne. Sipping it, an assistant approached and took me aside. 'There's someone here to see you.'

I had no idea who it could be. I knew no-one in New York.

In the dimmed backstage corridor, I was greeted by a woman. Even in the low lighting her extraordinary eyes were arresting.

'You asked for me?'

She opened her purse and from it extracted something else she'd buried all those years ago, and handed it to me.

'This belongs to your father.'

'And you are?'

'An old friend.'

Even then, I knew she was so much more.

'Ask him about the legend.'

'Legend?'

'He can explain.'

She was gone before I could ask anything more. I returned to the green room, as my father was ending a conversation. He saw the look on my face.

'Is everything all right?'

'A woman just gave me this. For you.' I showed my father what the woman had given me. My grandfather's gold signet ring.

'Where is she now?' His voice was suddenly agitated and urgent.

'She left.'

He pushed past me, almost knocking the glass from my hand. I followed and found him in the corridor, staring down its length. At the far end an open door cast a shaft of light that made the woman's figure a silhouette. A moment later, the door closed. In the darkness it echoed.

My father did not move.

'Who was that?' I asked.

No reply came. Not then.

He looked at the ring and slipped it onto the finger where it belonged. For the rest of his days, until it became mine, it never left his hand.

Author's note

*N*ight Lessons in Little Jerusalem is a work of fiction, told by a fictional narrator. It was inspired by the memoirs of my late father, Alex Held. Most of his adult years were lived in Australia, where he migrated after the war. Like Jakob, he became a yarn agent in the textile industry. And like my fictional hero, he was no tzadik – he had three marriages, made and lost fortunes, loved to gamble and lived life large. Also like my hero, he was a romantic and a risk-taker who made a real difference to the lives of others. It was with his help that his first cousin, the internationally celebrated conductor Robert Rosen, also made a new life in Australia. I like to think my father would be pleased to share with him the role of hero in a story that recalls the times they both lived through, and the marvellous city where they shared the years of their youth.

Acknowledgements

T here are so many people without whom this book would not have been realised, beginning with my oldest friend, Peter Wyllie Johnston, whom I've known since I was six. He convinced me that my late father would not merely have approved of my vision – a fictional re-weaving of his lived life – but that he would have been proud of it. As a hugely gifted composer, academic and author, Peter also became the key creative contributor to the musical aspects of the text. From the earliest stages there was another rock, too – my late sister, Toni Dale-Coote, who through the most difficult of her own times gave me constant encouragement and support. My other true believers were Amanda Lyons, Brad Creese, Michael Dye, Jo Moulton – my first reader – and cherished mates from the screen trade: Barbara Bishop, Alison Nisselle, Bevan Lee and

Sarah Walker. At various times they each contributed insightful feedback and creative input – thank you all.

For historical research I thank Professor Konrad Kwiet of the Sydney Jewish Museum, in whose 'bunker' I spent many hours and who introduced me to the eternally youthful Maurice Linker, who as a child lived through the times of my story, in the marvellous city where it is set. Through Maurice I became connected with a global community of other survivors, and their descendants. I am especially indebted to one member of that circle, Berti Glaubach, who from Israel responded swiftly and unfailingly to almost every group email I fired off, whether it was to do with the broad sweep, scale and timing of historical events or the minutiae of on-the-ground daily life.

My thanks also go to Professor Michelle Kelso, based in the US. Her special area of knowledge – the history of the Romani people during the Holocaust in Romania – could not have been more relevant.

For her input on the Yiddish, thank you Freda Hodge.

Thanks also to Jon de Ruiter and Geoff Boccalatte for their technical input re architectural details and photography of the times respectively. And, in Czernowitz itself – today known as Chernivtsi – to the two women who gave so generously of their time, when I was there and then afterwards, by email, when I had many follow-up questions: Zoya Danilovich and Iryna Yavorska.

Lastly, my heartfelt thanks to the true believers at Hachette: Andy Palmer, who introduced my work; Elizabeth Cowell, who tackled the first pass edit with such intelligence and attention to detail; the brilliant Rebecca Allen, who took over that baton and who, with patience and passion, worked with me through what effectively turned out to be a further two drafts; and, of course, Vanessa Radnidge, my publisher, who from the moment she read the story, and the first few chapters I'd written, loved it, nurtured it, and made it all happen.

hachette
AUSTRALIA

If you would like to find out more about Hachette Australia,
our authors, upcoming events and new releases you can visit
our website or our social media channels:

hachette.com.au

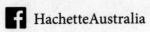 HachetteAustralia

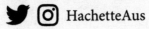 HachetteAus